"What on earth . .

Carina muttered to herself as she unwrapped the fabric. She stared at the assortment of metal tools in her hands. A scalpel, a pair of forceps and a surgical saw. And as if that wasn't bad enough . . . the instruments were covered in blood!

She tried to escape the only conclusion she could come to. But it was no use. Carina knew now that Malcolm Spencer had been murdered and that the one with both the motive and the means was none other than her lover . . . Damian Fleming!

ABOUT THE AUTHOR

Of the various jobs Elaine Stirling had before
launching her writing career, perhaps the one
she liked best was box-office manager of the
Sudbury Theatre Centre. In fact, it was this
job that inspired the setting and characters
for *Foul Play*. Though none of the cast or
crew went quite as far as Malcolm Spencer,
Elaine insists she'd never met a more colorful
bunch of people or had so much fun. She
always knew she'd write a book about her
experience one day. Having done so, Elaine is
now busy working on a Superromance and
plans to follow up with her fourth Intrigue in
the fall.

Books by Elaine K. Stirling

HARLEQUIN INTRIGUE
28–UNSUSPECTED CONDUCT
35–MIDNIGHT OBSESSION

These books may be available at your local bookseller.

Don't miss any of our special offers. Write to us at the
following address for information on our newest releases.

Harlequin Reader Service
901 Fuhrmann Blvd., P.O. Box 1397, Buffalo, NY 14240
Canadian address: P.O. Box 603,
Fort Erie, Ont. L2A 5X3

FOUL
PLAY
ELAINE K. STIRLING

Harlequin Books

TORONTO • NEW YORK • LONDON
AMSTERDAM • PARIS • SYDNEY • HAMBURG
STOCKHOLM • ATHENS • TOKYO • MILAN

To my editor, Marmie Charndoff,
for her sense of humor, her tenacity
and her unflagging ability to
"tell it like it is."

Harlequin Intrigue edition published November 1986

ISBN 0-373-22053-7

Chapter One

It seemed obvious that the frizzy-haired woman had long since drawn her last breath. Her complexion was sallow, nearly gray. Hands once graceful and eloquent now dangled from the chaise lounge on which she lay, while tiny slippered feet pointed rigid to the ceiling. Around her neck a rope of pearls was wrapped so tightly it might have been a noose.

Carina Rawlins stepped inside the office, took one look at the recumbent woman in the portrait and sighed. "I should've known you'd play dead today, Sarah." She hung up her coat and marched over to the photograph of actress Sarah Bernhardt hanging askew on the wall. "So far this morning, I've lost my gold locket and put a toe through a pair of ten-dollar panty hose. But of course, you must already know that, since every time I find you like this, something goes wrong."

It was Monday, and the start of a new season at the Myrmidon—proof positive that the grand old theater had once again beat the odds to survive another summer. That alone should have been enough to send Carina's confidence soaring, since summers in Dunn's Pond, Illinois, were notoriously difficult for the theater. There were no plays to produce, no money coming in. Crew members had to scramble for seasonal work—detasseling corn or whatever they could get—and there was always the chance that some of them might find steadier jobs and not return in the fall.

But, lo and behold, everyone had shown up for last week's production meetings, eager and ready for work. Later that morning, the cast would be arriving to begin rehearsals for *Fate of the Popinjay*, the season's opening play. Things couldn't have looked rosier, so why on earth was she fretting about Sarah hanging crooked on the wall? No reason to be superstitious, she told herself sternly. No reason at all. Still, if she just gave the picture a quick nudge...

Several times, Carina tried to right the tilting photograph. But each time she did, the actress's pose of flagrant seduction slipped into one more closely resembling death by strangulation. Carina tossed back her silky auburn hair in frustration.

"What are you trying to tell me, Sarah? It's been seventy-five years since you played at the Myrmidon. You can't possibly know when...oh gosh, listen to me, talking to a photograph as if it were alive." Even though she knew she was alone in the theater, Carina glanced over her shoulder to be sure no one had heard. "I think I've been working in this place too long," she muttered to herself.

Granted, there had been those other occasions when Sarah had seemed to—no, no, no! They were just coincidences! There was no such thing as an omen, bad or otherwise. The only thing wrong around here was a case of nervous jitters—the same one she suffered every fall at the start of a new season.

"So there, Miss Bernhardt," she couldn't help saying as she dropped to her knees to look under the desk for her locket. "Go ahead and hang that way. See if I care!"

Half an hour later Carina had abandoned her search for the locket and was laying out cream and sugar for coffee. The necklace would probably turn up, as soon as she stopped worrying about it.

Just then, a couple came in through the front doors to the lobby. They were in their mid-to-late sixties, the woman with silver curls and periwinkle-blue eyes, the man fit and natty in a tweed sports coat. Energy radiated from them both like sunbeams, making them seem much younger than their years.

The woman tossed the end of a long silk scarf over her shoulder and twirled about on one foot. "Oh look, Len, it's been eight years, but everything is exactly the same. I knew it would be—the lovely old pillars outside, the wainscot in the lobby—isn't it wonderful to be back?"

"If you say so, dear," her husband answered, enthusiasm and an English accent less noticeable in his speech than his wife's. "It seems to me that the Myrmidon possesses a few more sags and wrinkles than she used to. Not unlike us, I might add."

Amused by the intimate exchange, Carina went to the open counter that divided her office from the lobby. "I couldn't help overhearing your remark about sags and wrinkles, Len, and I disagree. The two of you have never looked better."

The couple turned to the young woman, their eyes lighting up at the sight of her. "Carina!" they exclaimed in unison.

Kate rushed to the counter and leaned over to give Carina a theatrical buss on the cheek. "I couldn't believe it when Malcolm told us you were still here, clever young thing that you are, but I must say I'm delighted. Now it really is like coming home, isn't it, Len?"

Her husband echoed his agreement and slipped an arm around his wife's waist. "Anywhere with my Kate is home. We've been apart for six months. Kate's had obligations in California, while I was stuck in Scotland doing *King Lear*. We're getting much too old for that sort of thing, I'm afraid."

Carina took Len's hand. "I'm pleased that we could do our part to bring you back together again. It was certainly one of Malcolm's wiser casting decisions." She immediately regretted her unkind remark about her boss, the theater's artistic director, but Kate and Len Kramer were courteous enough to overlook the slip. And they knew what the man was like.

"Let me think," Kate said, "the last time we were here, you were a blushing twenty-one-year-old fresh out of college and the shyest creature we'd ever laid eyes on."

Now it was easy for Carina to laugh at the memory of those awkward early years, but at the time they'd been dreadful. "You're right, Kate, I was. It was sheer agony for me whenever a play closed and I had to greet a whole new cast for the next one."

"Well, you certainly seem to have come out of your shell," the older woman said. "Was it Malcolm's merciless taunting that did it, or the influence of actors' bravado?"

"It was a combination of both, I think. One thing I learned quickly about theater was that you have to make yourself heard or get trampled in the chaos." Carina was not exaggerating. For better or worse, the past eight years had taught her more about life than her first twenty-one ever had.

Len peeked around Carina to the serving cart in her office. "I can hardly believe these tired old eyes. Blueberry muffins, whipped cream cheese and—" he paused to take a deep whiff "—mmm, I thought so, Javanese coffee. Bless your heart, child, you haven't forgotten a thing."

Carina allowed herself a small sigh of relief. Keeping files on actors' idiosyncracies and favorite foods never failed to pay off. "I'm glad they're still your favorites. Come in, please; the coffee's ready." She motioned them to enter her office through the side door around the corner. So far, things were going quite nicely.

After she'd hung up their coats Carina poured coffee while Kate moved about, reacquainting herself with the small cozy room. "When we were here before, you hadn't decorated your office yet, but I see now that you have a fine eye for antiques." She picked up a snuffbox that Carina used as a paperweight.

"Thank you," Carina replied, handing Len a cup and offering the plate of muffins. "I seem to spend most of my time here, so I thought I'd make it as homey as possible. Even the crew likes to gather in here instead of the green-room—"

"Oh dear, what's this?" Kate interjected dramatically as she stared at the old photograph behind Carina's desk. "Poor Sarah looks as though she's staging a death scene. Why is she hanging like this?"

Carina's growing self-satisfaction instantly deflated. In an otherwise impeccable office, the portrait did look ridiculous. "I tried to fix it, but I couldn't seem to..." Her words faded away when Kate returned the portrait to its proper position with a single nudge.

"There, that's much better," Kate announced, taking the cup that Carina offered. "Have I ever told you that my mother once met Miss Bernhardt at a cast party in London?"

Still feeling rather wilted, Carina said, "No, I don't think so. What was she like?"

"Quite eccentric, from what she could gather, and vain. If I recall correctly, Miss Bernhardt also enjoyed dabbling in mysticism." Pursing her lips, Kate shook her head. "I shouldn't be at all surprised if her spirit chose to rain havoc on the Myrmidon for displaying her so unflatteringly."

Carina's face must have registered the shock she felt at the way Kate's remark echoed her own musings about Sarah. And Len had obviously noticed, for he gently chastised his wife. "Now, Kate, you're frightening Carina. Not everyone appreciates your singular sense of humor."

"It's all right—" Carina began.

"But I'm not joking," the actress insisted. Then she turned to Carina with a look of remorse. "Oh dear, I have frightened you, haven't I? I'm so sorry."

Carina waved her hand in a gesture of denial. "No, you haven't frightened me, really." A change of tactics was definitely in order here. She couldn't let the Kramers feel as though they were dealing with a child. She set her own coffee down beside her. "Now that you mention it, Kate, the most remarkable things have happened with this portrait. Just last season, I—"

To Carina's relief, she was prevented from finishing her story by the appearance of a stunning brunette in a full-length mink coat. The woman was drumming manicured fingers on the counter, looking decidedly bored. "Is this really the Myrmidon or have I come to the wrong theater? This place is a dump."

Summoning her most professional smile, Carina stood up to introduce herself. She'd dealt with performers like this before. There was nothing to do but ignore everything they said or did.

"You must be Judith Deveau. Welcome to the Myrmidon. I'm the artistic director's assistant, Carina Rawlins."

Lackluster dark eyes appraised Carina briefly, then moved away to take in the surroundings. Carina followed Judith's visual path around the lobby and felt her own defenses rise. She knew what Judith must have been thinking. In the harsh gray light of morning, the Myrmidon looked every one of her hundred or so years. The carpet was fraying and faded, the plaster walls crumbling; a dieffenbachia, once magnificent, stood in dire need of repotting. But, dammit, the lobby wasn't what patrons came to see; the quality of plays was what mattered. Couldn't Judith understand that?

Carina forced attention back to Judith and realized the woman hadn't said a thing for some time. In fact, she was now smiling—quite maliciously, it seemed to Carina.

"So this is where the unsinkable Malcolm Spencer came to rest," Judith remarked. "How appropriate." She turned to Carina once more. "I'm sorry. I didn't catch your name. Did you say you were box office?"

No one could have detected that Carina was seething. Every shred of professional courtesy was in place as she repeated her name and her job title, then invited Judith into her office for coffee. Being an assistant had its occupational hazards; certain performers automatically assumed you were an insignificant gofer, lackey to the superior talents of the person in charge. Judith was dead wrong, but of course she couldn't possibly know that.

The actress floated into the office on an overpowering cloud of French perfume, and it occurred to Carina quite irrelevantly that the woman hardly needed the flamboyant fur coat, the makeup and the killer scent in order to be noticed. Who, in this dusty little town, was she trying to impress?

Carina offered to take her coat. "Have you met the Kramers?"

"Hi, guys," Judith said to the couple as if Carina hadn't even spoken. "I hope your mattress wasn't as lumpy as mine. I made them change it three times." Hugging her coat, she sat down.

The Kramers murmured some reply while Carina poured coffee. On second thought, Judith's snobbery shouldn't have surprised her. Less than a month before, the actress's television sitcom had been canceled, a show known more for loud laugh tracks and bouncing bosoms than quality scripts. Actors were an insecure lot at the best of times, but bad ratings and cancellations only made things worse. Now Judith was probably bemoaning the fact that she was in Middle America at a small run-down theater, about to earn in three weeks what she'd earned in three hours back in Hollywood.

Determined to wear Judith down with persistent courtesy, Carina held out the plate of muffins. "Would you care for one?"

Judith peered at them and wrinkled her nose. "Blueberries give me a rash, and anyway I'm on a diet." She glanced around at the others. "Why are we all sitting in here? Where's Malcolm?"

No one answered. Carina wondered why the mood in the office suddenly felt strained. It was as though Judith had not merely asked a question. She'd projected it like an actor delivering a line. Had someone missed his cue?

But that was nonsense, Carina told herself. More than likely, no one had answered because no one—herself included—knew where Malcolm was. Her imagination was simply running amok under pressure, and obviously, she still wasn't completely over her fear of dealing with a new cast.

Carina glanced at the clock on the wall. Malcolm *was* late. They should have started rehearsal by now. It wasn't exactly unheard of for Malcolm to make himself scarce at inopportune times, but this was different. A new season, an impressive cast: he should have been there strutting and preening. Nonetheless, Carina was accustomed to covering for her employer. "I'm sure he'll be here any minute," she assured them blithely, "and we're still waiting for one more cast member to arrive, so there's no hurry."

Len snorted in disgust. "Leave it to a reprobate like Malcolm Spencer to be late for his own play."

"Leonard!" his wife scolded. "A little respect, if you please, for our august playwright and director." Her sarcasm was subtle, but unmistakable. Kate's lips dallied with a smile, then she lowered her voice. "Just between us," she told the group, "Len and I would never have come back to the Myrmidon after our last experience with Malcolm, but the truth is, *Fate of the Popinjay* is simply the most wickedly brilliant play we've read in years. Of course it's incomprehensible to me that Malcolm could write anything, but who am I to question the mind of a genius?"

Judith's eyebrows lifted over her coffee cup. "Genius? Is that what you'd call Malcolm?"

Kate tipped her head. "Certainly. Wouldn't you?"

The younger woman's laugh was deep and throaty. "Why not? Let's give dear Malcolm Spencer his due. The man is clearly a genius."

Kate and Len joined in the laughter, and to Carina it seemed a harsh discordant sound. She held no great love for her egocentric employer, either, but ridiculing him behind his back was not something she could bring herself to do. When the laughter died down, she felt a sudden urgency to change the subject.

"Did all of you know each other before you came to Dunn's Pond?"

Judith delicately wiped a tear of laughter from her eye and shook her head. "Malcolm and I go way back, but I've only known the Kramers by reputation—and admired them greatly, of course. We met for the first time last night when Malcolm hosted a dinner for us in the hotel dining room."

"Oh," Carina said. "So Malcolm took you out for dinner. How nice." And how typical, she added silently. She should have expected that the Kramers and Judith Deveau would rate dinner in the town's finest establishment. Malcolm—on the pretext of his artistic obligations—could never be bothered with such mundane trivialities as operating budgets. He loved to spend the Mrymidon's money lavishly, leaving Carina to juggle a drawerful of accounts payable. Whether or not it did any good, she was going to have to waggle the budget under Malcolm's nose before his spending got out of hand. Their deficit was bad enough as it was.

"Carina," Kate said, interrupting her worrisome train of thought, "you were going to relate a tale about Sarah Bernhardt's portrait when Judith arrived. Why don't you tell us about it now?"

Nonplussed, Carina lowered her gaze. Bad enough that she'd brought up the topic at all, but now, out of context, it would sound more ridiculous than ever. "No, it was nothing really, just a couple of silly coincidences."

"But you must tell us," Kate insisted. "I do so love anything to do with life's little mysteries."

"Let her be," Len argued. "Can't you see you're embarrassing Carina?"

"Oh, please," Judith added. "Tell us your ghost story. I could use a good diversion right now."

Carina's eyes turned to the younger actress. "They're not ghost stories, Judith."

The woman shrugged a shoulder of her mink, making Carina wonder how she could wear a coat like that indoors without visibly sweltering. "Whatever it is," Judith said, "go ahead and tell us."

Carina drained the last of her coffee, reminding herself that they were just anecodotes, nothing more; there was no reason to attribute significance to them.

"All right," she conceded, "I'll tell you. The first time it happened it was last season. I came into my office one morning and found Sarah's portrait hanging crooked on the wall. Normally, I suppose I would've just straightened the picture and thought nothing of it, but when Sarah tips over at a certain angle, she looks as though she's been, well...strangled."

"Like this!" Kate exclaimed, jumping up from her seat and wrenching the portrait to the angle it had been when she'd entered the office.

Judith's eyes widened. "My God, I see what you mean. It's quite grotesque, isn't it?"

Carina tried to disregard the shudder that passed through her, but when Kate returned the portrait to its proper position, she felt an undeniable sense of relief.

"What happened when you found her like that?" Judith asked, apparently as intrigued with the tale as Kate was.

"Well, we'd been working our tails off for weeks because the governor and his wife were to visit Dunn's Pond for the first time and attend a preview performance of *Cat on a Hot Tin Roof* at the Myrmidon. Things had gone smoothly until the morning before the performance—

which was when I found Sarah hanging crooked. That day, half of our cast and crew came down with the flu, one of those instant viruses that knocks everyone flat for twenty-four hours. It was horrible.''

Kate clasped her elegant hands together. "And Sarah warned you about it. How marvelous! Tell me," she said, leaning closer, "did Malcolm fall victim to the dreaded bug?"

"He was the sickest of us all," Carina replied, "and spent the entire performance in one of the rest rooms throwing up. We had cots set up backstage for the cast so they could lie down between scenes. I don't know how we ever got through it, but somehow we did."

"I'd hardly call that portentous on Sarah's part," Len muttered. "Isn't the set designer's workshop on the other side of this wall?"

"Yes, it is," Carina said.

"Well, there you have it. The picture gets jostled by all the hammering. Simple enough, isn't it?"

Thank heaven there were still some levelheaded people left in this world, Carina thought. "I'm sure you're right, Len. As I said, they're just coincidences."

"But there have been other incidents, haven't there?" Kate said, refusing to let the matter drop.

"Only one," Carina reluctantly admitted. She got up to offer them more coffee, but everyone declined. She poured herself a second cup anyway, knowing she'd soon regret the extra caffeine.

"Are you going to keep us in suspense forever?" Judith asked. "What else happened?"

Carina sighed and gave a tight smile. *Humor them,* she grumbled to herself; *just tell the story.* Then everyone could forget about it and get on with the business of theater. "Last spring, I was working at my desk one morning when Malcolm came in. He was furious about something or other—I don't remember what—and suddenly he noticed that the portrait was crooked. I hadn't realized it because, as you can see, when I'm at my desk, my back is toward the picture. But I was so annoyed at being interrupted that I said something foolish, like you'd better watch what you say because Sarah has a way of predicting trouble. He thought that was a great joke, and that afternoon he drove his car into a tree. He needed forty stitches to his head." Lamely, Carina chuckled.

This time, the reaction was total silence. Kate and Len and Judith exchanged meaningful glances.

"It was just a coincidence!" Carina cried out. "Malcolm drives like a maniac. It was bound to happen to him sooner or later."

"Yes, of course, dear, you're absolutely right," Kate said soothingly, patting Carina's hand. "But what about this morning? I take it you walked into your office and found her like this again, a third time, no less."

Carina could have kicked herself for not taking the dumb old picture off the wall entirely. She nodded in response to Kate's question. "Though nothing unusual has happened."

"So we ought to prepare ourselves for some sort of ill fortune," the actress intoned as she played with the ends of her long silk scarf. "I wonder which of us it will be. Perhaps that explains Malcolm's absence—"

"That's enough, Katherine!" Len shouted in a surprising display of temper. "I insist we change the subject at once. The last thing any of us needs is groundless paranoia." He got to his feet and began pacing the office. "What the devil is keeping Malcolm and Damian? We ought to be getting started."

"What did you say, Len?" Carina thought she must have heard wrong.

"I said we ought to be getting started."

"No, before that. I thought you mentioned the name Damian."

He looked at her oddly. "Certainly I did. There are four of us in the play, and Damian Fleming is the fourth. Why would you ask about that?"

Carina glanced expectantly around, waiting for one of them to deliver a punch line. But no one did, and she didn't like the uneasy feeling she was getting in her stomach. "Tim Myers was the other actor cast in the play," she insisted. "I typed up the contract myself."

"Who's Tim Myers?" Judith asked. "He wasn't with us last night."

"I haven't the foggiest," Kate said.

"He's an actor from Chicago," Carina explained. "He's played at the Myrmidon twice before, and audiences love him." There was no reason for her to defend Tim's acting abilities, except that the others were staring at her as if they found her hopelessly ill informed—or somewhat dim. She felt the unmistakable stirrings of anxiety as she stammered out, "This is one of Malcolm's practical jokes, isn't it? You're supposed to tell me Damian Fleming showed up, but Tim's actually here, right?" *Answer me, somebody.*

Len put a hand on her shoulder. "Kate and I would never stoop to involve ourselves in one of Malcolm's pranks, my dear."

"Of course we wouldn't," his wife assured her.

Carina's eyes moved to Judith who raised her hands and said, "Don't look at me. I had nothing to do with it."

"This is ridiculous." Carina stood up and fluttered her hands through the air in a display of nervousness. "Damian Fleming would never come to Dunn's Pond...and even if he did, I'd know about it. Who am I kidding—the whole world would know about it!''

The lack of response from the others made Carina suddenly aware of how shrill she sounded. But in a case like this, she was surely entitled to hysteria. *Damian Fleming?* He was considered by many to be the finest dramatic actor alive. And he was no more likely to walk into this theater than was the president of the United States. Carina prided herself on always being prepared for any of the emergencies and eventualities of theatrical life. But this was unheard of! *Damian Fleming* at the Myrmidon? And everyone but Carina seemed to know about it. What had Malcolm perpetrated this time?

"I can't imagine how..." she mumbled ineffectually.

"It's all right, dear," Kate consoled. "I'm sure there's a perfectly logical explanation that Malcolm will offer the moment he arrives. In the meantime, try not to worry about it. Damian seemed quite comfortably settled in the hotel last night, and he's a delightful fellow. I'm certain you'll get on with him splendidly."

"But I should've—" she wailed.

The creak and thump of the front door swinging open silenced Carina. Which was just as well, she thought wryly. She'd have begun to babble in a hopeless effort to draw attention away from her scarlet face. Malcolm had taken pleasure in debasing her with his pranks before, but this was the worst. Humiliating her in front of the cast—she'd never forgive him this time.

But it wasn't Malcolm's booted feet crossing the lobby. Malcolm didn't walk; he shuffled, and this was a self-assured male stride. The footsteps came to a halt at the counter, and there was a sudden aura of tension in the office. Judith was staring fixedly at the new arrival. The Kramers were staring at Carina, no doubt awaiting her reaction. She couldn't postpone the inevitable for much longer, but Carina had the sudden inane feeling that if she concentrated very hard, she might turn around and discover Tim Myers standing there.

Seconds ticked away, or perhaps they only seemed to. With great force of will, Carina turned around and in the space of an instant, she was sixteen years old all over again. There in the flesh was the man whose initials she used to inscribe in her diary with pink ink and hearts, the man whose posters used to line her bedroom wall, who had filled her vague adolescent dreams with passion and romance.

It was preposterous. It was impossible. *But there stood Damian Fleming.*

Chapter Two

Reality had a harsh way of shattering even the best-rehearsed fantasies. It was supposed to have happened on an enchanted evening in a crowded room. Damian would be in black tie and tails, of course, and Carina would be wearing some frothy strapless creation, her shoulder-length hair wafting in the breeze, just so. Their eyes would meet, and the world would fade away. Damian would thrust his Manhattan into the hands of his unsuspecting date and cross the room boldly, parting the crowd that surged around them. He would take Carina into his arms, gaze into her eyes and murmur—

"Is something wrong?"

Carina started at the sound of his deep resonant voice and blinked several times. "Um...I, uh...w-why do you ask?"

"You look as though you're staring at a ghost."

Her blood pressure shifted into overdrive, and she blushed, hard. "Aren't I? I mean, I...that is, er—" Carina cleared her throat and gave up. What was she supposed to say, and what on earth was going on?

Mercifully, Kate stepped in to save her. "Apparently there's been some sort of a mix-up," she told Damian.

"Carina had been expecting another actor to arrive, and your sudden appearance has caught her off guard."

"I see." He turned vivid slate-blue eyes back to Carina. "Hasn't Malcolm explained things to you?"

"I . . . uh, I haven't seen Malcolm since Friday," she replied, grateful that her stammers were subsiding.

Damian might have stepped off the set of a period piece. His dark blond hair, longer than current fashion trends, curled at the collar and fell across a high broad forehead as if raked by impatient fingers. In the windowless lobby of the Myrmidon were no arc lights to soften the chiseled lines of his face; he wore no layers of theatrical makeup to mask the hollows beneath his cheekbones. He was undeniably handsome—genetic good luck had seen to that—but he looked as though he hadn't slept in days. There was stubble on his chin, and his eyes were bleary. His haggard physical state merely added to Carina's confusion. What was he doing there, looking like a highwayman fresh from a night of plunder?

"Our dear director hasn't shown up yet." Judith's voice cut rudely through Carina's musings. "What do you make of that?"

Damian arched an eyebrow, his smile cynical. "Hasn't he? Isn't that strange, considering Malcolm so specifically instructed us to arrive promptly?"

"Excuse me if I sound obtuse," Carina blurted out, "but it seems to me that Malcolm's tardiness is hardly matter for concern. He isn't that late yet. What I would like is for someone to explain to me why the Myrmidon has been blessed with the unexpected presence of Mr. Fleming."

"Damian," he corrected. "And your name is?"

Carina brought a self-conscious hand to her throat to finger the locket that should have been there, but wasn't. "M-me? Oh, I'm Carina Rawlins, Malcolm's assistant."

"Ah, yes, I have heard a great deal about you."

"You have?" Such a remark coming from a man like Damian was more than a little heady. "From whom?" her skeptical side wanted to know.

"From Malcolm. I should've recognized you at once from his description of you. Hair the color of cinnamon, a sprinkle of freckles across a perfect nose. Now, he described your eyes as being the color of amontillado sherry, but I'd be more inclined to compare them to Calvados, a fine, fiery apple brandy." His gaze danced lightly over her face, not quite mocking, not quite challenging, but disturbing somehow.

Time had faded Carina's earlier raging blush to a faint bloom, but inside she was a torrent of emotions. It would be so easy to let herself respond to this gorgeous man's flattery. She considered herself reasonably attractive, but she was hardly the kind of woman men wrote sonnets about. So why was he suddenly waxing poetic? And he still hadn't explained what he was doing at the Myrmidon.

Carina gave up trying to think of a suitable response to Calvados and decided instead to deal with the unresolved problem at hand. With a hint of desperation, she yanked open a desk drawer, relieved to find the file folder exactly where she'd left it the week before. She pulled it out and riffled through the yellow sheets of legal-size paper.

"Yes, here it is, a contract for Timothy Myers to play the part of Jasper Garnet in *Fate of the Popinjay*." She jabbed her finger emphatically at the signature on the dotted line. "Signed and delivered." She looked up, and as she met Damian's unyielding expression, she realized how completely futile it was to insist on legalities when Tim was obviously nowhere near the Myrmidon, and Damian was standing right in front of her.

Despite the whiskers and the red-rimmed eyes, he didn't appear the least bit ruffled. "I can understand your confusion, but I assure you there's a simple explanation."

She exhaled slowly. "I hoped there would be."

"Malcolm and I have known each other a long time."

Carina's mouth dropped open. "You have? I didn't know that!"

For a moment it seemed as though Damian didn't believe her. His eyes narrowed and turned dark, piercing, but then the look subsided and he was coolly self-possessed once more. "We were young starving actors sharing a loft in Greenwich Village when *Fate of the Popinjay* came into being. I imagine Malcolm must have forgotten how much I'd always wanted to play the role of Jasper, because when he finally got around to producing it, he called someone else—namely, this Myers fellow."

"But you live in England," Carina said in her employer's defense. "It probably wouldn't even occur to Malcolm to ask you after all these years, and even if he did, he might have been too intimidated. After all, your careers have diverged a bit." Who would have believed that she'd someday be defending Malcolm? Not even Malcolm himself, she thought with wry amusement.

"Perhaps you're right," he conceded.

"How did you learn he was even doing the play?"

Damian's shrug was noncommittal. "Theater's actually quite a small world. I must have heard about it somewhere or other in passing. When I phoned Malcolm and told him how much I'd like to have a part in it, he was quite cooperative. We made arrangements for Tim to get another suitable role...and here I am. It was all quite simple, really."

Almost too simple, Carina thought. Thanks to a relentless and adoring press, she knew almost all there was to know about Damian's professional life—not to mention a fair bit of the private stuff. American by birth and upbringing, he'd risen to fame in the early days of television as a handsome young lawyer on the side of the underdog. Later he'd moved to England to train in classical drama, soon astounding the critics with his perceptive interpretations of the great Shakespearean roles. By then he was free to choose only the parts that appealed to him, moving with ease between film, stage and television. In addition to acting, the forty-one-year-old actor was artistic director of his own theater in London's West End, a small but typically successful enterprise.

His explanation of why he'd come to Dunn's Pond wasn't in itself so implausible—except that this was Damian Fleming. Any other moderately successful stage actor might vie ambitiously for a role at the Myrmidon, but not a mega-star like him. He would arrive, it seemed to Carina, with fanfare and publicity, or not arrive at all.

"Aren't you going to find it terribly anticlimactic to play for small Midwest audiences?" she couldn't help asking.

His grin, a combination of dry wit and roguishness, was the very one that turned her knees to jelly in all the movies she'd ever seen him in. "I think I'll find it a wonderful change of pace, an escape. And, needless to say, it will give me a chance to become reacquainted with my old friend Malcolm."

Carina studied his drawn face, his guileless smile, but she knew she was wasting her energy. One thing she'd learned over the years was that you could seldom tell what an actor was thinking. You only saw what he wanted you to see. And, doubtless, Damian would be a consummate master at that game.

She should have been ecstatic, considering how dull life in Dunn's Pond could be, to have a celebrity—her forever idol—in their midst. But she wasn't. Everything felt so awkward, so off balance somehow.

Damian must have sensed her discomfiture. "If it would make you feel better, I can go back to my hotel room and get the copy of my contract. Malcolm sent it to me air-express last week."

Carina's ever-practical business side told her it would be prudent to verify the legalities of the casting change—it might even dispel these unsettling feelings of hers—but the star-struck swooning teenager inside told her to forget it. One did not ask Damian Fleming, of all people, to prove that he had the right to be in a shabby small-town theater like the Myrmidon, of all places. "No, it's not necessary," she said. "If you think of it, you can bring it in some other day, but—"

"I'll do that."

"But what I don't understand," she pressed on to say, "is why Malcolm didn't tell me about the change in casting, especially since I'm the one who always draws up the contracts."

"Perhaps he wanted to surprise you," Kate suggested.

Carina turned to the older woman, who was smiling complacently at her. She realized that no one else seemed the least disturbed by this turn of events.

"Perhaps he did," Carina said quietly, though she knew it was highly unlikely. Anyway, these were not the people with whom she ought to be discussing the matter, nor was this the place. But the very instant Malcolm Spencer poked his head through that door, he was going to get dragged by the ear to some private corner where he'd be forced to explain the whole story word for word! She'd taken all she could from that man.

"What does a person have to do to get a cup of that fantastic-smelling coffee?" Damain asked.

Resigning herself to the situation, Carina pointed toward the entrance of her office. A moment later, when Damian sauntered in through the doorway, she felt an irrepressible urge to stumble back a step or two. He was even more overwhelming close up than she thought he'd be, a tall man with a strong rangy build. His well-worn leather coat was full-length and hung open to reveal a fisherman's knit sweater and tight faded jeans tucked into dusty riding boots. Carina's quiet gasp, she knew all too well, was purely physical; it was the same reaction she experienced every time she saw him on screen.

His thighs were what always did her in. The visual media had provided ample evidence of Damian's flawless physique, but Carina was hopelessly fixated on those long, lean, muscled, incredibly sexy thighs. She could forget the plot and everything else when his thighs were displayed. Now, suddenly, here they were, so close she could reach out and touch them. Not that she'd ever dare—he probably sizzled on contact.

Instead, she picked up a cup and saucer, which started to rattle in her hand as if there were an earthquake. She grasped them quickly with a second hand and asked, "How do you like your coffee?"

Damian looked down at her shaking hands and, almost as though he'd issued some silent instruction, they suddenly went still. Then his gaze moved slowly upward, pausing at the feminine curves of her breasts beneath the blouse of topaz silk. When his eyes met hers and held, he said in a husky voice, "Black...please."

He took the coffee she handed him, thanked her and sat down to chat with the others. Carina listened to their conversation, which was mostly about the play, but she was listening less to the words themselves than to the way they were spoken. Judith and the Kramers must have worked with Damian before; there was no other explanation for the camaraderie between them, the kind one generally found among actors who'd been rehearsing together for weeks.

Damian seemed much more modest than she'd have expected; he seemed almost self-effacing, in fact, with no apparent need to flaunt his status. Yet the man could and did command millions of dollars for his film roles and television appearances. Carina remembered reading that he only rarely abandoned his own theater to do stage work for another company, and this was what continued to trouble her. If he needed a break, if he craved anonymity, why not rent a secluded villa, charter a yacht? Why take on a role in an unknown play in Dunn's Pond, Illinois? And if he and Malcolm were such great friends, why had Malcolm—an inveterate name-dropper—never mentioned him? That last unanswered question in particular lodged itself in Carina's mind like a burr, and she couldn't shake it. If only Malcolm would show up. What could possibly be keeping him?

Just when she'd decided to call Malcolm's apartment, Len stood up and stretched his arms. "If you folks don't mind, I'd like to rest awhile until our director arrives. Could you show us to our dressing rooms, Carina?"

Her hand still on the phone, she got up. "Yes, certainly." She decided to call later in the morning, and actually it did seem wiser to wait until she got the actors comfortably settled—and out of earshot. What she planned to say to Malcolm was best said in privacy.

As Carina led the four of them down the hall, she pondered the dilemma of dressing rooms. Assigning them involved a pecking order that was every bit as complex as army logistics. The bigger the star, the bigger the room; failing that, it was age before beauty, and so on. The Myrmidon had only three dressing rooms: one of star quality and two that were little more than broom closets. When the cast was large, other arrangements were made, with workshops doubling as dressing rooms, but this time she'd had no advance warning. The Kramers had to have the larger room, since it was the only one that could accommodate two people. Judith and Tim would have been given the small rooms, but now there was Damian. She didn't want to offend him by asking him to put up with a cubbyhole, but for the time being there wasn't much else she could do.

As it turned out, Damian wasn't the problem. The Kramers were quite happy with their dressing room, but when Carina brought Judith to hers, the actress let out a wail of protest.

"You can't possibly expect me to use this gloomy little niche!" Judith's mink was draped over her arm as she stood outside the room in an attitude of stubborn defiance. "My coat won't even fit in there."

Carina was terribly tempted to remind Judith that fur coats were seldom needed in Dunn's Pond in September. But a remark like that was out of the question. For one thing, Carina preferred to maintain congenial relations with the actors, and sarcasm hardly served her purpose. For another, Judith obviously still thought of herself as a star, and stars did like their trappings.

"I know it's small," Carina tried to explain, "but—"

"Small! It's microscopic! If I had known things were going to be this primitive, I'd never have bothered coming."

Damian stood a short distance away, and from the corner of her eye Carina could see that he winced every time

Judith's voice reached a shrill pitch. Inexplicably, Carina found that amusing, even though the situation was far from funny.

"Why don't you let Judith have my dressing room?" Damian suggested.

Carina smiled at him wanly. "Because yours is exactly the same size as hers," she explained, waiting for the explosion. None came. Carina pushed open the adjacent door to reveal the matching closet-size room and watched as Damian stepped inside.

"They're adjoining," he called out.

"Yes, they are," Carina replied.

He came back into the narrow hallway. "Let Judith have both rooms and pretend it's a suite." He smiled at the actress, who seemed to have lost her belligerence. "Is that all right with you?"

"Well, it's certainly better than the original arrangement."

He spread out his hands in satisfaction. "Then it's settled."

"But where will you go?" Carina asked, surprised to discover her authority so neatly undermined.

"Why don't you let me camp out in Malcolm's office for now? Does he have a sofa?"

"Yes, but—"

"Then I'm sure he won't mind if I borrow it for a while. I just need a place to recover from a massive dose of jet lag."

Carina didn't immediately answer him. Too much had happened too fast, and her head was muddled as she tried to anticipate Malcolm's reaction—would he mind if she allowed Damian to use his office? But then, so what if he did? Dammit, after all the confusion he'd caused so far, it was the least he could put up with.

She looked at Damian, who seemed to be aware of her every thought; there was such probing intensity in the way he was watching her. Or was it just that he was a born observer of people, the kind of person destined to be a great actor, a great director? She'd never been this close to someone so highly revered in the theatrical profession, and the experience was strangely bewildering. She had an idea that when Damian Fleming wanted something, a person would be hard pressed to refuse him.

"Follow me," she said. "I'll take you to Malcolm's office."

BY NOON, Carina was genuinely worried about Malcolm. She had called his apartment numerous times, but there was no answer. She called the diner where he ate breakfast every day, but he hadn't been in, they said. She talked to the wardrobe mistress, the set designer, the stage manager; no one in the crew had seen or heard from Malcolm since Friday.

The only person she hadn't talked to was Gerry, the property master, because she'd hoped to run into him in the halls or the auditorium or on the stage. She hadn't, which meant she had to go down to the props room to find him.

The sound of Carina's heels clicking across the floorboards of the stage echoed through the empty auditorium. She came to the trapdoor at center stage that was camouflaged, except for a small iron ring recessed into the wood. She tried knocking on the door, first with her knuckles, then with the heel of her shoe, but it was no use. Gerry would never hear her.

With a sigh, she lifted the heavy wooden door to rest against its hinges. "Gerry, are you down there?" She listened carefully for a moment, but didn't hear an answering shout. "Okay, okay," she muttered, gathering her pleated skirt and lowering one leg onto the top step.

As soon as both feet were on the stairs, Carina firmly grasped the edges of the doorframe. She wasn't particularly claustrophobic, but the stairs to Gerry's storeroom were steep and rickety, and the lighting was terrible. She'd ruined at least three pairs of panty hose on the rough wooden steps and snagged a hand-knit sweater on an errant nail. Paying social visits to Gerry was simply too hard on her wardrobe.

She descended the stairs carefully, holding on to the stage floor as long as she could. There was no railing and when she let go to take the last few steps, her hand swept through a thick cobweb. "Oh, how disgusting," she muttered, trying to shake off the sticky fibers.

Gerry was nowhere to be seen amid the clutter of props. Recessed nooks held floor-to-ceiling shelves crammed with everything imaginable. There were dishes and books and footstools, dressmakers' dummies and hat racks and mannequins. It would have looked like complete confusion to anyone except Gerry.

Carina could hear him rustling something in the back room that he used for cleaning props. She'd give him a minute; maybe he'd come out soon. Meanwhile, she paused to examine an ornate antique wheelchair, made of rattan and equipped with a fascinating recliner mechanism. It squeaked when she pushed the back down, but otherwise, the chair was still in remarkably good condition.

Gerry came through the door of his workroom and grinned when he saw her. "Hello, Carina, it's been a while since you've been down here to visit."

She smiled affectionately at the bandy-legged little man. He'd worked at the theater since she was a little girl, and she used to defend him against other children who called him a troll. He was odd, a little deaf, but harmless. "Hi, Gerry," she said, being sure to speak loudly. "This is quite a chair. Where did you find it?"

"At a flea market across the border. It's the second one, actually. Malcolm wanted an antique wheelchair for the play, and I got him one, but then he said he needed one that reclined. I tell ya, I had some trouble finding it. Had to pitch the other one." Gerry was carrying a stuffed owl in his arms. "Whaddya think of this beauty? I've waited twenty-eight years for the chance to use her in a play; I was just in back cleaning her up."

Carina thought the bird looked rather moth-eaten, but she'd never tell him that. Gerry was as protective of his props as other people were of their pets.

"He looks quite…wise," she finally answered, for lack of anything better to say.

"Yeah, I think so, too. Was there something you wanted to see me about?"

"Yes, I've been looking for Malcolm all morning, and I was wondering if you'd seen him."

Gerry's mouth turned down in a pout. "Why would you wonder that? Him and me don't exactly get along."

That was an understatement, if ever there was one. Malcolm treated Gerry with appalling rudeness, as he did anyone whom he didn't consider his intellectual or artistic peer. Carina wished she'd had some other reason for coming down.

"I know that, Gerry, but I thought you might have run into him somewhere…on the way to work, maybe."

Gerry stroked the feathers of his owl and shook his head. "I ain't seen him."

"Okay, thanks anyway. I'm sorry to bother you about it, but I am starting to worry." She turned to go, then paused. "Do you like blueberry muffins?"

The little man grinned. "Sure."

"Then come up to my office for coffee this afternoon, and I'll save you some."

Carina was relieved to reach the top of the stairs without a single snagged thread, cobweb or run in her stockings, but she was also feeling increasingly uneasy about Malcolm.

What if he didn't show up? What if he just disappeared from the face of the earth, never to be seen again? She tried out the supposition as if it were an alien taste on her tongue. Her reaction came as a shock. If Malcolm didn't show up, she'd be free to run the theater herself, the way it ought to be run. Everyone on the board of directors liked her; they wouldn't hesitate to make her Myrmidon's artistic director. She'd do a much better job than he ever had, and she'd finally get the credit she knew she deserved. No more of Malcolm's nagging, no more tirades, no more of his bumbling mismanagement to repair—it'd be heaven! Then, scarcely recognizing the galloping thoughts as her own, Carina promptly reined them in. What a horrible, ungrateful reaction! Malcolm Spencer could be lying sick or injured somewhere, and all she could think about was how wonderful life would be without him!

THE ARTISTIC DIRECTOR'S OFFICE revealed less attention to harmony than Carina's. The desk and chairs were mismatched, and a layer of dust had settled over the cluttered wall unit. Damian closed the door firmly behind him and studied the room with interest. It had the look and feel of Malcolm Spencer, he thought—his harried, almost tormented way of coping with life.

Damian crossed the room to a cluster of framed photographs arranged on a low table. They were all of Malcolm; in each, he was posing with someone illustrious or renowned. There were actors, writers, even a politician or two.

"What's the matter?" Damian said to the likeness of his old friend. "Am I not famous enough to rate a place in your collection?" The dark-haired, mustachioed man seemed to stare defiantly back at him from the photograph.

Damian's mind churned with long-forgotten memories. He and Malcolm had grown up holy terrors in an eastern steel town, their friendship based on a shared and burning passion to escape the fate of their fathers. They had no intention of growing up to work in a foundry, work that sucked the lifeblood from a man, made him old before his time. They were going to turn the world upside down, Malcolm used to say, grow rich and famous by their wits and thumb their noses at the rabble once they'd done it.

Looking back, Damian could almost laugh at the course they'd set for themselves and at the way their lives had turned out—if only there was humor in any of it. Granted, he could now afford to buy whatever he wanted. Except for the things that couldn't be bought, the things that really mattered, like the loyalty of a true friend, a woman who could look beyond his name, the luxury of walking down a street unrecognized.

He drew back the curtain from the window and gazed out on an abandoned railyard littered with rusting boxcars, its terminal building boarded up and neglected. It was nothing like the view of the Thames River he enjoyed from his own theater in London, a city vibrant with culture and sophistication. Damian found the contrast suddenly disquieting and released the curtain.

Had the years of struggle, the uncertainty and loneliness been worth it? Finding no answers, Damian shrugged
and turned away. At this stage in his life, he hardly thought
about his achievements anymore. He tried to measure
success in other, simpler ways. Perhaps that was what it
meant to grow up. Funny how some people, like Malcolm, never did.

But enough of this maudlin reminiscing. He hadn't
come all this way to wallow in nostalgia. Spotting a collection of liquor bottles on one of the wall-unit shelves,
Damian lifted the bottle of Chivas Regal and poured himself a glass. He sniffed it and shook his head with a rueful
smile. Leave it to Malcolm to pass off cheap Scotch as the
real thing. Nevertheless, he picked up the glass and walked
toward Malcolm's desk. He sat down, then began me-
thodically opening the drawers. In a matter of minutes,
he'd found what he was looking for—the director's copy
of *Fate of the Popinjay*. It was no longer the original, but
he really hadn't expected it to be. He thumbed quickly
through the script, pausing now and again to read Malcolm's notes.

There would have to be some changes made, especially
in the blocking. Malcolm had the characters moving
around too much in the first and third acts, blurring the
entire focus of the play. Watching Malcolm's version, the
audience would miss the needle-sharp dialogue, the sub-
tler aspects of characterization seen in an arched eyebrow, the nervous drumming of an actor's fingers. Instead
of the satire it was meant to be, the play would sink to the
level of crude slapstick.

Damian tossed the script onto the desk and folded his
hands behind his head. Then, in a reckless flash of inspiration, he leaned forward to read the list of telephone
numbers on a desk pad. When he found what he was

looking for, he picked up the receiver and dialed three digits that would connect him with an extension down the hall.

The intercom buzzer sounded only once before a person on the other end answered. "Hello?"

"It's me," Damian said. "Just checking to see if you're settled in all right."

"Oh, yes, everything's just fine. How about you?"

Damian leaned back and put his feet up on the desk. "Things couldn't be better. I'm sitting at Malcolm's desk, drinking his cheap Scotch, script in hand. I always knew I wouldn't regret this."

"I wouldn't be too optimistic yet." The voice on the other end was tense. "In fact, I don't think you should be on the phone like this. Someone might be listening in."

"So what? Let them listen." Damian swirled the pale amber liquid around in the glass. "Everyone's going to find out what's happened soon enough."

"But if they find out too soon, it could ruin everything for you. Slow down, Damian. You've waited all these years; a few more days aren't going to hurt."

"You're right," the actor replied. "I am getting ahead of myself. But what about Malcolm's expression when I walked into that hotel dining room last night? Was it priceless?"

The person on the other end laughed softly. "For a minute, I thought he was going to take a bite out of his glass. I've never seen a man look so terrified. But, Damian—"

"I know, I know. I shouldn't be talking about it. Anyway, I thought I'd let you know that I'm going to wait until this afternoon before offering my services as the new director of *Fate of the Popinjay*. It won't seem quite so obvious."

"That's a good idea. Now you get some rest." The voice was stern, but unmistakably tender.

Damian promised that he would and hung up the phone. Who was it who'd said revenge was a dish that should be eaten cold? Whoever said it was right. He'd waited for the first fires of anger to die down, waited long years for his bitterness to cool. And now, revenge was pure and sweet. Never in his life had he tasted anything quite so delectable.

Chapter Three

Before leaving her office, Carina slid the wooden partition across the counter. It was nearly two in the afternoon, and still no word from Malcolm. She was more certain than ever that something had happened to him, and though she didn't particularly like the idea of going to his apartment alone, she had no choice. Everyone else wanted to take full advantage of the opportunity to work without the artistic director breathing down their necks.

As she was walking out the front door she nearly bumped into Gwendolyn Dunn Pennell. Carina's first instinct, as usual, was to look the other way and pretend not to see her. But it was too late; Gwen was already plucking at Carina's coat sleeve.

"I'm so glad I caught you before you left!" Gwen exclaimed, her voice slightly breathless, her pale eyes saucers.

Carina made a production of looking at her wristwatch. "Actually, I'm in a bit of a hurry—"

"But I simply have to talk to you...it can't wait...I shouldn't even be here, but I had to come and warn you." The frenzied words poured from Gwen's mouth in one nonstop sentence.

Carina pulled her arm out of Gwen's grasp and tried to summon tolerance. It wasn't really Gwen's fault that she aroused irritation in people instead of friendship. Heaven knew she meant well.

As the sole surviving descendant of Patrick Dunn, the town's founding father, Gwen should have had everything going for her. She'd attended the best schools, traveled extensively, been tutored in deportment, music, dance. But despite her pedigreed upbringing, Gwen was graceless and awkward, and part of the problem was her appearance. Designer fashions hung slackly from her gaunt frame, and cosmetics did nothing to soften the flat, uninteresting planes of her face. Her only saving grace was her position on the theater's board of directors, since she was devoted to the Myrmidon and regularly donated substantial sums of money.

It was a shameful fact, but the only way Carina could put up with more than a few minutes of Gwen's company was by reminding herself that the woman was their most important benefactor. "All right, Gwen, what did you want to tell me?"

Gwen's eyes darted around the lobby. "Couldn't we talk someplace more private?"

Carina knew that if she invited Gwen back to her office, she'd never persuade her to leave. "There's no one here but us. You can talk."

The woman glanced around the lobby and shifted nervously, obviously unconvinced. "Well, I guess if you're sure, but promise you won't tell my husband I was here. He'd kill me if he found out I told you anything."

"I won't tell a soul," Carina promised. "What's the problem?"

Gwen spoke in a conspiratorial whisper. "Harland wants to shut down the theater."

Harland, Gwen's husband, was her only success in life, if one could call him that. A slick Southern boy, he'd blown into town twelve years before, and in a remarkably short space of time, had swept Gwendolyn Dunn off her large, ungainly feet. No one had expected the marriage to last, but Harland was no fool. By marrying Gwen, he landed a trainee's job in her daddy's bank, and when the old man died ten years later, the position of bank president plopped, oh so neatly, into Harland's waiting lap.

Carina tried not to show her impatience. "Is that all? He's always wanted to shut us down."

Gwen twisted the belt of her cloth coat around a bony finger. "No, this time he really means it. He's had an offer, and they want to demolish the Myrmidon to—"

"Wait a minute," Carina cut in. "Did you say demolish? He can't do that!"

"Yes, he can. You know the bank has the power to call in your loan anytime."

"But the Myrmidon's a landmark," Carina protested loudly. "It's over a hundred years old. He'll never get away with tearing it down; the townspeople will fight him tooth and nail."

Gwen's facial muscles were moving with odd little jerks, no doubt in her effort to look sympathetic. "I wish I could say you were right, Carina, but the people in this town need jobs. Most of your patrons are people who drive in from Chicago, and they can always find other theaters to go to. But people in this town don't care about culture; they're only interested in getting regular paychecks."

"Yes, but once they have jobs, they'll want to go to the theater again, and if we let them tear down the Myrmidon, it'll be too late."

Gwen didn't answer, and her silence hit Carina like a blow to the stomach because she knew that Gwen was right. Ever since the two remaining mines had closed down and the railroad was diverted, the town had lost much of its vitality. In the past year alone, two restaurants had closed, along with the cinema and a gas station. Last she'd heard, nearly twenty families had moved away in search of work.

She had to brace herself to ask the next question. "What was the offer your husband got, Gwen?"

"It's for a shopping mall, the largest in northern Illinois. There'll be hundreds of stores, a skating rink, a children's zoo, a—"

"I get the idea," Carina said resignedly. "How soon is it supposed to happen?"

"I don't know exactly, but I expect Harland will call you in the next day or so." At the mention of her husband, Gwen's eyes grew large. "Don't forget, you have to act surprised when he tells you, otherwise he'll know I've been talking to you."

Carina nodded in understanding. "Don't worry, I won't let on a thing. But it seems to me you've taken a big risk telling me at all. I know how...well, how difficult your husband can be at times. Maybe you shouldn't be involved at all."

The woman looked away. "I love this theater as much as you do, and besides, I—well, let's just say, I have my reasons."

Gwen's loyalty was touching, but it did nothing to relieve the growing knot of tension in Carina's stomach. She moved toward the door with leaden steps. "I appreciate your coming, Gwen, but frankly I'm not sure it will do any good."

"Wait! Don't go yet! Tell me, is it true? Is Damian Fleming really here in Dunn's Pond?"

At first, Carina felt like shrieking at the woman for bringing up something so irrelevant when she had Malcolm's absence and the closing of the theater to worry about. But then she put herself in Gwen's position, and her heart softened. The woman worked hard for the theater; the least Carina could do was offer her a private audience with the resident sex symbol.

"Come on, Gwen—" she began, but clamped her mouth shut when she heard the floorboards squeak loudly in the hall around the corner.

Gwen flinched like a frightened rabbit. "I knew someone was listening!"

Carina darted to the corridor entrance in time to find Judith Deveau slinking along the wall, her face set in a grimace as she tried to make a noiseless retreat.

"Was there something I could do for you, Judith?" Carina asked, hands folded across her midriff.

The woman stopped dead in her tracks, turned to face Carina and hunched up her shoulders in embarrassed apology. "Squeaky darned floors, aren't they?" she quipped.

Carina didn't smile; she was in no mood to humor anyone. "You were eavesdropping," she said bluntly. "Why?"

Judith's nails looked like scarlet bullets as they waved through the air. "No, I wasn't—I mean, I know how it must have looked, but I...what I really intended to do was come down and find out if you'd heard anything from Malcolm. Then I realized you were having a private conversation, so I tried to go back to my dressing room without disturbing you."

Gwen took a hop-skip to Carina's side and glared at Judith. "Don't you mean you tried to sneak back?"

Carina looked at Gwen in surprise. The viciousness of the remark was quite uncharacteristic for the normally unassertive Mrs. Pennell, and apparently Judith had taken strong exception to it. The actress tossed her dark hair and tapped a stiletto-heeled pump on the floor in an indignant rhythm. "Listen here, you, I can't help it if you choose to have your so-called private conversations in the middle of a public lobby! I'm not a criminal. Unfortunately, I'm working here for the time being!"

Gwen blanched, but stood her ground. "How much did you hear?"

"I don't know," Judith snapped. "Most of it, I suppose, but hey—your financial problems are the least of my concerns, as long as I get the few measly bucks spelled out in my contract."

Carina placed a restraining hand on Gwen's arm. "Let's not make an issue of it. Judith's right; the theater's problems are of no interest to her, and I'm sure she'll keep whatever she heard to herself."

Her dignity restored, Judith was once again the haughty television star. She spun around on one foot and sashayed back to her dressing room without another word. But the set of her shoulders told Carina that the next little while with Judith might be very trying indeed.

"What's someone like her doing in a place like this?" Gwen hissed, her face pinched in anger. "I don't like her one bit."

"Don't be too hard on her, Gwen," Carina said as she led the way to Damian's office. "Her ego's undergone some battering lately, so we'll just have to be patient." Still, she admitted to herself Gwen had a point. Carina had been so busy wondering why Damian had come, and where Malcolm was, that she hadn't really stopped to think about Judith. There were literally thousands of starving stage actors out there who would kill for a role, no matter how poor the pay or how run-down the theater. And even though Judith was unemployed, she could have found work in Las Vegas or Atlantic City, someplace that appreciated her glitz. What kind of hold did Malcolm have on the woman that would bring her to the Myrmidon, of all places?

The agenda for her next meeting with Malcolm was growing by leaps and bounds, but Carina pushed this latest puzzle to the back of her mind as she came to the door of Damian's—or should she say, Malcolm's—office. She was about to knock when she heard loud rumbling snores emanating from the other side.

"He's asleep, Gwen. I don't want to wake him."

The woman bounced up and down on her toes like an aging teenybopper. "Oh, please, Carina, just this once! I would die for a chance to look at Damian Fleming close up."

"There'll be plenty of opportunities. He's here for over three weeks—"

"But he'll be busy! Please?"

Gwen's expression was so pitiful Carina couldn't bring herself to refuse. She hoped Damian wouldn't bite their heads off; the poor man had just flown all the way from England.

"I'll knock once , but if he doesn't wake up, that's it. We can't afford to have the whole cast furious at us."

Carina knocked , and the somnolent splutters gave way to shallower snores, then stopped altogether. She had to suppress a smile. Somehow she'd never imagined her idol engaging in something as human as snoring; it was an oddly reassuring sound.

She could hear Damian mutter in a thick sleepy voice and cross the room with heavy footsteps. Then the door swung open, and he stood there, staring numbly.

It seemed as though a gust of wind had come and whisked away the last traces of Carina's self-consciousness. How could anyone be intimidated by a man with sleepy blue eyes, rumpled hair and a chevron pattern pressed onto one cheek?

"Hi," he mumbled, scratching his head. "I was studying lines."

Impulsively Carina lifted her hand to his cheek. "Yes, I can see that. The lines match the ones on Malcolm's couch perfectly."

His responding smile was rakish as his hand caught hers and held it against his face. "You dare to jest with me, sunshine?"

Sunshine? What an endearing name, Carina thought vaguely. But most of her attention was drawn to her palm, pressed warmly against his lean, whiskered cheek. When he released his hold, a moment later, and her hand fell to her side, Carina felt curiously bereft.

"I really was studying lines," he insisted. "It's a form of self-hypnosis. I read them over a few times and then go to sleep. It's virtually foolproof."

Carina couldn't help but laugh. "Another illusion shattered. I'd always pictured you rehearsing lines in a great hall with mirrors and wonderful acoustics—in full costume, of course."

The spontaneity of his laugh belied the seriousness in his eyes. "Illusions are bound to be shattered, aren't they, if we examine them closely enough."

It struck Carina as an odd thing to say, too melodramatic for the occasion, but then she shrugged it off as the propensity of a Shakespearean-trained actor.

Damian turned to Gwen and said hello, all traces of gloom banished. "Are you a friend of Carina's?"

He had to be one of the few people who had ever noticed Gwen without first being prompted. A glow of warmth rose in Carina at his friendliness.

As for Gwen, she looked as though she might faint. "I've seen all of your movies and every one of your miniseries and I even saw you in a play once in England...you were wonderful in every one of them." She said all that without pausing for breath, and then gasped at the end of it.

Carina decided to step in and help. "This is Gwen Pennell. She's not only one of our community's leading citizens, but she's on the Myrmidon's board of directors. We could never get along without her."

Damian took Gwen's hand in both of his. "It's a pleasure to meet you, Gwen, and thank you for the compliments."

Carina was duly impressed. He really did look flattered, though it had to be the millionth time he'd heard such words.

"Come on in," he said, gesturing them into the office. Carina was tempted to excuse herself so she could continue her search for Malcolm. But when Gwen trotted in like a delighted puppy, she decided to go along for a minute or two. It wouldn't hurt to be sociable.

Gwen asked for and received an autograph, and soon she was chatting amicably with Damian. Carina was content to sit and watch the two of them; the contrast was so startling. Gwen fidgeted and talked too fast and fluttered her hands needlessly, while Damian was relaxed, his long legs stretched out, his movements minimal and always in perfect balance with what he was saying. She'd never before known a man to be graceful—in fact, she'd never considered it a desirable male attribute. But Damian's physical elegance remained assertively masculine; he moved with a subtle, controlled energy that was remarkably compelling to watch.

Then she remembered Malcolm and chided herself for being so easily distracted. "If the two of you will excuse me, I really have to go."

Damian stood up beside her. "Anyplace special?"

"Malcolm's apartment. Someone has to find out if he's ill or something."

"Isn't Gwen going with you?"

"No!" This was uttered by both women in unison, much to Carina's surprise. She looked at Gwen, who had lunged forward in her chair.

"I mean, it's not that I don't want to," Gwen explained hurriedly, "but my husband doesn't know I'm here, and—" She swung her arm out widely and knocked over a desk set, spilling pens, pencils, paper clips and thumbtacks all over the floor. "Oh dear, now look what I've done. I'm so clumsy...oh, goodness." She fell to her knees, her lank hair covering her face as she tried to gather up the mess.

Damian and Carina knelt down beside her to help. "It's all right, Gwen, we can take care of this," Carina assured her. "You go ahead, and I'll talk to you later."

"That's a good idea," Damian said, "and I'll go with Carina to Malcolm's."

Gwen's worried eyes moved quickly from Carina to Damian. "Okay, I guess I'll leave. I'm so sorry about this...."

"Don't give it another thought," Carina said, "and thank you for coming to see me." *For all the good it will do,* she thought with a sharp stab of anxiety.

"Hope to see you again soon," Damian added. Gwen nodded to both of them and fled the room.

"Nice lady," Damian remarked as he picked up thumbtacks one by one. "She seemed a little nervous."

Carina sat back on her heels and looked at him in amazement. "Aren't you accustomed to that by now?"

"What do you mean?"

"Oh, come on, you must realize you can shatter a woman's self-possession just by walking into a room."

He shook his head. "I don't think she was nervous because of me; I recognize adulation when I see it, and this was something different."

"Believe me, I know the woman. Gwen's uncomfortable with most people, famous or otherwise. She's quite shy." Carina dropped a handful of paper clips into the appropriate compartment and began picking up pencils. "By the way, you don't have to come with me to Malcolm's, though it was nice of you to offer."

"I didn't offer just to be nice."

Carina looked up. "Oh?" His nearness was making her uneasy. Perhaps it was the awkwardness of their positions as they knelt, hunched over, on the floor. Or the fact that he hadn't explained why he wanted to accompany her to Malcolm's apartment.

"There," he said. "All cleaned up. Ready to go?"

She brushed off her knees and stood up beside him. "Like I said, you don't—"

He pressed a finger to her lips. He was standing so close she could smell his soapy scent and the faint essence of wool and leather from his clothing. His slender, slightly callused finger was against her mouth, and when he took it away, she instinctively licked her lips with the tip of her tongue. She was hardly aware of her actions until she saw Damian watching her through veiled eyes. Then her face flooded with hot shame for responding to his touch so brazenly.

"You don't know what you might find when you get there. I won't let you go to Malcolm's alone." He crossed the room, picked up his coat and ushered her out of the office and through the lobby. It was clear that he considered the matter closed.

They walked along Wood Street beneath a monochrome, overcast sky. Carina had always regarded this the least appealing time of year. September fell between seasons—summer had faded but autumn hadn't properly begun, and the leaves drooped lifelessly on the trees, as if waiting for frost to impart a last brilliance. She drew up the collar of her coat against the chill breeze and wondered what Damian thought of the rows of small aluminum houses with their identical clotheslines and their identical sheers in the windows. The street was clean, the yards well kept, but he would surely find it dull compared to London.

"How long have you known Malcolm?" Damian asked after they'd walked in silence for a while.

"Eight years, ever since I started working at the Myrmidon," she replied. "Malcolm took over as artistic director the year before."

"Do you like working for him?"

Carina thought a moment. "I like the job, and the fact that I can stay in my hometown."

His chuckle was barely audible. "Not quite the same thing, is it?"

She glanced up at him, but saw nothing in his expression to suggest that the remark was anything but casual. "He's taught me a great deal about the theater. I'm grateful for that."

"No doubt, but eight years in the same job is a long time."

Had Damian sensed her vague feelings of discontent? They'd only known each other for a matter of hours, yet he'd already seen through her polite fictions about Malcolm. "It would be nice," she found herself admitting, "to have the chance to run the theater myself, but that's not likely to happen for years." Their conversation was beginning to seem strangely disquieting, and she was relieved when they came to the walkway of Malcolm's apartment building. "We're here," she said.

Her employer lived in a three-story brick walk-up with a small front yard and a fire escape at one end. Damian stopped and studied the building with great interest, but said nothing. When they were inside the cramped lobby, he asked, "Do you have a key to Malcolm's apartment?"

"No, why do you ask?"

He shrugged. "No reason. It would have been convenient, that's all."

Carina led him to the second-floor apartment and peered through the peephole, but naturally she couldn't see a thing from the outside. She knocked on the door and they waited, but there was no answer. With growing frustration, she knocked louder, as though she could somehow will Malcolm to come to the door and put an end to her worries.

She pounded so hard her hand was beginning to hurt. Then Damian caught her fist and drew it away from the door, rubbing her knuckles with his thumb. "Take it easy. Injuring yourself isn't going to solve a thing."

A voice from the ground floor called up. "He's not there."

Carina glanced at her hand, still wrapped in the incredible warmth of Damian's, and she wondered whether the rapid beat of her heart was fear or something else entirely. Pulling her hand away, she leaned over the banister. Malcolm's landlady, frail and white-haired with bright piercing eyes, looked up at them.

"How do you know he's not here?" Carina called down.

"He didn't come home last night."

"Are you sure?"

Muttering to herself, the lady clutched her shawl and began climbing the stairs. When she reached the second floor, she said, "I wake up when my cat rolls over in the kitchen. When Mr. Spencer clomps up these stairs, I hear him—don't matter what time of the day or night."

"I'm sure you must be right," Damian said, "Mrs...?"

"Lucid."

"Mrs. Lucid, we're colleagues of Mr. Spencer's, and since he didn't show up at the theater, we're quite worried about him. Would you mind letting us have a look in his apartment?"

The woman mulled over his request, then shook her head. "Nope, Mr. Spencer pays his rent on time, and he's entitled to his privacy."

"I appreciate your concern," he pressed on, "but you must understand he may be lying somewhere injured. We have no way of knowing unless we can find some clue in his apartment. Surely you'd want to help us any way you can."

Damian was persuasive, and the landlady was clearly weakening. She pulled a large key ring from the pocket of her apron. "I'd have to hold you fully responsible," she warned.

"That goes without question," he replied, deftly taking the key she held out in her palm.

Downstairs, a phone started to ring. "Oh, that'd be my sister calling from Dubuque. I have to go, but you bring back that key the minute you're through—and don't forget to lock up!"

Damian promised that he would. When Mrs. Lucid was gone, he turned the key in the lock and pushed open the door. He stepped inside the apartment as Carina followed a hairsbreadth behind, scarcely breathing. Sour-smelling air assaulted her nostrils, and one thing was apparent from the outset: whenever Malcolm was last in his apartment, he hadn't been alone. The place was a shambles.

Chapter Four

Malcolm's taste in decor ran to the spare, contemporary lines of smoky glass, chrome and black leather, but there was nothing upscale about his living room now. Empty wine bottles lay overturned on the floor; the coffee table was littered with overflowing ashtrays and dirty dishes. The foul smell seemed to waft from the remnants of food—cocktail-olive pits, dried cubes of cheese, kolbassa sausage left uncovered. Nearby, a man's shirt and tie were tossed onto a chair. More intimate male apparel lay in a heap on the carpet.

"Did Malcolm invite the four of you here for a party last night after dinner?" Carina asked, waving her hand in front of her face in an effort to dispel the odor.

Damian stepped gingerly over an empty bottle. "No, the last I saw of him, he was staggering out of the hotel sometime after two, belting out a tune from *Fiddler on the Roof*. He was in no shape to continue with his hosting duties."

Trying to breathe as little as humanly possible, Carina went to an end table and picked up one of two wine goblets. There was lipstick on the rim, a brilliant shade of violet red that would have looked horrible on Carina.

"I wouldn't touch that if I were you," Damian suggested.

Carina put the glass down. "Why not?"

"Don't you ever watch cop shows? You might be tampering with evidence."

She wrinkled her nose in disgust. "The only evidence around here is that Malcolm's party was of the intimate variety." She replaced the glass on the table, shuddering slightly.

"You seem annoyed," Damian said.

"I am. I come here, worried to death, expecting to find Malcolm unconscious or worse, and all I find is this...this pigsty."

Hands thrust in his pockets, Damian moved through the room with typical ease. "Maybe you should hold off on casting judgment until we've checked the rest of the apartment. Which door is the bedroom?"

"I think it's that one," Carina answered, pointing to the far end. "And I guess you're right. There's no reason for me to believe he would be lying here in the front room for our convenience. It's just that this place is making me queasy, and I can't think straight."

"Then you wait here. I'll check the bedroom."

"Oh, would you?" Carina murmured gratefully. "I'd really appreciate it."

The opportunity was too good for Damian to pass up. "And to think, a little while ago you didn't want me to come." Only his rakish grin prevented Carina from tossing back a suitable epithet.

Damian went through the door to the bedroom. A moment later, he called out. "It's all right! There are no bodies, but come in and take a look. You ought to find it interesting."

Reluctantly Carina walked into the bedroom, and the sight that greeted her was appalling. Whenever the bed was last used, it clearly hadn't been for sleeping. Rumpled red satin sheets covered the king-size mattress, and the bedspread that had fallen to the floor was of some tacky fake fur. The headboard was ornate brass and looked like something from a baroque bordello.

Damian pointed to the ceiling. "Nice added touch, huh?"

Carina looked up. "Ugh, I can't believe it—mirrors." Her growing fury with Malcolm made her want to rip the lurid sheets apart and smash the obscene mirrors. But being the irrepressibly organized person she was, she contented herself with gathering up the fur spread and throwing it onto the bed.

"You're bound and determined to restore some order to this place, aren't you?" Damian observed with amusement.

"I can't help it," she said as she straightened the sheets. "Malcolm's slovenly behavior irks me no end."

"You seem well acquainted with the man's personal habits."

Carina slid him a sidelong glance. Was he insinuating something? It was hard to tell beneath that calm exterior. "Malcolm and I have to work long hours together," she explained, "and he's just as sloppy at the theater."

Damian seemed satisfied with her answer and continued to look around the room. "Did he have a steady girlfriend?"

"No, he prefers actr—" Carina stopped herself. "The women in Dunn's Pond weren't…aren't his type." She had been about to say he preferred actresses, but that would have sounded unnecessarily catty—even if it was true.

Actresses came and went with assured regularity, which was precisely the way Malcolm liked his women.

Carina went to a pile of dirty laundry near the bed and tossed it into the closet. Not that she was accomplishing much, but at least there was a bit of floor space now, and the place looked a little less offensive. But the stale smell of seduction hung heavy in the room, mingling with the nauseating odor of leftover food. Carina feared she was going to be ill.

"He's obviously not here," she said, "and he hasn't left us any notes, so could we just go?"

"In a minute, but let me check the bathroom first, just to be sure."

Carina didn't argue when Damian went through the adjoining door, leaving her with her imagination to keep her company. Where could Malcolm have gone? And who was this woman he'd so enthusiastically entertained in his bedroom? Whoever it was, maybe she'd drugged him and left his body somewhere else. He might have passed out, and—

"Carina!" Damian called from the bathroom. "What size dress do you wear?"

"Ten," she replied absently.

He emerged a moment later, holding up a delicate black camisole of silk with silver threads running through it. "This wouldn't be yours, by any chance?" he asked, smirking.

Carina let out a gasp. "Where'd you find that?"

Damian's expression of shock matched her own. "You mean it *is* yours?"

"Yes, but—no, I mean..." She took a deep breath and tried again. "It's mine, yes, but I have no idea how it got here."

Much to her consternation, Damian threw back his head and roared with laughter. "Are you telling me Malcolm stole it? As what, a gift for his lady friend?"

"That's not funny! Where did you find it?"

He motioned to the bathroom between guffaws. "Near the tub, next to the incense burner."

Carina tapped her foot impatiently. "Well, for your information, I have never been in Malcolm's bathroom before, much less his bedroom. Where's the rest of it?"

Damian raised his eyebrows. "The rest of what?"

"There's a slip that goes with it. Are you sure it wasn't in the bathroom, too?"

"I didn't see it." He was leaning against the doorjamb wearing a bemused expression.

Carina began pulling apart the bedclothes she'd just finished straightening.

"What are you doing?" he asked.

"Looking for my slip."

"Why the bed? A minute ago, you were telling me you'd never been in here before."

Her head shot up. "I haven't, and stop looking at me like that. Malcolm and I have never...I mean, we're hardly even—oh, for heaven's sake, just get that thought right out of your head! I'm checking the bed because I have to start somewhere." She noticed the camisole dangling provocatively from Damian's finger and snatched it from him. "Here, give me that! You're holding it like it's some kind of weapon."

He chuckled. "With the right woman, it probably is. But while we're on this fascinating topic, do you mind telling me how you suppose your lingerie ended up in here without your consent?"

Carina continued to shake out sheets and toss pillows; it helped release the adrenaline. "I bought the set last spring in Chicago, but before I got a chance to wear it, I loaned it to wardrobe for *Cat on a Hot Tin Roof*. It must have slipped my mind, what with the summer break and everything, because I never got around to getting it back." *Damn, where was that slip?* Even on sale, the lingerie had cost her a small fortune.

Damian's grin was infuriating. "I've heard some interesting alibis in my day, but I must say, yours is unique. Why are you so adamant about denying a relationship with Malcolm? I mean, these things have been known to happen in the theatrical world. I wouldn't be shocked."

Carina tossed back the swath of auburn hair that had fallen across her face. "Oh, wouldn't you? Well, if you must know, for one thing Malcolm Spencer couldn't be further from my type, and if I were going to be unjustly implicated in an affair, I'd at least want it to be with someone desirable." She paused to take a breath but found that it caught in her throat. Mere mention of the word *desirable* in the company of Damian was like lighting a match near explosives. Still, she pressed on. "And secondly, while I'm well aware that theater people have been known to indulge in recreational sex, I have never been one of those people." And what a topic to discuss, her first day with Damian.

It was difficult to tell whether Damian believed her or not, but he seemed to be enjoying her embarrassment. "All right, sunshine, I won't torment you anymore on that topic, but just out of curiosity, what—or should I say who—would inspire Miss Rawlins of the pleated skirts and sensible heels to buy such seductive apparel?"

His question caught her completely off guard, even more than the appearance of the camisole had. Did she really want to admit to him that she bought exciting intimate apparel because her life at present was so lacking in excitement and intimacy? Was there something strange about wanting to feel seductive underneath pleated skirts and sensible heels? She honestly had no idea and gave what she hoped was a look of nonchalance. "Whom I bought it for is none of your concern. Now why don't you start helping me look for the slip?" Carina jammed the camisole into her shoulder bag.

Damian glanced at his watch. "Much as I'd like to help you with this dilemma, I don't think we have time. We can't have Mrs. Lucid coming in to find us tearing up Malcolm's apartment any more than it already is."

Carina sighed deeply. "I guess you're right." She turned and led the way back to the front door, feeling disturbed and somehow violated.

As Damian followed her through the apartment, he wished he hadn't been quite so glib with Carina. He knew from the flashing amber in her eyes that he'd upset her, and he hadn't meant to, but the story about lending her lingerie was pretty incredible. Unfortunately, he didn't know her well enough to judge whether or not she was lying. It would be easy enough, he supposed, to find out from wardrobe if the camisole was hers. That might confirm her story, as far as it went, but it wouldn't explain how the thing could have ended up in Malcolm's apartment. If she was lying, if she'd left the lingerie behind herself, it raised a whole new set of questions. Were they lovers, and if so, was she protecting him? Betraying him? Or like most people who'd known Malcolm for any length of time, did she just despise the man? In any event, only two things were certain: the artistic director was missing, and the lingerie found in his slovenly apartment belonged to his assistant. Interesting . . . perhaps even expedient.

CARINA COULD NOT REMEMBER the last time her apartment had felt so inviting. She stepped inside shortly after eight o'clock that evening with a tension headache hammering behind her eyes, her nerves frayed from too much coffee. What she needed now was to be alone.

She lived about four blocks away from the Myrmidon, on the far side of the town's central park. Here, the houses were older and larger with mullioned windows and gables and wide front verandas. When her parents had sold their home and left Dunn's Pond for an Arizona retirement community, Carina had been lucky enough to find this apartment. It was a tiny bachelor on the top floor of a converted house, but it compensated for lack of space with a fireplace and its very own turret.

She placed her briefcase in the front closet, telling herself she'd go over the theater's financial records after she'd relaxed for a while. Right now, she didn't even want to think about work.

The turret with four tall windows had a southern exposure, making it paradise for plant life. There were ferns and dracaenas hanging from the ceiling, corn plants and palms reaching up to meet them. In the midst of this indoor jungle was a cozy sofa where Carina flopped down, closed her eyes and put everything out of her mind... except Damian.

She sat up quickly and pressed her fingers to her temples. As pleasant as it was to think about her day with Damian, she knew such thoughts would inevitably bring to mind certain unpleasant associations. Like Malcolm. After all, Malcolm—or rather, his disappearance—was the only reason Damian would choose to spend several hours in her company. Carina sighed wearily; she wasn't having much success relaxing. Her headache was worse, if anything, so she got up and went to the kitchen, little more than a corner of the sitting room set apart by a butcher-block counter. She found some aspirins and filled a glass with water. Leaning against the sink, she swallowed the pills and tried to rub the kinks from her neck and shoulders.

The balance of the afternoon had been fruitless, for Carina anyway. There was still no word from Malcolm, and though Carina had wanted to call the police, Damian had dissuaded her. They wouldn't even listen to her until Malcolm had been missing twenty-four hours, he said. He was probably right, but doing nothing seemed so callous.

She had also wanted to talk to Elsie, the wardrobe mistress, about the camisole and slip, but the woman had gone home early to take her child to the dentist. Perhaps now would be a good time to call her, Carina thought, and picked up the phone by the sofa.

"Elsie? It's Carina. Sorry to bother you at home, but something strange happened today, and I was hoping you might be able to shed some light on it."

"If I can. What's the problem?" the woman replied.

"Remember the camisole and slip I loaned the wardrobe last season—black silk with silver trim?"

"Hmmm, let me think. Oh, sure, I remember. Didn't I give those back to you?"

Carina had to struggle not to snap at her. The woman, for all her talents with a needle and thread, had a hopeless memory. "No, Elsie, I did not get them back."

"Dear me, I could've sworn I did, but let me think a minute now."

The minute seemed to take forever. "When was the last time you noticed them in wardrobe? Can you remember that?" By now, Carina wasn't holding out much hope.

"I wish I could remember, but it was last season that I borrowed those things. Last season is a long time ago."

I know it was last season. "All right then, can you tell me when Malcolm last came into the storeroom? Was he in wardrobe at all on Friday?"

Elsie chewed on the question a while. "He might have been—yes, now I remember, he definitely did come in, to make sure I'd gotten the fabric for the play. He was his usual self, you know, bossy."

That was a foregone conclusion, Carina thought with a sigh. "Did anyone else out of the ordinary come in either Friday or today?"

"No one except the cast. They were in this afternoon to get fitted for their costumes."

"Oh, I see." Carina didn't know what more she could expect from Elsie, but there had to be some way of getting to the bottom of this.

"I'm sorry I forgot to return your lingerie, Carina, but I can look for them tomorrow."

"Thanks, Elsie, I'd appreciate it. And by the way, it's only the slip that's missing. I have the camisole." Carina said goodbye and hung up the phone, reaching across to pull the scrap of black silk from her purse.

It didn't make sense. Why would Malcolm take her camisole? Could he possibly have lent it to someone, some woman he was trying to impress with expensive gifts? She remembered Damian's joking suggestion and the idea began to seem plausible. It was just the kind of cheap, underhanded thing Malcolm would do. Gerry, the prop man, had once complained that dishes were disappearing from his storeroom, and they later discovered that Malcolm had "borrowed" them to round out his cupboards.

Assuming this was a similar case, who was the woman? An image of Judith Deveau suddenly popped into Carina's head, if only because she was the younger of the two actresses currently in residence. Hadn't she mentioned that she and Malcolm knew each other a long time ago? It would have been simple enough for her to grab a taxi from the hotel and visit Malcolm after the others had retired to their rooms. And she was a size ten, so the camisole would fit even though she'd strain the bust seams more than Carina ever could. Examining the camisole for signs of wear and finding none, she got up, marched to the bathroom and dropped it smartly into the laundry hamper. She was going to have a talk with Judith soon.

THE PRESIDENT of Merchants' and Farmers' Bank had a face as pink and smooth as a baby's bottom, and when he smiled, cherubic dimples enhanced the image. His quiet voice with the soft Southern drawl was almost hypnotic to the unsuspecting, as was the unflinching gaze of his baby-blue eyes.

Carina sat down across from Harland Pennell's vast rococo desk in the chair reserved for loan applicants and defaulters, a chair that was low, uncomfortable and undoubtedly designed to make the person in it feel inferior. The tactic was subtle, but Carina believed it was as deliberate as anything the banker had ever done. He was leaning back now, his hands folded across a pinstriped vest, nails buffed to a blinding gloss. The man fairly oozed success, and he obviously wanted to be sure she'd noticed. Then he flipped open a thick file folder on his desk.

"I've been keeping a close eye on the Myrmidon's account, and frankly I don't like what I've been seein'."

Carina cleared her throat. "We, uh, we had a difficult season last year."

"Seems to me you've had yourselves a string of difficult seasons. Our records show you've abused your overdraft privileges consistently, and you've missed no fewer than four payments in the past year alone."

"But if you check further on, you'll see that we caught up with those payments by the end of the season."

Harland did not seem interested in the details. He blinked at her as if she hadn't spoken. "Banking is a business, and we're honor bound to our customers to keep it profitable, y'understand what I'm saying?"

"Yes, but surely you're aware that it's difficult for small regional theaters to—"

He waved his soft hand in dismissal. "Spare me your homilies. I'm much too busy to cry tears for some ragtag operation." Then his tone changed; words flowed from his mouth like oil, thick and cloying. "Now that's not to say that I don't care about what happens to you, Miz Rawlins, cuz I do. I know you work hard to keep your theater going, and I've watched you grow from a shy little puppy dog to a lovely young woman. Hell, you're the only one around with the guts to stand up to that artistic director of yours. I also know for a fact that there isn't a single person in this town who doesn't like you. You're a shrewd lady, and I admire that."

For a moment she was nearly swayed by his praise, until he'd called her shrewd. Coming from someone like him, it was hardly a compliment. "Why don't you tell me why you asked me here?" Carina tried to sound sufficiently uninformed to keep Gwen out of trouble.

Still, suspicion flickered in his eyes. "All right, let's get straight to the heart of the matter. Recently, I've been meeting with real estate developers who are interested in building a spectacular shopping complex in Dunn's Pond, the largest in the Midwest."

Carina remained impassive. "I see."

"They like the town's easy access to Chicago, Milwaukee, Rockford, and they've made us an offer—a substantial one—to buy up the old rail yards and the adjacent block, which unfortunately is where your theater now sits.''

Gwen had forewarned her, so there was no reason for the shiver of apprehension that ran along her spine. ''So, I suppose they'll want to tear down the Myrmidon.''

''They're gonna need a lot of room for parkin'.''

Carina swallowed the lump of emotion rising in her throat—to be replaced with blacktop was the final affront. Nevertheless, she was determined to voice the arguments she'd been rehearsing all that morning, ever since she got Harland's summons. ''The Myrmidon is one of only three remaining landmarks in this town. You wouldn't allow anyone to tear down the Victoria Hotel or Dunn's mansion, Mr. Pennell, would you?'' Her last reference was something of a dig, since the banker and his wife lived in Dunn's mansion.

But the man was too thick-skinned to take offense. ''You're overlookin' one vital difference, honey. I pay taxes—damned high ones—for the privilege of living in that mansion, and as for the Victoria, they've always paid their way. Which is more than can be said for the Myrmidon.''

''But it's a historically important building. The town council will never agree to its demolition.''

Harland's fleshy mouth turned up in a grin. ''The town council has nothing to say in the matter. The bank owns the land; in fact, it owns most of the town. So you see, I'm well within my rights to do with the property whatever I see fit.''

Carina paused long enough to make it look as though she was thinking quickly. ''What if we were able to come up with the money to pay back the loan?''

The banker laughed out loud. ''I must say you've got more moxie every day, but lemme put it to you this way. If you had a check in the briefcase of yours for the full amount of funds outstanding, then I, bein' an honorable businessman, would go straight to the developers and tell them they'd have to redesign their plans. But I know that all you got's a demand loan from Merchant's and Farmers' Bank, and as of this moment, I'm callin' that loan."

"Immediately?" she asked.

"This very minute."

Carina exhaled very slowly. He'd said exactly what she'd been hoping he'd say, and she reached into her briefcase to pull out the contract. Her fingers hardly trembled. "I don't believe you can do that, Mr. Pennell."

His eyes bulged. "What?"

"If you look on page three of the loan agreement, you'll see there's a reasonable notice provision. You have to give us fourteen days to come up with the outstanding balance."

He leaned back and hitched his thumbs into his vest. "Is that all? I've been in the banking business a long time, l'il lady, and I know all about those provisions. But they're set up for those with a reasonable chance of comin' up with the money. The Myrmidon hardly falls into that category."

"It may seem that way, but you are still required to give us two weeks."

His jowls quivered as he glared at her. "Like hell I am." It was obvious that Harland Pennell was unaccustomed to being challenged. His cheeks were flushed a sickly violet, and his eyes snapped with anger. Carina didn't think her own face revealed the panic she was feeling, but beneath her loose-fitting dress of rust-colored linen she was sweating profusely.

The banker stood up and leaned across his desk, emitting menace like a noxious vapor. "No one pushes Harland Pennell around and gets away with it. I don't intend to let some chickie who's still wet behind the ears mess things up for me with those developers.''

Carina forced herself to stand. If she stayed to listen to his bombast, she'd probably end up backing down. "If you make any attempt to close us down before two weeks are up, Mr. Pennell, then we'll have no choice but to sue. Good day, sir. We'll talk again soon." With a curt nod, she turned and walked out the door.

Harland Pennell sat staring at the door long after Carina had gone. Who'd have believed that little lady, who once used to blush and stammer just sayin' hello, could turn out so gutsy? He oughta be furious, except that she did have a case, in the legal sense.

So it would take a few weeks longer than he'd planned. So what? He could stall those guys from Chicago for a while. As long as he got rid of that polecat Malcolm Spencer in the process, that was the main thing.

A low chuckle rumbled from his throat as he pulled open the drawer of his desk and got himself a big fat illegal Cuban cigar. Quite the lady, that Miz Rawlins, sittin' there so calm and pretty. But he'd seen the perspiration on her upper lip. Yessirree, Miz Rawlins was mighty worried, and if there was one thing made him feel good, it was makin' a body—particularly a lady—sweat.

Chapter Five

When Carina got back to the office from her meeting at the bank, she was practically slithering up the walls with anxiety. Normally she could handle pressure; in fact, she thrived on the rise and fall of tension associated with putting on a series of live performances every season. But this was a different kind of tension. She felt as though something had infested the calm predictable waters of her life, churning up angry whitecaps that she could neither control nor predict, but could only buffer herself against.

The bank was eager to destroy the one place in Dunn's Pond that mattered more to her than anything else. Now she could look forward to two exhausting weeks of attempting to accomplish the impossible. And she didn't even have Malcolm there to help her through it. Worse, he'd been missing for thirty-six hours, and she'd been too preoccupied with her own future to call the police and report it. It should have been the first thing that came to her mind this morning. Carina sank wearily into her chair, resting her forehead on her folded arms. What was the matter with her? It was as if, subconsciously, she didn't want him to be found. Yet, like it or not, Malcolm—and not Carina—ran this theater. He was needed to direct *Fate of the Popinjay*, his own play, the play that he'd written himself and had wanted to stage for years. Two of his old colleagues, Judith and Damian, were there to help celebrate his success. But Malcolm was gone. If ever there was an inappropriate and unthinkable time for her employer to disappear, it was now. So why did she keep relegating his disappearance to the bottom of her list of priorities?

Before she could think too deeply about her own inexcusable behavior, Carina picked up the phone and dialed the number for the state police. That was the only respectable course of action—and the least she could do for her boss. Saving the damned theater could wait for five minutes.

A switchboard operator answered her call on the second ring. "Uh... good afternoon," Carina said, not knowing quite how to begin. "I'd, er, I'd like to report a missing person." Wasn't that how they always said it on television? Her call was transferred to a desk sergeant, so she must have been doing it right.

"I'd like to report a missing person," she repeated, this time to the officer who'd barked his unintelligible name into her ear. "He's an adult... male Caucasian." Good Lord, had she really said that?

"How long's he been missing?" The sergeant spat out the question.

"Since Sunday night—no, I'd guess you'd say early Monday morning, around two. Well, he might have had a woman with him, but—"

"Are you his wife?"

Carina blinked in confusion, then realized what the policeman must have been thinking. A spurned spouse bent on dragging back her unwilling husband. "No, I work for him. He's not married. He was supposed to show up yesterday morning at nine and didn't. No one has seen him since."

"Okay," the beleaguered-sounding officer said, "come down to the station and we'll fill out a report."

Carina nervously transferred the receiver to her other ear. "Excuse me, Sergeant, but things are kind of in an uproar around here, and I've been left in charge. Is there any chance you could send a man over here?" She braced herself, waiting for the crusty sergeant to chew her out, but to her surprise, he didn't.

"I'll send someone out. Your name?"

Carina gave him all the information he requested and was told she could expect an officer within the hour. As she hung up the phone, she was already feeling a little better. Now she could safely put the matter of her missing boss aside for the moment and concentrate on other things. She was about to call the box office manager with the dire news of the foreclosure when Gerry, the property master, bounded into her office, greatly agitated.

She put down the phone with a sigh and got up from her desk. "What is it, Gerry? What's wrong?"

True to his troll-like appearance, Gerry hopped from one foot to another whenever he got excited, as he was now. "The props, the props! They've been stolen!"

"What props?" she asked, putting a hand on his shoulder to calm him down.

"For *Fate of the Popinjay*! The taxidermist's tools, the ones that Mr. Tiggles uses in act one! They're gone!"

Carina frowned. "Are you sure? Have you checked everywhere?"

"Sure I did. I wouldn't be here bothering you if I hadn't." His leathery face was creased with worry. "I kept them wrapped up in flannel on the top shelf to keep them safe, but when I looked this morning, they weren't there. I've been trying to track 'em down all day."

"Have you spoken to Damian?" Funny how naturally she thought of Damian as the person in charge of the cast, and he wasn't even supposed to have been here. But he had, in any event, solved one problem for her—the afternoon before, he'd offered to begin rehearsals in Malcolm's absence. She returned her attention to Gerry. "They might have borrowed the props," she suggested.

"I asked them, too, and they don't know a thing about them."

The tension headache was back. Carina pressed her fingers to her temples and tried to will it away. She already had a vanished boss, a ruthless banker and a near-bankrupt theater to worry about, and now she was supposed to solve the riddle of a few misplaced props that had probably fallen behind a shelf somewhere.

Gerry must have sensed her irritation. "I know you're real busy," he said, "and if I could, I'd just go out and replace them, but I can't. I borrowed them from Dr. Sedgwick—you remember, the retired surgeon from Darlington who never misses a play. The instruments belonged to his father, and they're worth a lot of money. I promised him nothing would happen to them. What am I gonna do?"

Carina knew better than to think Gerry had been careless. He was one of the most reliable employees in the theater. If he'd been entrusted with articles of value, Gerry would move heaven and earth to protect them.

"What exactly is missing?" she asked, her tone gentler.

"A scalpel, a pair of forceps, and one of them saws— you know, the kind doctors use to cut through bone."

A shudder passed through her, a cold slippery shudder. "All three are missing?"

"Yup, and the flannel they were wrapped in. It's kinda like someone wanted them all for something real specific."

Carina refused to let herself be drawn into Gerry's overactive imagination. "I'll do what I can to help you find them," she said consolingly, "but meanwhile, don't worry about it. I'm sure they'll turn up. And until then, perhaps the actors could make do with some kind of substitute prop."

Realizing there was little else he could say or do, Gerry left the office with his usual bandy-legged gait. Carina sat down at her desk again and blinked back tears of fatigue and frustration. If something nice didn't happen to her very soon, she was going to scream.

A pair of feet landed with a thump beside her. Carina turned and there stood Damian, clean-shaven today, looking more gorgeous than ever, but blond hair still in endearing disarray. He also had a pencil smudge across one cheek, the sight of which seemed to tug at some latent maternal heartstring.

"Did you just leap over the counter?" she asked, trying not to grin.

"I did." His expression was serious, but his eyes glinted with laughter.

"Why did you do that?"

"Because it seemed more heroic than coming in through the door."

Carina had always envisioned Damian as eternally debonair. That he could be boyish as well came as a pleasant surprise. "Why did you want to seem heroic?"

He plopped himself down on the sofa and lifted his foot onto the opposite knee. His cambric shirt was of a soft, teal blue that conformed to the contours of his upper body and made his eyes seem even bluer, if such a thing were possible. "Whenever the hero rescues a damsel in distress, the script calls for a dramatic entrance. I'm just sorry you didn't have a chandelier."

Now Carina couldn't help but laugh. "I shudder to imagine. Thank you, by the way, for taking over rehearsals until Malcolm returns. It's quite a load off my mind knowing his play is in such good hands."

A look that seemed out of place momentarily crossed Damian's features, but it was gone before Carina could identify it. "Don't thank me," he said. "It was the least I could do. Something tells me the play is not your biggest worry right now. Were you thinking about Malcolm?"

"No—I mean, yes, I was; I just called the police and reported him missing. But something else has come up, as if we needed another problem around here."

Damian patted the empty space beside him on the sofa. "Why don't you sit over here where it's more comfortable and tell me about it?"

His concern seemed so genuine and her emotions were so precarious that the invitation was too good to pass up. So she rose and crossed the short distance to the couch. But when she sat down, there was much less space between them than she had intended. Was it something she'd done without realizing, or had Damian slid closer? His arm lay stretched across the back of the couch and rested lightly against her shoulder. But it was his thigh that held her rapt attention. Aligned with hers from hip to knee, his denim pressing against her linen, their body heat mingling. Good grief, she realized with a start, he really does sizzle on contact. It occurred to her somewhat belatedly that she ought to edge away and create some space between them. But when she tried to shift, his fingers curled around her shoulder.

"Don't move, sunshine. I like you right where you are."

Carina looked up into the face of the man who was so achingly familiar, yet so much a stranger. What did she really know about him that the rest of the world didn't know, too? With a sudden flash of resentment for the rest of the world, Carina decided not to edge away after all.

"I had a meeting with the bank president today," she began.

He looked at her with understanding. "Yes, someone told me you'd gone there. I take it the meeting didn't go well?"

Carina knew she shouldn't be discussing the Myrmidon's financial problems with someone from outside the theater—especially a visiting actor—but she'd already taken the gamble by saying this much. So she unburdened herself the rest of the way by telling him what had happened with Harland Pennell.

"How much do you have to come up with in the next two weeks?" he asked.

She named a six-figure sum to which he replied with a low whistle.

"Two weeks doesn't even take us to opening night. Where are you going to get the money?" His question was indisputably logical.

Carina tried to make light of it with a laugh, but she was hardly convincing. "I'm not sure yet. I was so busy trying to come up with a way to stall them, I haven't had time to work it out any further."

Damian pulled her closer in a hug that felt wonderfully reassuring. "Something tells me the indefatigable Miss Rawlins has a trick or two up her sleeve. I'm told you're the only one who's ever matched wits with Malcolm. That's got to have been good training for you."

Toppling on the verge of despondency despite Damian's enthusiasm, she stared straight ahead. "People in theater exaggerate. I'm not that clever." The rudimentary ideas she'd come up with the night before now seemed so hopeless and farfetched. Maybe it would have been easier just to let the bank have the place and then let the actors sue for breach of contract. It would have been a lot less work in the long run.

Damian lowered his head and breathed softly in her ear. "Are you still with me?"

The ripple of excitement that coursed through her brought Carina rapidly back to the present. Her stomach was fluttering in nervous anticipation. She knew what Damian was doing and where it was meant to lead. She also knew that these distracting sensations were totally out of place in a discussion about the theater's financial future—but what was a woman to do? There was such an aura of fantasy about Damian's presence. She still couldn't understand why he was there, but questions like that were so easy to overlook when his body was touching hers.

"I, uh, I'm planning to have a press conference as soon as possible," she said, staring into his eyes, aware that her own were wide as saucers. "We'd invite all the major dailies in the area...TV...radio..." Was she imagining things or were their mouths moving closer? Oh, gosh...

"Sounds good so far." He *was* moving closer, and he was studying her mouth as if he definitely intended to kiss her.

Sudden shyness washed over her like a tidal wave, and she leaped to the edge of the couch. She sat there stiffly, her back rigid despite the tempting softness of the upholstery, her hands held carefully in her lap. "It would only be effective," she said in the most austere tone she could manage, "if you and the other cast members agree to speak on our behalf."

Inexplicably he laughed. "You want me to talk at your press conference?" Damian didn't seem the least bit perturbed that she'd jumped away like a skittish colt. He had that way about him, as though he felt there was all the time in the world for whatever he wanted.

"Yes, but what's so funny?" she demanded, feeling awkward and childish and defensive. Why hadn't she let him kiss her? Would it seem foolish for her to change her mind now?

"Nothing, really," he said, taking her hand and coaxing her gently back to his side. "I was just thinking about how strange life is, sometimes." He traced the length of her arm with a fingertip, rekindling her as though he knew the fire had only temporarily gone out. "I'd be happy to help out at your press conference."

"Even though you came here to get away from publicity?" Carina asked.

"Where did you get that idea?"

Carina looked at him curiously. "Why, from you. Isn't that why you're—"

"Yes, yes, of course," he said quickly, "I did say that, but then this is a worthy cause, saving a landmark theater. I'll also do what I can to persuade the others to help out."

"Oh, would you?" Carina flung out her arms, about to wrap them around his neck in sheer gratitude. But deeply ingrained propriety stopped her, and her arms hung in the air for a moment like limp wings. "Thank you," she uttered awkwardly, "I don't know how to show my appreciation, but—"

He caught her upper arms and lowered them gently. "I wouldn't worry too much about that." The warmth of his hands through the crisp linen sent waves of sensation along her arms; her heart was pattering madly. Carina blinked, but her eyes stayed closed a moment too long, as if to savor this new and exciting contact. The backs of this thumbs were very nearly resting beside her breasts. All she had to do was bring her arms closer to her sides...like so... Her eyes sprang open when she realized what she'd unconsciously initiated, and she found Damian's face even closer than before, his look even more intense.

"What happens after the press conference?" he asked, the words pouring from his mouth like warm, sweet honey.

Carina, trying hard not to lose herself in his hypnotic gaze, replied, "A party...we'll invite everyone to a gala opening-night party." Dear God, the suspense was killing her! She had to find out how his lips felt on hers, or she'd die. But he was holding back deliberately, making her yearn for him. It was cruel, deliciously, undeniably cruel. "If we charge two hundred dollars a person for opening night and sell out for the rest of the week, we...we just might make it."

One hand came up to cradle her cheek; she could feel the calluses against her skin. His other hand enfolded hers and brought it to his lap, to his thigh where the worn denim hugged his flesh like velvet. Her fingers shyly, tentatively grazed the taut ropy muscle of his leg. Carina thought she'd never experienced anything even remotely resembling these exquisite, exciting sensations—and he hadn't even kissed her yet.

"Sounds...ambitious," he said, and moved his tongue across his lower lip tantalizingly.

Carina couldn't keep her eyes off his mouth. "Mmm-hmm," she replied.

"There isn't much time," he warned an instant before his lips brushed hers.

"I know that, too," she gasped, squeezing her eyes shut as if she might lose her equilibrium. Could a single feathery kiss really feel that incredible?

"We'd all have to work extra hard...." Damian punctuated his statement with another kiss, this one more leisurely as he took the time to slowly, thoroughly taste her lips. "There'd be no guarantees—" both hands held her face, and his tongue met hers for one brief erotic instant "—and we'd need a lot of luck to pull it off."

Carina could scarcely whimper as she was swept away by the passionate onslaught of his mouth on hers. He pulled her to him, and she clung to the blond tendrils at his collar.

Somewhere off in the distance she vaguely heard a commotion, the annoying sound of clumping feet. The intrusive noises came closer, and finally Carina managed to free herself from Damian's bewitching embrace and turn around. Her irritation gave way to shock when she discovered a uniformed policeman leaning against the counter, watching them.

He flipped open his badge. "Lieutenant Chapman. I'm looking for a Carina Rawlins."

She leaped off the couch as if springs were attached to her bottom; her hands flew to her hair to restore a businesslike appearance, if a little late. "I'm Carina Rawlins." She tried to match the policeman's authoritative tone, but her voice came out sounding rather squeaky.

His arrogant smirk made it obvious that he knew why she couldn't talk properly. He pulled out a notebook and pen from his tunic. "You wanted to file a missing-persons report?"

"Yes, that's right." From the corner of her eye Carina could see that Damian was taking his time getting to his feet—unruffled, unembarrassed. Just like a man, she thought with a tinge of pique. "My employer, Malcolm Spencer, has been missing since yesterday."

Lieutenant Chapman's beefy neck and squashed nose suggested a history of playing varsity football and breaking up brawls; obviously, he was a man any criminal would be foolish to tangle with. Still, that was no reason for Carina to feel as though she were suddenly under investigation. His steady, impassive gaze was probably something he was taught at the police academy.

"He's your employer, you said?"

"That's right."

"And I understand Mr. Spencer has no wife. Any family in the area?"

"None, and I don't know how to contact the relatives he does have."

He stopped to take down some notes, then turned his attention to Damian who, despite his lean build, towered over the sturdy policeman. "Hey, I know who you are!" the officer exclaimed. "You're that actor...that what's-his-name Fleming, right?"

Damian nodded, the very essence of civility. Without so much as moving a muscle, he managed to make Lieutenant Chapman look clumsy and bumbling. "I am," he said.

"The missus drags me to all your movies," the officer went on to say. "Hey, not that I don't like your stuff—just that she gets all soppy and romantic every time she sees your face. You know how women are."

The actor smiled in a way that might have been either sarcasm or assent. The policeman naturally took it to mean the latter. He waved a thick forefinger back and forth between Damian and Carina, chuckling heartily. "Guess all the ladies get a little carried away when you're around, huh?"

Carina felt like crawling away in embarrassment. But Damian finally chose to make his opinion known, his voice clipped and rather cold. "Women may be infatuated with the characters I play, Lieutenant, but I assure you, I have neither the time nor the inclination to reciprocate their affections as often as you might think.''

The policeman seemed almost disappointed. For her part, Carina decided this was not the time to ponder the nuances of Damian's remark. ''Could we get back to the matter of Mr. Spencer's disappearance?'' she suggested firmly.

Lieutenant Chapman's grin bordered on the lascivious. ''Sure, why not? Who was the last person to see him?''

Carina turned to Damian, silently inviting him to speak first, though she would have sworn his look darkened for an instant before he answered. ''Neither of us can really be certain, but my last sight of the artistic director was late Sunday night. Malcolm hosted a dinner party at the Victoria Hotel for the cast, and I intended to walk him home when it was over.''

''You intended to?''

''Yes, I changed my mind halfway there when Malcolm's behavior became more than I could tolerate.''

''How so?''

''His off-key baritone was waking up the entire town,'' Damian explained.

''He'd been drinking?'' the policeman asked.

''We all had, but I suppose you could say that Malcolm had overindulged more than the rest of us.''

The officer turned to Carina. ''How about you? When's the last time you saw the missing party?''

''Friday afternoon.''

''You weren't at this . . . shindig at the hotel?''

''No,'' she said, ''Malcolm does not include his employees when he entertains the cast. But on Friday, I saw him leave the theater sometime after six as usual.'' She paused, then added, "He was in a particularly good mood that day."

"Why do you suppose he was in a good mood?" the officer asked, scribbling as he spoke.

"Probably because Monday was the start of our new season, and he was finally going to stage the play he'd written years before. That's why I found it so hard to understand why he didn't show up yesterday. This is a big occasion for him."

"Where does Mr. Spencer live?" Carina gave him the address, and the officer looked up. "Has anyone been to his place to check on him?"

Neither Damian nor Carina answered right away. The policeman's eyes narrowed; finally, Damian spoke up. "Miss Rawlins and I visited his apartment together yesterday afternoon to make sure he wasn't ill or unconscious."

"You didn't touch anything, I hope," Lt. Chapman challenged hastily, glancing from one to the other.

Carina didn't dare look at Damian when they both answered, "No." What possible good could come of her admitting she'd taken her camisole home with her? She could have kissed Damian for backing up her little white lie.

"Did you find anything out of the ordinary?" the officer asked.

This time, Carina replied. "It did look as though Malcolm—Mr. Spencer—had been entertaining a female...guest in his apartment, but there was no way of knowing what night that would have been...or who the woman was."

Lieutenant Chapman apparently found the item sufficiently interesting to write it down. "Did he have a steady girlfriend?"

"No, he didn't," Carina said, feeling strangely guilty for baring her employer's secrets to an officer of the law.

"Did he date local girls?"

She was just about to blurt out that Malcolm dated mostly actresses, but that would have been tantamount to accusing Judith of being the unknown female guest, since the happily married, silver-haired Kate was safely out of his league. "As far as I know," Carina hedged, "Malcolm preferred to date women from out of town."

Lieutenant Chapman issued her one of his finest interrogatory looks, and when she miraculously managed not to flinch, he turned his attention back to Damian. "You mentioned a dinner party. Who else—besides you and Mr. Spencer—was there?"

"Len Kramer and his wife, Kate, and Judith Deveau."

It looked as though the policeman's eyes were going to pop right out of his head. "You don't mean *the* Judith Deveau, the one with the..." He held his hands out in front of his chest to approximate the actress's generous measurements. Carina had to clench her teeth at the man's deplorable lack of taste.

"Formerly of *Pairs and Misfits*," Damian explained tactfully. "Were you a devotee of her show?"

"Are you kidding? I never missed it." The officer pushed back his hat and leaned closer, comradelike. "Hey, do you think I could get a couple of autographs? One from you for the missus, and one from Miss Deveau for me?"

"I don't see why not," Damian replied.

The officer grinned at Carina askance. "It must be pretty exciting for you, Miss Rawlins, hobnobbing with the rich and famous here in your little theater."

Something, and she couldn't quite determine what, put Carina on her guard. Perhaps it was the officer's lightning-quick way of coming back with questions or the slightly exaggerated dumb-macho-cop routine he affected. Whatever it was, she suddenly got the feeling that Lieutenant Chapman was not what he appeared to be. She considered her answer very carefully before she admitted, "Working in the theater does have its rewards."

"Do you have any more questions for me?" Damian asked the policeman.

"Not at the moment."

"Then would you excuse me? I should have been back in rehearsal ten minutes ago."

"Go ahead," the man in the uniform answered. "I'll probably saunter on down later to meet the other actors, if that's okay."

Damian gave him a tight smile. "Anytime. Carina can point you in the right direction."

Carina was wishing she'd had the forethought to invent a pressing appointment, but it was too late to escape. Now she was alone with Lieutenant Chapman, who didn't appear to be in any hurry to leave.

"Have you known Fleming a long time?" he asked after a long probing look.

"No, I met Damian for the first time yesterday." *And, yes, you caught us kissing in my office today,* she added silently. *Care to make something of it?*

"Lucky guy," the policeman observed. "Doesn't have to waste a lot of time getting to know the ladies."

Carina was sorely tempted to hurl a few choice epithets in his direction, but she refrained. Perhaps a scathingly worded report to his boss would have more clout anyway. "I don't believe my relationship to Mr. Fleming has anything to do with the disappearance of my employer, Lieutenant."

He shrugged. "I have no way of knowing that for sure, Miss Rawlins. But let's get back to your boss. Do you know whether he had a history of emotional problems, anything that might trigger a sudden disappearance?"

"It would depend on what you define as emotional problems. Malcolm is temperamental, but so are most people associated with the creative side of theater. He has his tirades, his tantrums, but nothing serious enough to be described as . . . well, emotional instability."

"Was he in any kind of trouble that you know of?"

Carina shook her head.

"Any enemies?"

Despite the fact that she'd initiated this investigation, Carina was beginning to get annoyed with the officer's line of questioning. She had to struggle to keep the irritation from showing in her voice. "Malcolm Spencer has never been an easy man to get along with. You'd probably have a hard time finding someone who said they genuinely liked him, but I can't think of a single person who would actually want to harm him."

The policeman wrote furiously. "How long have you know him, Miss Rawlins?"

"Eight years."

"Know anything about his past?"

"Not much, except that he grew up somewhere in Pennsylvania and started as an actor in New York City."

"So you really have no way of knowing whether someone from his past holds enough of a grudge to wanna get rid of him."

Carina's grip on the back of her chair tightened defensively. "No, I guess I haven't," she admitted.

He had a few more questions about Malcolm's position with the theater and then asked Carina to point him in the direction of the rehearsal room. She was more than happy to send him on his way.

"Would you mind if I took a look around this place? I'd like to chat with the cast and crew, see if they got any ideas."

"By all means," she replied, busying herself with a stack of papers on her desk. "Go wherever you like. I'm sure you'll find everyone cooperative."

He touched his fingers to his hat and was about to turn down the hall when he stopped. "One more thing: would you mind giving me your home address and phone number? Since you're the one who filed the report, I'd like to be able to call you at home if we find anything."

Carina felt a prickly sense of unease that was probably due to an overactive imagination more than anything else. After all, it wasn't as though she were hiding Malcolm's body somewhere. She gave the policeman the information he requested.

"Thanks," he said. "I'll be talking to you."

She watched him saunter down the hall, then he turned, paused and walked all the way back to the counter. Carina was still standing where he'd left her.

"You don't have to answer this if you don't want to," he mumbled apologetically, "'cause it's really none of my business, but when I first came in, I overheard Fleming say something about needing a lot of luck to pull it off. What did he mean by that?"

Carina giggled, but it was all she could do not to start screaming at him. "We were talking about saving the theater. We're in a...well, some serious financial trouble, and I'm hoping to put on a fund-raising gala to come up with the money we need." She made a concerted effort to look the lieutenant boldly in the eye, to stare him down with her confidence.

Lieutenant Chapman broke the stare first and scratched his head. "Yeah, I figured it must be something like that."

Then to Carina's fury, he had the audacity to chuckle. "Guess I've been a cop too long, huh? I smell rats wherever I go."

Chapter Six

It had been a horrendously long day. Carina finally shut off the lights in her office sometime after eight and slid the partition across the counter. That afternoon she had called an emergency meeting of the entire crew to inform them of the Myrmidon's financial crisis. To her relief, everyone had been more than willing to pitch in and help.

The wardrobe mistress had offered to organize a raffle, with some of their more exotic and illustrious costumes as prizes. The set designer would try to persuade the lumber dealer to donate his material and the box-office manager would do the same with the printer. They were small contributions—in all, not amounting to much more than a few thousand dollars—but every bit helped.

As for planning the gala opening, everyone knew it was a calculated risk. If patrons did not respond quickly, their work would be in vain; there wouldn't even be an opening night. But despite the uncertainty, all of them were willing to put in long hard hours to make the event happen. As Carina slipped on her coat and left her office, she felt both drained and elated.

Rehearsal had finished for the day an hour or two earlier, but Kate and Len were just now coming down the hall on their way out. Carina was glad to see them. She enjoyed the Kramers and hadn't had much opportunity to visit with them yet.

"How would the two of you like to come to my place tonight for dinner? I know it's short notice, but—"

Kate was tying a bright square of silk over her hair as she walked beside her husband. "We'd love to, dear," she said, "but Len and I have made other plans."

"Oh, you have," Carina replied, feeling childishly disappointed. "How nice."

"We're going to do something we haven't done in years," Len said. "We're playing bingo at St. Michael's. Would you like to join us?"

Carina gave them a pleasant smile. "Bingo...no, I don't think so, thanks anyway."

"Some other time, perhaps." Kate waved on her way out the door. "Have a nice evening."

Carina stood there for a few minutes, uncertain of what she wanted to do, knowing only that she could not bear the idea of going home to her apartment alone. When she saw the stage manager coming toward her down the hall, she brightened. Here was a fellow who was always available for a free meal.

"Henry!" she called out. "What do you say to pizza and beer at my place?"

He gave her shoulder a brotherly punch as he walked by. "Sorry, babe, but I'm meeting Judith at the hotel for a drink. Not that I don't think you're gorgeous, too, but you know how it is." He winked suggestively as he stepped out the door.

Carina sighed. "Yes, I know how it is. Have fun." She was pleased for Henry. He was just getting over a breakup with his girlfriend. What better medicine than an evening with Judith Deveau?

She had just turned out the foyer lights when she heard Damian's voice coming from the hallway. "Does the invitation extend to visiting directors or is Henry the only one who rates?"

Carina spun around, her heart bouncing to her throat with excitement. "I didn't know you were still here."

He stepped out from the shadows, his face illuminated only by the reflected amber light of the streetlamps outside the lobby. "I didn't think you were, either."

She leaned back against the door, feeling suddenly shy, but pleasurably so. "I might as well move in to my office permanently, considering all the work there is to do."

Damian came closer until he was only a pace or two away. His leather coat was hanging open, his hands thrust in the pockets. "You might be more comfortable in my office, or should I call it Malcolm's? There'd be more privacy."

His words were like a potion. One sip and she was transported to a world of adolescent fantasy, of long-forgotten softly-lit scenes with a dream lover, with the Damian Fleming whose photographs had adorned her room. But those dreams didn't even come close to the heart-stopping reality of standing in a darkened theater lobby with Damian himself.

"I think I'd find the distractions a bit much," she admitted coyly, knowing the risks involved with flirting, but choosing to ignore them.

Damian took one last step to close the distance between them. "So would I . . . with you there, but it would be a delightful way to waste time, wouldn't it?" His hands moved up her arms and came to rest at her shoulders, pressing gently. The subtle influence of his fingers was like a wordless question. The intensity of his gaze, the rhythm of his deep and steady breathing, all seemed to demand a response from her.

Common sense told her she should take the opportunity to say something or even to pull away completely, but she did neither. Carina stood where she was, unmoving, though she knew it was akin to giving him an engraved invitation. Damian kissed the side of her neck, and her only response was a quiet gasp as she instinctively dropped her head back. She wanted to remind him they'd only met yesterday, but all she could think about were his lips hot and moist against her skin. She wasn't in love with the man, she insisted to herself; she was living out a fantasy. And when his tongue flicked her earlobe, her body should not have responded the way it did, with an echo deep inside that suggested her feelings were stronger than fantasy.

"Damian, don't...please." She jerked her head away. He was an actor, doing what actors liked to do to pass the time in a strange town. And she, who had always abided by her self-imposed rules, was only relenting now because he was Damian Fleming. Her behavior was as shameless as his.

He took her head in his hands and buried his face deep in her silky auburn hair, crushing it with his fingers. "Don't ask me to stop, sunshine. You feel so good...and you smell good...and you taste wonderful." Then his mouth covered hers, and there was no gentleness, no hesitation in his kiss—just the raw honest hunger of a man wanting a woman.

If he had paused even a few seconds, just long enough to consider her protests, Carina would have had the upper hand. She wouldn't be slipping her arms around his neck, as she was now, and returning his kisses with a passion to equal his. She wouldn't be moving her hips as he pressed against her, making her ache with a desire that was almost terrifying. She'd be telling him she wasn't interested, period. She'd be lying, but . . .

Finally, somehow, her well-trained defenses resurfaced, and Carina managed to unwrap her arms and pushed them against his chest. "I do mean it, Damian . . . please stop."

She was as limp as a rag. He could have ignored her plea, and she probably would not have had the strength or the desire to resist him. But he didn't. He stepped back and released her. As she looked up at him, she realized with a strange sinking sensation that if he'd forced his attentions on her, at least she could have had the luxury of hating him for his insensitivity. Damn, but the man knew how to make things difficult!

"Why didn't you stop me," he asked, "when I kissed you this afternoon?"

Carina had wondered the same thing and wasn't proud of the answer she'd come up with. She couldn't very well tell Damian that she wanted to know how it felt to be kissed by him, any more than she could admit to an even stronger yearning to find out how he was as a lover. So, for both their sakes, she lied. "I didn't have to. The policeman stopped us, remember?"

Damian frowned. "That's not an answer."

Grateful for the partial darkness, she looked away. "I know it isn't, but I told you before I don't—"

"Yes, I remember, you don't sleep with actors, but considering you work night and day in a theater, it must get lonely, since you've categorically eliminated the prime source of men from your life."

Carina began buttoning her coat with fingers that trembled. "In the long run, I still think it eliminates a lot of emotional aggravation."

Damian pushed the door open, inviting her to step outside first. "And contributes its fair share, too, I don't doubt."

Carina did not bother to argue the statement since protesting too much would give her away completely. She concentrated instead on locking up the theatre, careful to avoid glancing in Damian's direction. Intentionally or not, he had touched a sore spot. It hurt to be twenty-nine and alone. Not that she felt the driving need for a husband, the way most of her friends did. She liked her independence, her solitary life-style. But in Dunn's Pond, she was considered an oddity. Most Midwest girls still grew up and got married as a matter of course, even if there was college and some travel tucked into the plan somewhere. The few who were career-oriented or aggressively feminist sought the anonymity of Chicago or other large cities. Carina probably should have done the same, but she like Dunn's Pond. She liked the people there, and she loved her job. The only thing she hated was the loneliness, the lack of intimate companionship.

"Am I competing with anyone else in your life right now?" Damian asked after they'd walked along the street in silence for a while.

His question not only broke through her maudlin self-analysis, it surprised her. Why would an actor, who was only in town for three weeks or so, care whether he had any competition? Most of them looked upon such escapades merely as sampling the local wares before moving on. Whatever devastation they left behind was the least of their concerns.

"There's no one," Carina admitted almost wistfully.

Damian turned her around to face him in the semidarkness. "Then listen to me, Carina. Maybe it's not the most original line in the world, but I really don't want to hurt you. I don't want to frighten or offend you, either; I only want to make you feel special . . . because you are. There's a freshness about you, a vitality that I seldom find in women anymore. When I look at you, it's as if the sun is shining and all is right with the world."

Carina hardly recognized the soft moan that escaped her throat. "But you've dated heiresses and movie stars and royalty. You can have your pick of the world's most beautiful women—"

"Hush." He put a finger to her parted lips. "You see what my publicist wants you to see. Most of it's box office hype, and more often than not, I'm holed up in my theater, putting in the same long hours that you do. Or I'm on location, sweating in a 120-degree desert."

The manly essence of Damian's worn leather permeated the crisp, chilly air of autumn. Carina could feel his breath, moist and steamy, on her face. He had captured her fingers lightly in his, as one would hold a butterfly, fearing to harm it, fearing it might fly away. But as tremulous and timid as she felt, Carina knew she wouldn't fly away. She couldn't. She was much too captivated.

"Why have you never married?" she couldn't help but ask.

"Because most of the women I've met wouldn't be able to take a honeymoon without eighty pieces of luggage and three hairdressers," he answered with a tinge of bitterness in his voice. Carina didn't press him to elaborate. "Now what do you say to a room-service dinner in my hotel room?" Before she could object, he added, "Nothing will happen . . . unless you want it to."

Giving in completely to the ripples of excitement he inspired, Carina nodded. "I'd love to."

The Victoria Hotel, which evoked a sort of faded elegance, was an even grander structure than its pillared limestone contemporary, the Myrmidon. The hotel still managed to convey a sense of warmth and gentility that Carina felt whenever she stepped inside the spacious lobby. As they passed bowls of cut flowers and Romanesque statuary to the brass elevator, she found it comforting to know that Dunn's Pond, despite its recent setbacks, still held the capacity to charm.

Damian's two-room suite was typical, with its high ceilings, ornate moldings and plush upholstery of royal blue velvet. Double doors opened to a bedroom through which Carina could see an exquisite four-poster bed with a blue-floral spread. Such a warm, inviting bed.

"May I fix you a drink first?" Damian asked.

Carina spun around, feeling guilty and embarrassed, as if he'd been reading her thoughts. "Yes. Yes, thank you—a gin and tonic, please."

He crossed to the ornate bar at the far end of the room. "That's a good Englishman's drink. Have you ever been there?"

Carina sat down rather primly on the couch. "England? No, but if I had the chance, it would be the first place I'd visit. And I know what I'd do the minute I stepped off the plane."

Pouring a splash of tonic expertly over the ice, Damian grinned. "I hope you're going to tell me."

"I'd buy tickets to every single show in London and wouldn't see the light of day for a month."

His answering laugh was relaxed and spontaneous. The man was really so easy to like, Carina mused.

"It sounds like the kind of thing I've always wanted to do, but when I had the time, I lacked the money. Now it seems to be the other way around." She watched Damian prepare himself a drink made up of vermouth, bourbon and bitters—a Manhattan. Why was it that Carina had always imagined he would drink Manhattans? She couldn't recall reading it anywhere. She quickly dismissed the thought as irrelevant. Knowing a man's drink did not imply knowing the man.

He came over and sat beside her. "Cheers."

"Cheers." Carina took a sip of her cool tingly drink as her eyes met his. A week ago, she would never have believed that she could sit in a hotel room with *Damian Fleming*, and not babble or choke on an ice cube. Yet here she was, no less excited than any other woman would be, but surprisingly comfortable nonetheless. The man wore his fame as easily as he wore his brown leather coat and, like the coat, he seemed capable of leaving it at the door.

"Would you like to see the room-service menu?" he asked. At the moment, even reading a menu seemed like too much of a distraction. "No, it's all right. You can surprise me."

Damian set his drink aside and got up. "All right, I'll do that. I don't want to rush us, but the kitchen closes in an hour. If you want to freshen up, the bathroom is that way." He pointed through the door of the bedroom.

Carina rose and thanked him. It would feel good to freshen up.

Damian watched Carina leave the room, her shoulders held back, hair swinging. There was a self-possession about her that intrigued him. He sensed that her confidence was hard won, that her struggles had been like his own. He'd always liked self-made, independent women. Women who didn't sit around and wait for men to see them through their troubles. Women who didn't—

Dammit, he had only a few minutes to set the scene, and there he was, frittering away the time like some half-wit stagehand. Damian strode to the front closet and lifted a cardboard box from the top shelf. He had to find out how much Carina really knew about Malcolm's disappearance. He also had to know whether she was suspicious of his own reasons for being in Dunn's Pond. So far, she didn't seem to be.

He placed the box on the sofa, quite close to where Carina had been sitting. Then he picked up a menu, sat down in a nearby chair and waited.

She emerged from the bedroom a moment later, smiling. "Have you made up your mind yet?"

Ignoring the part of him that was enchanted with her looks, he watched her resume her seat on the sofa. She reached for her drink, glanced at the box, but didn't say anything. She did, however, appear mildly curious.

"I'm toying with the idea of Mississippi catfish," he said evenly, "but since I've never had it, I thought I'd get your opinion first."

"Oh, it's delicious," she answered, leaning forward with her usual enthusiasm. "You should try it; it's always fresh in this part of the country."

Her bubbly mannerisms amused him. No, it was more than amusement. Carina had a way of crawling deep inside, to the man who was once young and innocent of the real world. She even made catfish sound like an alluring experience.

"I'll try it. Would a California chablis do catfish justice?"

Her cheeks turned an appealing shade of pink. "I think so."

Damian phoned in the order, then returned this time to sit on the sofa. The box was between them now, and finally Carina pointed to it.

"Aren't you going to show me your scrapbooks?"

Damian stared at her curiously. Then realizing she was serious, he threw back his head and laughed. "Is that what you think this is?"

"Well, I . . . that is," she stammered with embarrassment, "most actors bring scrapbooks with them. I just assumed . . ."

Wishing he hadn't laughed, he said, "I didn't bring them with me, but I thought you might like to see this before I give it to Gerry tomorrow. I thought we could use it in the play."

"Oh, it's a prop." Carina leaned closer with her hands clasped in her lap. "I'm sure Gerry will be thrilled, whatever it is."

Damian lifted the lid and brought out a large stuffed parrot with a brilliant plumage of blue, yellow and emerald green. Holding it up, he said, "What do you think?"

Carina looked as though she didn't know quite what to say. "He's, uh, he's certainly very ornery looking."

He watched her reaction closely as he spoke. "They say he was a real scrapper in his day. See where his beak is chipped? Apparently it happened in Shanghai when he got in the way of a switchblade intended for his owner's ribs."

"Oh, my." Carina touched the bird's feathers almost reverently. "Did he belong to a sailor?"

"A merchant marine who was a friend of my grandfather's. The parrot and his owner traveled all over the world together, and in his will, the sailor stipulated that if he were to predecease the bird, my grandfather was to have him. Not only that, he wanted the parrot preserved and passed down in our family since the sailor had no relatives of his own. That's how I ended up with it."

"How fascinating," Carina remarked. "So your grandfather had him stuffed."

"Actually, no, he did it himself. My grandfather was a taxidermist in New York for over forty years."

"Really? Just like the character Len portrays in the play. So that's where Malcolm got his inspiration."

Carina's eyes were bright and animated, her expression pleasant. There was nothing in her demeanor to suggest she was involved in any way. Still, he couldn't be sure; perhaps she was just covering well.

"I suppose that's true," he said. "Malcolm got acquainted with Pop when we shared a place in Greenwich Village."

"Pop?"

"That's the bird's name. Pop is short for popinjay, another word for parrot."

"Hence, the play's title—*Fate of the Popinjay*," Carina said with a smile. "But doesn't popinjay have another meaning?"

Damian's grin was humorless. "It can also mean someone who's vain and contemptuous."

"Like Malcolm," Carina blurted out.

"Yes, quite. Like Malcolm." Her spontaneous remark about her employer forced Damian to reconsider his earlier opinion. Carina's antipathy toward Malcolm was obvious, so perhaps she *was* involved somehow. If he'd been wrong about her, didn't it make sense to take advantage of the situation? He still hadn't figured out how she might be involved, or even how much she knew, but it didn't matter. With Carina Rawlins as an unwitting, silent partner, his success in this venture was virtually guaranteed. Malcolm Spencer would never work at the Myrmidon—or any other theater, for that matter—again.

CARINA HUGGED HER COAT tightly around her as she took the shortcut home through the town's central park. Once part of the Dunn family estate, it boasted an archway of stone at the entrance and a formal stand of evergreens surrounding the pond itself. A network of paths was lighted by converted gas lamps in translucent yellow globes, and overhead a million stars reached to infinity.

Damian had offered to walk her home but she'd refused. The night had been perfect just as it was; she didn't want to complicate things with awkward goodbyes at her door. Besides, Damian had looked tired and drawn toward the end of the evening. She supposed he still hadn't adjusted to the time difference between England and the Midwest.

True to his word, he'd remained a gentleman. He'd held her in his arms, kissed her; he'd murmured delicious endearments. But he hadn't pressed her to make love. She needed more time, and he seemed to understand that. What a warm, wonderful man Damian Fleming had turned out to be.

Majestic boughs of foliage reached out at either side as Carina walked along the gravel path. The air was spicy with the heady scents of spruce, pine and juniper. She would have to make a point of bringing Damian out here some evening; the setting was so utterly romantic.

But her pleasant thoughts were interrupted by a strange sound. Carina stopped and tipped her head to listen. The park, in fact the whole town, was perfectly safe to walk through at night, but she hardly ever encountered anyone else this late on a weekday evening. She strained to hear more, and sure enough, someone was nearby, crying softly. The sorrowful sound urged Carina closer. Her instinctive reaction was one of concern; it didn't occur to her to be frightened.

She rounded the corner and came to a wrought-iron bench at the pond's edge, and there was Judith Deveau, mink coat and all, hunched over, shoulders heaving with the effort of her sobs.

"Judith?" Carina stretched out a hand to touch her.

Startled, the woman whipped her head around. Her face was ravaged from crying, and even in the darkness she looked twice her age. "It's you!" she rasped. "Why don't you get out of my sight and leave me alone?"

Carina caught a whiff of liquor on Judith's breath and wondered if the distraught woman had perhaps mistaken her for someone else. There could be no other explanation for her violent outburst.

"It's only me—Carina. What's wrong, Judith?"

This time, the actress leaped up from the bench and staggered back a step or two toward the pond. "I told you to get away from me," she snapped. "I know what kind of person you are. You're a murderer. Malcolm's been missing for two days, and it's because you killed him!"

Chapter Seven

"Judith, look out!" Carina barely had enough time to lunge forward and grab the woman's coat an instant before she backed into the frigid pond.

Judith was anything but grateful at being rescued. Her hands came up like talons, and she tried to claw Carina's face. The younger woman ducked, avoiding the worst of the scratches as she pulled the actress up the bank to safety.

When the immediate danger for both of them had passed, Carina let go of the coat and felt her face to make sure she wasn't bleeding. "What in heaven's name are you talking about, Judith?" she cried with anger and frustration. "I haven't killed anybody!"

Judith stared at her, swaying slightly and looking positively wretched. "Then why would Malcolm disappear the very night he bragged to us about the play? I know that something horrible must have happened to him, and I know all about you being in his apartment."

"I never—" Then she decided to rephrase her denial. "Well, I was there, but only with Damian."

The actress's laugh was caustic. "Oh, sure, Damian told me your cock-and-bull story about loaning your lingerie to wardrobe. Well, he might have fallen for it, but I sure as hell didn't. I know what a skirt chaser Malcolm was.

That's probably why you killed him, too. You caught him with some other woman, didn't you?''

The night air was chilly, but Carina was feverish with indignant rage. "Listen, Judith," she broke in. "I don't know how my camisole ended up in his apartment, and as a matter of fact, I'd intended to confront you about it. You've admitted knowing him—and Malcolm has always preferred the company of actresses." She would have loved to storm off just then, leaving the woman to her alcohol-induced ravings, but part of her needed to know what had triggered that wild accusation of murder.

But to her surprise, her protests brought on a fresh spate of tears from Judith. For a few moments the actress could barely catch her breath from crying, her face buried in her hands. Then, wobbling on precariously high heels, she returned to the bench and sat down heavily.

"I should have known it was wrong for me to come here. Things have gotten so complicated, but I only wanted to tell him..." Her voice faded tearfully.

"Tell him what?" Incensed as she was, Carina's instincts reached out to the woman whose carefully cultivated facade had crumbled before her.

"I...I wanted to tell him that if it hadn't been for him, our child might have t-turned eighteen this year."

"Oh, my God." Carina's mouth dropped open, and she sank down on the bench beside Judith. "I had no idea, Judith, honestly...and I swear I had nothing to do with Malcolm's disappearance." As she waited for the woman's tears to subside, it seemed as though Judith found her presence almost comforting—a few short minutes after her incredible accusation. The complete change of emotion prompted Carina to press on. "I know he can be a terribly selfish man. What did he do to you?"

Her emotions spent, Judith looked up. "Are y-you sure you didn't kill him?"

"Very sure," Carina answered soberly.

The dark-haired woman wiped her eyes with the back of her hand, then she laughed raggedly. "I suppose, given half a chance, I might have done him in myself, but as usual, he didn't stick around long enough."

Hoping the woman was only speaking figuratively, Carina waited for her to continue.

"We were practically engaged for two years, Malcolm and I," Judith finally said.

That poor woman, was the first thought that sprang to Carina's mind, though admittedly the man did seem to possess some freakish charm that appealed to certain women. "When was this?"

"A long time ago, when the three of us were young, naive and living in New York."

"The three of you?" Carina asked.

"Yes, Damian, Malcolm and I. The men had an apartment a few doors down from mine in Greenwich Village, the place for young, struggling artists to be in those days."

Learning that Damian formed part of this scenario caused a silent warning to flash in the back of her mind, but she ignored it for now to concentrate on what Judith was telling her.

"The three musketeers, Damian used to call us," the actress recalled quietly. "We were inseparable, and probably if we'd all stuck it out there long enough, we'd have made it. Damian did. But Malcolm was too greedy, too ambitious. He wanted Hollywood—the movie contracts, the glitter, the phoniness. I would have been content to sing and dance in a Broadway chorus, but he had bigger plans for me. He was going to make me a star, he said." Her mouth turned up in a shaky smile. "Guess it's not the first time a woman's fallen for a line like that, is it?"

Carina smiled, too. "Women have been falling for lines a long time, probably always will as long as there are men around."

"Yeah, I guess that's true," Judith agreed.

"Did you go to Hollywood with him?"

"No, he wanted to go on ahead without me, make some contacts and set us up in a little apartment. I didn't mind at the time because I had found a good steady job dancing, and I wanted to save some money. Before he left I gave him five thousand dollars, everything I had in my savings account. Seemed like a fortune at the time."

"I suppose you never heard from him again," Carina offered, knowing Malcolm well enough to predict his behavior.

"You're right, I didn't, but that wasn't the end of the story. A month after he left, I found out I was pregnant. I did everything I could think of to get in touch with him, but it seemed as though he'd dropped off the face of the earth." She paused and took a deep breath, as if bracing herself for what she had to say next. "The doctor warned me I'd have problems carrying the baby to full term if I didn't rest, but I was so sure that if I could just find him, we could work things out ... and be a family."

Carina's heart wrenched at the woman's anguish, and she felt a surge of hatred for Malcolm rising in her own chest. "What happened?" she asked gently.

"I sold everything I had to raise some money and took a bus to California, but I only got as far as Missouri. In the rest room of a truck stop, I had a miscarriage."

Sympathetic tears welled in Carina's eyes for the young mother and the unborn child. But Judith just sat there like a pillar of stone, no energy left for emotion.

"Did Malcolm ever know about the baby?" Carina asked.

The woman shook her head. "I was planning to tell him while I was here, but I never got the chance. I stopped loving him years ago. I don't even hate him anymore. But I still want him to know about the baby."

This was one of the rare occasions when the truth simply would not do. "I'm sure Malcolm would have been devastated to learn what you went through," Carina said, knowing full well the man wouldn't have given a damn.

Judith turned to look at Carina, and the expression in her eyes said she knew it was a lie, but that it was appreciated. "When I recovered from the miscarriage, I swore no man would ever deceive me again. Eventually I made it to California, and after a few years of waitressing and guest spots on TV I landed the part in *Pairs and Misfits*."

"How did you find Malcolm again after all these years?"

"I saw the ad for *Fate of the Popinjay* in a theater rag. There was his name, bold as brass, listed as playwright and director of a bright new play. He was looking for experienced actors. I figured enough time had passed for me to get in touch with him. At first, I wanted to make him suffer for what he'd done, but once I got here, I only wanted to tell him about the baby. More for my sake than his, I suppose. But now he's gone again, and he still doesn't know." Her tone was sad, wistful; the anger was gone.

"How did he react when you contacted him?"

Judith shrugged. "Typically, I guess. The man's always been good with surface polish. But I knew he was jittery having me around, and then when Damian showed up—" Suddenly she stopped, as if realizing she'd said something she shouldn't have.

"What about Damian?" Carina's nerves sent up a signal of red alert.

The woman shook her head and looked away. "Nothing, I was just . . . never mind, it's nothing."

Carina sighed and a kind of heaviness settled over her. One set of questions answered, another—even more puzzling—raised. *What had Judith wanted to say about Damian? What was he hiding?*

But Judith merely sat there, tight-lipped; obviously, she'd retreated to her own private world. Carina got up, knowing there was no point in pursuing the topic. Damian was the one with the answers.

"I have to be getting home. Are you going to be able to find your way back to the hotel?"

Judith nodded. "I'll be fine." She paused, and when she spoke again, her eyes were downcast, her voice low and hurried. "I'm sorry, by the way, for the awful things I said earlier. I had no right to accuse you. Overreaction, I guess, what with the drinks I'd had and sitting here thinking about the baby. And Malcolm. It was all so long ago, but it changed so many things in my life. Anyway, I'm sorry."

"It doesn't matter."

The woman's expression softened. "I had a nice time with Henry, your stage manager, tonight. Small-town men are nothing like the ones in California."

Carina smiled, but her mind was racing with disturbing thoughts of Damian. "No, I don't suppose they are. Good night, Judith."

THE NEXT MORNING Carina was in her office with Gwen Pennell, making plans for the opening-night gala. She'd been out soliciting donations when Damian came in, and now he was locked away in rehearsal. She wouldn't be able to talk to him for the rest of the day. With great effort she was able to put the troublesome matter of Judith's confession aside while she concentrated on the task at hand.

"Are you sure Harland isn't going to have a fit when he finds out you're raising funds for the theater he wants to tear down?"

Gwen was gnawing ungracefully on the end of a pencil. "He's already had a fit, but as I told him, I was working for this theater long before he came along, and he's not going to stop me now." Suddenly she slammed the desk with her fist. "I've got it! Let's make the gala a masquerade ball! People love getting dressed up in costumes, and we'll beat Halloween by a month."

"I don't know, Gwen. It doesn't give people much time—"

"Oh, please, Carina, say yes! People who can afford to come to this party have a dozen costumes sitting in their closets, and it doesn't take any time to rent one. It would be such fun!"

Her enthusiasm struck Carina as a little excessive, but Gwen was influential in society circles. "All right, if it means that much to you. How are we going to get the invitations out in time?"

The woman smoothed out the wrinkles in her designer shirtwaist. "No problem. We'll put fancy ads in all the major papers—you know, scrollwork, the whole bit."

Carina planted both elbows on her desk and wished she had half of Gwen's exuberance. "You're a genius," she remarked, meaning it sincerely. She couldn't help wondering, however, what the designer of Gwen's dress would say if he saw her in it. No doubt designed to make a slender woman look svelte and tidy, on Gwen the long-sleeved dress hung as if puckered in a hot-water wash.

Just then, a young man wearing a messenger's uniform came to the counter. Carina turned to him. "May I help you?"

"I have a telegram for Carina Rawlins," he said, holding up an envelope.

Carina's stomach constricted. It had to be from Malcolm's relatives back east, announcing his death. She was sure of it. People always seemed to send announcements like that by telegram. "I'm Carina Rawlins," she said, taking the envelope. Gwen stumbled up behind her and gave the young man a tip.

"Thanks, Gwen," Carina said absently as she scanned the message for some sign of a tragedy. Finding none, she read it a second time, and now her fear subsided and righteous anger took its place. "Why, that—" She bit off the words, reading the cable once more to be sure she wasn't seeing things.

> Sorry for worrying you. Pressure too much. Thanks to you, play sure to shine. Complete rest in Majorca just what doctor ordered. Will be back 6/10 for *Dames at Sea*. Break a leg!
>
> > Malcolm

"How dare he!" Fuming, Carina tossed the telegram onto her desk. "That no-good, conniving bastard!"

"Carina, your language!" Gwen clucked as she scooped it up. "After all, he is your boss."

Carina snorted in disgust. "Boss, hah! That's a laugh. To think, I actually worried he might be dead. Now I'd give anything for the chance to strangle him with my bare hands!"

Gwen clamped a bony fist to her chest. "You can't mean that. Didn't you read this? Poor Malcolm is suffering from nervous exhaustion. He did the only thing he could think of under the circumstances.''

Carina turned to stare at the woman. "How can you defend him? No one in his right mind disappears when there's a show to do. He could've ruined us, if he hasn't already."

"But you have Damian," Gwen argued. "If there's going to be a play at all, it couldn't be in better hands."

"Yes, but what if Damian hadn't shown up? I can run a theater, but I don't know the first thing about directing. Majorca! Doctor's orders! The man has been bumbling along all these years as a neurotic. Why pick now to go off the deep end?"

Judith came down the hall from the rehearsal room and caught the end of Carina's tirade. "My, my, what's gotten into you?" She was friendlier now, having bared her soul the night before.

Carina dropped the telegram onto the counter. If anyone could sympathize with her rage, it was Judith. The actress read the cable, suppressing an unnamed emotion by biting her lower lip. "The weasel hasn't changed at all, has he?"

Carina shook her head. It didn't feel right somehow, the message, the timing, the unexplained suddenness of Malcolm's defection. "I can't understand it. There've been plenty of occasions when things were so desperate around here that even I considered leaving, but this should have been the one play Malcolm would want to be totally involved in. Now he's missing the whole thing. Why?"

The actress shrugged. "If I could understand the reasons Malcolm Spencer does what he does, I'd probably be just like him. I honestly haven't got a clue what makes the man tick." She turned to walk away.

"Oh, one more thing, Judith," Carina said.

"Yes?"

"Would you please tell Damian and the Kramers that we won't be holding memorial services for our dear departed director after all?"

Judith's smile, full of irony, mirrored Carina's. In Malcolm, it seemed, they'd found a link, a kindred feeling. "I'd be happy to," she replied.

THE PRESS CONFERENCE was held that afternoon in the Myrmidon's ballroom, a setting that was both practical and designed to show off the theater's grandeur to maximum advantage. The floors were of highly polished oak, and a pair of crystal chandeliers glistened like giant snowflakes from the ceiling. Half the room had been cordoned off to make the noisy gathering of press corps seem intimate. At one end stood a linen-covered table with five chairs and, nearby, a podium. Carina perched stiffly on one of the chairs, watching the assorted grips and technicians clamber over each other to set up cameras, microphones and lights. She wished fervently that she were somewhere else. Anywhere else. This had seemed like such a brainstorm a couple of days before, when all of her indignation was directed toward Harland Pennell. The way she'd felt then, she couldn't wait to humiliate him in the media by disclosing the Myrmidon's plight, making him regret the day he decided to pick on a poor defenseless cultural institution.

Now she was angrier at Malcolm for letting her face this mess by herself. She was not a public speaker; she got stage fright talking to her own reflection in the bathroom mirror. If Malcolm were there, he'd be able to step up to the microphone and make mincemeat of the Harland Pennells of this world. The man, for all his failings, could coax blood out of stones when he put his mind to it. She, on the other hand, would be doing well if her palms didn't start to drip the moment she stepped up to speak.

Thank heavens everyone in the cast had agreed to be there, even though their vested interest in the theater did not extend beyond the current production. Carina wasn't deluding herself. They wouldn't have had a quarter of the turnout from the press without the attraction of show-business names.

Even now, Kate and Len were mingling contentedly with a couple of well-known theater critics from Chicago, one of whom was known to be a crusty old geezer except when it came to performances by the Kramers. For them, he could not sing praises high enough.

Judith was reigning over her own entourage, consisting mostly of libidinous male reporters, and enjoying every moment of it. Carina almost envied her ability to gesture gracefully and laugh easily, oblivious to what lay ahead. Wondering what was keeping Damian, Carina glanced at her watch. They were due to begin now, but she couldn't possibly do anything without Damian's reassuring presence. She simply couldn't!

"We're ready to go," a handsome young technician told her, gesturing for her to approach the microphone.

"But I . . . but we're still . . . Damian's not here," she moaned, her feet unwilling or unable to wrest themselves from their spot on the floor.

"Sorry," the man said, holding up his hands, "we gotta get started."

Carina glanced at the door, but it remained stubbornly closed. Dammit, what was keeping that man? What with Malcolm in Majorca and now Damian God-knows-where, she was rapidly losing faith in her fellowman. Kate, Len and Judith had already taken their places at the table and were watching Carina expectantly. She had no choice but to start without him.

On legs that felt distinctly wobbly, Carina walked the short distance to the podium. She leaned into the mike, said, "Testing," and was nearly thrown back against the wall when it responded with a deafening shriek.

"Oops, sorry about that," a soundman wearing headphones said as he leaped up to correct the problem.

By this time, Carina's whole body felt like a mass of wriggling worms, and she wasn't altogether sure she wouldn't faint. But even fainting might be effective, she told herself firmly as she stepped up to the microphone once more.

Carina took a slow look around the room and counted to ten. Society columnists, critics, assorted TV and radio journalists began to take their seats, tape recorders and pens at the ready. *This was it, her only chance.* If she could survive this ordeal, she could survive anything. With one final inhalation of tortured breath, she began.

"Welcome, ladies and gentlemen, to the Myrmidon Theater, and thank you for coming on such short notice. I'd like to think that your presence here today is an indication of concern for our rich and varied heritage, one that's threatened daily with extinction by what we call progress."

Good grief, Carina thought with a shudder, any more purple prose like that, and people are going to start retching. She hadn't trusted herself with cue cards, certain that she'd either drop them or sound insincere. At the moment, dropping cue cards seemed preferable to trusting her memory.

She folded her hands and continued explaining that she and each of the four cast members—*please, let there be four*, she silently prayed—would take turns speaking, and then they would open the floor to questions from the press.

A kind of numbness began to settle in her limbs, and as she spoke, she felt the strength of her convictions taking over where stage fright left off. Her voice was calm and clear when she said, ''Well over a hundred years ago, an enterprising young Irishman escaped the potato famine of his own country and came to America. An unscrupulous speculator sold him a parcel of land in northern Illinois that turned out to be little more than swampland. But Patrick Dunn did not discourage easily. He found himself a wife, sired twelve robust children and, in fifty years, turned Dunn's Pond into a boomtown.''

Off to her right, Carina could see the door opening slowly. She continued to tell the story of the town's railroad, farms and lead mines, but another vital part of her was following Damian's entrance.

She automatically noticed that he was dressed in a navy blazer, gray flannels, white shirt and red tie. Out of the corner of her eye she could see that his hair was still rumpled, which only added to the enticing image of disreputability he wore so well. More than anything, her body ached with the urge to turn around and stare openly, but no—she had to continue this infernal history lesson!

''...Enrico Caruso has sung here, Sarah Bernhardt played Camille, and President Grant's box seat is just the way it was when he and his wife used it over a century ago.'' Carina paused while some of the slower reporters scribbled notes, but uppermost in her mind was the knowledge that Damian was standing somewhere just beyond her field of vision, watching her. There was no other accounting for the way her body prickled with low-key excitement beneath her charcoal sweater dress. She could almost feel his eyes taking in her slim waist cinched with a wide black belt, her legs clad in dark textured stockings.

Enough of this! If she wasn't careful, the most important part of her speech was going to get fluffed, and even the possibility of another night with Damian wasn't worth that. So she gamely persevered, pleading with the press to support the Myrmidon's cause. She urged subscribers to show continued faith and asked single-ticket buyers to call the box office right away to ensure a sell-out crowd. In short, she begged everyone, public and press alike, to dig deep into their pockets and their hearts. Finally she announced the masquerade gala, to be held on opening night—the opening night that Harland Pennell's bank was so determined would never take place. "Together," she said in closing, "we can ensure that the Myrmidon will continue to provide first-class entertainment and culture for our children and our grandchildren." The long sigh she exhaled at the end of her speech was less than eloquent, but miraculously, it was drowned out by the sound of reporters getting to their feet and applauding.

She must have stood there like an idiot for the longest time because finally Damian came up to lead her back to her seat. The dear man, he made it look to the others as though escorting was part of his job, but Carina knew better. Still, her awkwardness hardly mattered at that moment. *She'd done it!* Never mind that her brain was now jelly and her nerves mush—she'd actually gone up there and done it!

Belatedly she realized she was supposed to have introduced Kate and Len, but Damian was ready for that, too. He strode calmly back to the podium and presented the veteran actors as if it were truly an honor. Then he returned to sit beside Carina.

Damian leaned over to whisper in her ear. "I've never seen you looking this sexy." His hand moved to cover her thigh, and Carina thought she might faint after all—but not from stage fright.

She turned to thank him, surprised to find his face so close their noses were practically touching. Carina drew in a sharp breath and whispered back, "I was thinking the very same thing about you."

He seemed genuinely flattered, which amazed her. She'd always assumed that men who became the objects of women's fantasies developed an immunity to women's affections. After all, how many times could a man stand hearing he was gorgeous?

"You were remarkable up there," he said. "You had them eating out of your hand." As if to emphasize his point, Damian took her hand under the table and drew circles on her palm with his fingertip.

Her body went instantly limp. "Damian, don't... besides, we're supposed to be paying attention," she protested weakly.

He nodded as if properly chastised, then turned to listen to Kate. But his fingers continued their seductive exploration of Carina's arm, rendering her a little more helpless with each calculated motion.

Kate was winding down her speech. "...the Myrmidon has always been like home to us ever since we left our repertory roots in England. There are times when Len and I feel ancient after forty years on the stage, but then we come here to this theater that has aged so gracefully...and we feel young again." The actress bowed deeply, and the reaction was, of course, tumultuous. Carina felt terrible that she'd missed so much of what Kate had said, but that didn't prevent tears of sheer gratitude from welling in her eyes.

Len, typically, did not try to upstage his wife. Instead, he confined himself to a short anecdote, relating their first bumbling efforts to speak with American accents on stage. It took him no time at all to have even the most jaded of journalists rolling in their seats with laughter.

Carina felt as though she were on an emotional roller-coaster ride. There was no other way to describe the effect of Kate's panache, Len's dry wit, her own astounding success at the microphone and Damian's devastating proximity. She was about to return his affections under the table with an aggressive move or two of her own when her attention was caught by the door opening once more.

Her first reaction was annoyance. She had made it explicitly clear to everyone in the theater that no one was to be allowed into the ballroom during the conference. Not even an irate bank president, if it came to that. They couldn't risk the consequences of an all-out brawl on the evening news.

But it wasn't Harland who slipped in through the door. It was a beefy dark-haired man Carina couldn't immediately place, though he looked familiar. Damian saw him too and leaned closer.

"It's our old friend, Lieutenant Chapman, in plainclothes this time," he whispered.

The officer looked around leisurely and caught Carina's eye just as she was replying with an obvious, "What's *he* doing here?"

"Probably looking for Malcolm. Did you remember to call them and cancel the missing-persons report?"

Carina wished Damian would stop conferring with her in front of the policeman. He was watching the two of them with great interest and making her nervous, as if they really were conspiring in something illegal.

"Why does he have to come looking for him here? If Malcolm had shown up, I'm sure one of us would have noticed by now. And no, I didn't remember to call the police. Obviously I should have."

Damian squeezed her knee under the table. "Calm down. He's probably just interested in the press conference...or he's here to catch Judith's act."

The stunning brunette was now making her way to the podium, and it occurred to Carina that if every good story needed a sexual angle to capture interest, Judith was definitely doing her part for the Myrmidon. The actress's wraparound dress of crimson silk jersey looked as though it had been hand-painted onto her body. Carina glanced across the room of pathetically lusting men and had to swallow a smile. Judith would probably do more for the theater's cause than the rest of them put together, simply by displaying her assets for the cameras.

Her discourse on the future of the Myrmidon was uninspired but mercifully short. Judith's vow to attend the opening-night gala to "greet her many fans," however, was vintage Deveau. Carina could now appreciate the woman's talents. She was far from empty-headed and knew precisely what button to push with her listeners and when.

Now it was Damian's turn to speak. Carina could not imagine how he could possibly come up with something new to say, but he had specifically requested that everyone else speak first. As he walked to the podium, Carina watched the roomful of eyes following his every move. One society columnist from a prominent Chicago daily, a woman in her sixties, was dabbing her florid, heavyset face with a handkerchief, proof positive that age was no barrier to Damian Fleming's charms. He'd had that very effect on Carina often enough, she recalled with mixed emotions.

She could still feel Lieutenant Chapman's eyes on her and was relieved when Damian began to talk. Even the policeman seemed interested in hearing what he had to say.

"It is unfortunate," Damian said after a brief introduction, "that the Myrmidon's artistic director has chosen this particular time to be away, but I must assure you that his absence will in no way affect the quality of our current production—and as I understand it, he will be back to direct the second play of the season."

Carina had to stifle a groan. Who but Malcolm would have the nerve to come back after pulling a stunt like this? But she banished the thought for the moment and concentrated on Damian.

"I've looked forward for years to acting in this particular play, and, yes, directing it. I'm especially proud that its world premiere will take place in such an illustrious theater as the Myrmidon. I'm convinced that the presence of those who've trod her stage before us somehow lingers on. But then we actors are notorious for being a superstitious lot."

There were several restrained chuckles, but the atmosphere in the room had perceptibly changed. Damian was definitely leading up to something. The tension in the room seemed to increase with each word that he spoke. Carina found herself sitting forward in her chair, clasping her hands tightly in anticipation.

"There is, however, one significant item that I feel needs to be clarified at this time. Barring any untimely action by those who control the Myrmidon's purse strings, we will be staging *Fate of the Popinjay*. It is generally accepted that Malcolm Spencer is the playwright of this somewhat irreverent social comedy. I am here to tell you that it's not true. At the present time, my solicitors in England are preparing the documentation necessary to sue for infringement of copyright. You see, ladies and gentlemen, it is I, not Mr. Spencer, who authored *Fate of the Popinjay*."

Chapter Eight

For a moment, all was silent. Then the room burst into a maelstrom of noise and confusion, reporters leaping from their chairs, cameras whirring, everyone shouting at once.

Carina sat motionless, stunned by what she'd heard. Damian's shocking announcement formed and reformed itself in her mind. Infringement of copyright . . . solicitors in England . . . the play was Damian's . . . the crime, Malcolm's. All the awkward, ill-fitting events of the past few days suddenly snapped into place. Damian hadn't come to Dunn's Pond for the sake of old friendship; he'd come to reclaim his play. And now Malcolm's disappearance made so much more sense. He'd been caught in his lie by the one person who could ruin him. What else could a coward like Malcolm do but run?

Carina turned to Judith seated at her left and when they exchanged glances, Carina knew this came as no surprise to her. But why should it? Judith, of all people, would know what Malcolm was capable of. Carina then turned to Kate and Len. They were whispering, their heads close together, and she could tell from their composure that they too knew why Damian had come.

Carina hardly knew what to feel. On the one hand, it was good that the truth, however odious, had come out, but the ensuing scandal could be disastrous for them. Malcolm had muddied the reputation of the entire theater by what he'd done. And he'd left her to handle the consequences. She was now the official spokesperson for the Myrmidon. How would she explain what had happened? Would people believe that Malcolm had acted alone, or would she and the crew be suspect, too?

Her thoughts jumped back to the cast. It could be no coincidence that Judith and Damian were both there. Each had cause to hate Malcolm, to want justice done, and their presence would certainly fuel Malcolm's urge to flee. But Judith, at least, had confided in Carina. Why hadn't Damian? Perhaps she was wrong to assume too much at this stage of their relationship, but they'd seemed to be growing so close. She shouldn't have found out like this.

No, that's not true, said a rational voice inside her. To Carina, it might seem that they'd known each other a long time, but that was because Damian had been her idol for years, and she'd adoringly followed every step of his career. But, in reality, they'd only just met. Damian had no way of knowing whether or not she was somehow involved with Malcolm's deception or whether she'd assisted in his escape. Even if he didn't doubt her innocence, it made sense not to tell her about his real intentions. He wasn't keeping secrets from her; he was protecting her. A delicious feeling of warmth crept through her as she watched him fielding questions from the press. With Damian at her side, they would get through this—she was sure of it. And meanwhile, she could hardly wait to be wrapped in his strong, loving arms again.

Half an hour later, the press conference was over. As miles of cable were being wrapped up and lights dismantled, Carina headed toward the door. The event had left her frazzled; she'd do anything for a cup of coffee right now.

"Excuse me, Miss Rawlins," a voice said from behind her.

Carina spun around, intending to remind whoever it was that the conference was finished. But it was the policeman whose presence she'd somehow managed to forget.

"Lieutenant Chapman," she exclaimed guiltily. "I saw you come in a while ago, and for a minute I thought you were one of the reporters."

He grinned and looked down at his baggy sports coat. "I've been assigned to some undercover work for a while. I just came here to find out if you'd heard anything from your boss. Obviously, you have. I had a word with Fleming a few minutes ago, and he told me Spencer's in Majorca. Right?" He tucked the notepad into his pocket, which for some reason put Carina more at ease—as though he were closing the file.

"Yes, that's right. I'm sorry I didn't get in touch with you right away, but the telegram only arrived this morning. With getting this press conference off the ground, it's been utter chaos here. But I did mean to call you as soon as it was over." *Honest,* she felt like adding.

"Hey, no problem. I was in the neighborhood anyway. Saved you a phone call, I guess, huh?"

Carina smiled, itching to get away. "Yes, I guess you did. Thank you so much for your trouble, Lieutenant."

"Don't mention it," he said with a shrug. "That was some announcement your friend made, wasn't it?"

"You mean about the play being stolen? Yes, it certainly was."

An expression of contentment settled on the officer's face. "Sure hope they nail him good." Whistling, the of-

ficer sauntered off, leaving Carina to wonder why she felt
so relieved to see him go.

"THIS SPAGHETTI SAUCE is sublime, Carina," Len said as
he twirled a huge portion of pasta onto his fork. "If I'd
known you were such a fine cook, I'd have foregone last
night's bingo."

"Thank you." Carina's elbows were propped on the table, and she held a glass of burgundy lightly between her
fingers. Her appetite was virtually nonexistent; she'd given
up trying to eat after the first few bites.

"It certainly is delicious," Kate agreed. "Pity that Judith couldn't join us. She's quite a nice girl when you get
past the brittle outer shell."

Damian tore off another slice of garlic bread. "She
seemed quite anxious to spend another evening with
Henry. It's probably the best thing for her right now."

Everyone was deliberately steering away from the one
topic Carina most wanted to discuss. She'd thrown together this impromptu dinner party, hoping that her questions would be cleared up once and for all, but so far no
one had volunteered any information. Finally she couldn't
stand it any longer. Tossing etiquette to the wind, she
blurted out, "Would somebody please tell me how Malcolm managed to steal Damian's play?"

The expressions and gestures around her suddenly froze;
for what seemed a long time, no one said a word. Then
Kate turned to Damian.

"Perhaps you ought to tell her."

Damian nodded and set down his wineglass. "I wanted
to tell you earlier, Carina, but I had to be sure where your
loyalties lay first."

"I understand," she said, having already come to that
conclusion herself.

"When Malcolm took *Fate of the Popinjay*, there was only one rough draft and a pile of research material and he made off with all of it. Proving ownership is largely going to be a case of his word against mine. I'm sure he's long since destroyed anything with my handwriting on it."

"When did he actually take it?"

"The same time he 'borrowed' Judith's money and headed for California." One corner of his mouth turned up in a grim smile. "He always had a knack for stretching the bounds of friendship."

"That must have been nearly twenty years ago," Carina said. "Why didn't you press charges right away?"

"I couldn't do anything until Malcolm actually tried to stage the play. Well, I guess I could have laid a charge of larceny, but none of us knew where he was. Then, as luck would have it, a couple days after Malcolm's disappearance, my agent called to say they wanted me to do a screen test in California for *Drake Kelly, Attorney-at-Law*. From then on, there were too many things going on in my life to worry about a play I'd written mainly as a catharsis."

"For years none of us knew what had become of Malcolm," Kate went on to say, "but then he made the fatal mistake of casting Len and me in a play at the Myrmidon eight years ago, unaware of our relationship to Damian."

Carina raised her brows. "Your relationship?"

This time it was Len who spoke. "Damian's father, Corporal Fleming, and I were part of the allied troops that invaded Normandy. After the war the pair of us went on a two-week bender and became fast friends. Then it was the steel mills for him, stateside, and back to the repertory in England for me, but not before we'd promised to act as godfather for each other's firstborn child."

"You're Damian's godparents?" Carina exclaimed. "I had no idea!"

Kate cast her godson a remonstrative though loving look. "Damian has always been reluctant to admit it to anyone. Sometimes I wonder if he's embarrassed about it."

Damian's face was suddenly stubborn. "You know better than that, Kate. I just never wanted it said that I rode on the coattails of the Kramers' success, being something of an idealist in my younger days."

Kate took his hands in hers. "You might call it idealistic, my dear. I call it foolish."

"Now, now, Katherine," Len chided. "We've had this discussion a hundred times, and we always end up deciding that it probably didn't do Damian any harm to come up the ranks the hard way."

"The only thing he ever allowed us to do," Kate explained, "was to lend him the use of our flat when he moved to England. The rest he accomplished on his own." Her smile shone with pride. "But to us he's been like the son we never had."

The love that flowed between the Kramers and Damian was so unmistakable, Carina wondered how she'd ever missed seeing it before. "Then you must have known about the stolen play," she said to Kate.

"Oh, yes," Kate replied, "we knew all about the unscrupulous Malcolm Spencer, so you can imagine our surprise when we found him here in Dunn's Pond. We let Damian know his whereabouts immediately, but he asked us not to say or do anything unless Malcolm tried to stage *Fate of the Popinjay*. Of course, we realized he was right, that he'd have a much stronger case against Malcolm. So all these years, we've been waiting and watching."

"But how did the four of you come to be cast in the play? It could never have happened coincidentally."

"No, you're right," Len said, "but fortunately, the roles of Mr. and Mrs. Tiggles in the play are ideally suited to Kate and me. Malcolm jumped at the chance to have us back."

"You must remember," Damian said, "that Malcolm had never learned that the Kramers were my godparents. He had no reason to distrust them."

"But what about Judith?" Carina asked.

"Now that was a little different," Damian admitted. "She was the only other person who knew the play was mine, and of course, Malcolm would have realized that himself. When she called him and asked for the part of Bettina Tiggles, she threatened to expose his crime unless he agreed to cast her. As you know, she had her own reasons for wanting to see him again, but she also wanted to be present when I finally exposed him."

Up until now, Carina had been reluctant to take sides, despite her own feelings about Malcolm. But Damian's oblique reference to Judith's tragedy somehow swayed the balance. What the cast had done still struck her as conspiratorial, almost shady, but then perhaps those were the only appropriate methods to adopt with a man like Malcolm. In any event, her sympathies for him were dwindling rapidly.

"How did you get the male lead?" she asked Damian.

"I didn't exactly have it handed to me," he said, "but as soon as I received word from Judith and the Kramers, I set out to dissuade Tim Myers from accepting the part of Jasper. Tim didn't care one way or the other where he worked, so he was quite happy to receive financial compensation for this role, along with the promise of a part in my next theater season."

"And you got Malcolm to draw up a contract?"

Damian swirled the burgundy in his glass and glanced uneasily around him. "Did I say I had a contract? Well, to tell you the truth, I don't. My appearance at the dinner party Sunday night came as a complete surprise to Malcolm. Are you going to report me to the Actors' Guild?"

He smiled when he asked her the question, but Carina knew the challenge ran deeper than the simple breaking of a union rule. He was asking her to see things from his point of view, to empathize with his actions. His eyes sought hers and held them.

"No," Carina said finally. "I think it would be better if I drew up another contract tomorrow, listing Damian Fleming as the new male lead." Her decision gave her a strange feeling of exhilaration...and danger. It was the closest she'd ever come to breaking the rules; Damian's powers of persuasion were amazing.

Later, when they were cleaning up the kitchen, Kate asked Carina, "Have you read *Fate of the Popinjay*?"

"No, actually I haven't. I prefer to see plays for the first time opening night. To me, it's the most exciting thing about working in a theater."

"I'd just as soon she didn't read it," Damian remarked as he dried the dishes and placed them on the counter.

Carina glanced at him and noticed that his jaw had tightened with a tension that seemed inappropriate to the conversation. "Why not?" she couldn't refrain from asking.

Damian dropped the glass he was holding, and it bounced on the linoleum floor. Surprisingly, it didn't break. He bent quickly to pick it up, avoiding her eyes as he said, "No reason. Just writer's insecurity. It comes across better on stage."

"Tell me, Carina, how have you managed to tolerate Malcolm all these years?" Kate cut in. "He must be quite unbearable at times."

Suddenly uncomfortable, Carina toyed at her throat with nervous fingers. She didn't like discussing Malcolm anymore. "I don't know," she said. "I've gotten used to him, I guess."

"Haven't you ever wanted to work elsewhere?" the actress asked pointedly.

"Well, I was offered a position a few years ago at the Court Theater in Chicago—"

"Fine place," Len mutterd. "Excellent reputation."

"Yes, it has," Carina agreed. "Unfortunately the job fell through a week before I was to move." She smiled wistfully. "The crew chipped in and bought a lovely monogrammed locket as a going-away gift and ended up giving it to me in commiseration instead."

Kate's sharp eyes must have noticed that Carina had a habit of reaching automatically for the locket at her throat. "Why aren't you wearing it?"

"I misplaced it and haven't had time to look for it. The clasp was loose. I should have had it fixed."

"Oh, dear, isn't that a shame?" Kate murmured with her usual theatrical flair.

Not long after that, Damian and Carina stood at the door waving good-night to the Kramers. It was raining, but the couple had brought umbrellas and insisted they would enjoy the walk, joking that a leisurely stroll on a rainy night would remind them of England.

Carina closed the door and turned to Damian. His eyes were a warm blue-gray, smoky and languorous. A woman could get lost in the deep dreamy mists of those eyes and never find her way back. No doubt, it had happened to many.

Slipping his arms around her waist, he drew her closer. "Alone at last. I was beginning to wonder if they'd ever leave."

"Yes, so was I." Yet Carina had spent the evening alternately wishing the Kramers would go and hoping they wouldn't. There was a certain inexplicable comfort in being able to hold off the immediate future, if only for a few hours and if only in one's mind. Part of her wanted badly to be alone with Damian, to share his feelings, to fall asleep in his arms until morning. What she wouldn't give to be the only woman in his life for a few precious hours! But a small, weakening part of her still sought the safer route.

"Would you like a brandy?" she asked, her palms moving across the lean muscular contours of his chest. The red tie and blazer had been tossed aside hours earlier, and now the top buttons of his shirt were open to reveal a fine sprinkling of dark blond hair. Brandy was a stalling tactic. With a heightened sense of clarity, she knew that. Her words were in direct opposition to what her hands and her heart were doing. Why couldn't she just admit to Damian how much she wanted him?

"I hardly need a brandy when I can look into intoxicating Calvados eyes," he said, his voice low and seductive.

Carina dropped her gaze. "Someone once told me my eyes were the color of weak tea," she joked.

Damian lifted her chin with his finger. "Listen to me, sunshine. I realize we've only known each other a few days, but I have to tell you in all honesty that I haven't been this captivated by a woman in years. I love the way you talk and the way you move. I love your stubbornness, the way you dig your heels in without giving up, no matter how tough the odds. And I already know I'm going to miss you terribly when these few weeks are over. Let's not pass up this opportunity we've been given.''

For a moment Carina teetered indecisively at the edge of his words. But then she glanced at the fire in the fireplace, now little more than a single glowing ember; soon it would die out and grow cold. But at least it had been a raging blaze once. She wanted to—no, she *needed* to feel that way about herself, to look back and know that once there had been a raging blaze. Taking his hand, she led him away from the door.

Neither of them spoke. The only sounds in the room were the rhythmic patter of rain on the roof and the fevered beating of two hearts. They walked slowly to the sofa, still hand in hand. Then Damian gently released her fingers and leaned over to open the curtains on the turret windows. As he switched off the lamp, all extraneous clutter disappeared; the room became an intimate, shadowed place. Plants glowed with a soft golden light from the streetlamps outside. Water glistened on the windows like dewdrops, then slid down in tiny silver rivers.

Damian took Carina's face in his hands, and he kissed her. They were delicate, searching kisses, each one isolated from the next by a subtle change in the angle of his mouth. Unique, delectable samples—first lips alone, then his tongue skimming her teeth, their tongues meeting to touch and caress, to dart in and around as if ritually courting. Together they kept pace, following the rising intensity of the kisses. Carina wrapped her arms around his neck and curled her fingers in the hair at his collar. Damian's hands sought out the gentle curve at the base of her spine and drew their bodies together. For a moment, time was suspended.

Then it was as though they couldn't get enough. Damian's tongue plunged deeply into her mouth, and Carina welcomed the invasion. Her senses drank in the lingering essence of wine, the musky male scent of him, the roughness of his whiskers at the edges of her mouth. Hesitant desire was washed away by the tide of passion, a full-blown stormy passion that demanded unequivocal response from its captives.

When the first wave reached its peak and subsided, Damian released her, using the respite to feast his eyes on her body. Then his hands boldly followed the outline of her neck, her shoulders and her breasts. First his palms, then his fingers rasped over her nipples, with a gentle friction that made them rise and harden. A small wanting sound escaped her throat and drifted into the night.

Still, the magic continued. Damian's hands followed the curve of her hips and came together over the softly rounded plane of her stomach. He buried his head between her breasts, and her body swayed with the exquisite torture of his mouth hot and moist against the soft texture of her dress.

When he tried to pull her dress upward, his movements became suddenly awkward. The garment with its clingy lines did not make things easy for a man. With a secretive smile on her face, Carina drew up the skirt a few provocative inches at a time. At this moment her need for him was not quite so overwhelming as his for her and she was in control. But with innate feminine wisdom, she knew it would not always be so. Lovemaking was fluid, a matter of ebb and flow, rise and fall...power and surrender.

She lifted the dress over her head and heard Damian's soft moan. The sound filled her with an icy-hot tingle, and she knew that she pleased him. She was wearing a lace teddy of pearl gray, her textured stockings held up by matching garters. Perhaps it was her slightly wanton attire or the man who stood before her, his gaze almost worshipful, but she'd never felt so completely a woman until this moment. With an elusive sense of déjà vu, she wasn't surprised that Damian Fleming would be the man to make her feel this way.

Carina began to undress him, opening the rest of his buttons and slipping the shirt from his shoulders. The tawny expanse of his broad shoulders, his tapered waist and flat stomach were so flawless, so intrinsically male. Her fingers began to tremble. She fumbled with the buckle of his belt and knew it was time to relinquish control.

With swift sure motions Damian stepped out of his pants and briefs. Then he helped her with the bows and the garter and the stockings. It seemed to take forever, but at last they were both naked.

Locked in each others arms, they fell to the couch. Damian fit his body over hers, and Carina arched up, moving her hips in a seductive sway beneath him. She felt him shudder with anticipation while her own body seemed to melt and grow weak in need of him.

"Please, Damian," she whispered, "don't make me wait."

"Don't worry, love," he answered in a voice ragged with desire.

He pulled back slightly, then thrust himself deep inside her. Carina's responding cry was explosive, a guttural sound emanating from the most womanly part of her. For a moment they lay quite still, their bodies responding to the perfect fusion; then they assumed a unison rhythm, a heated dance. The pulsing, driving fire of their passion rose and quickened and rose again, until together they reached the peak, a powerful white-hot burst that consumed them both with a fierce sweet agony and left them clinging to each other, breathless and replete.

Wrapped in Damian's arms, Carina drifted off into a misty, dreamlike state, aware of little more than her complete contentment. She couldn't bring herself to worry about the day's events or what tomorrow would bring. She and Damian had the whole glorious night to themselves; nothing else mattered.

Much later, Carina was half awakened from a deep sleep by the sound of persistent knocking. Rolling over, she tried to ignore the intrusive noise, but it wouldn't go away. Damian groaned, and when he tried to bury his head in her shoulder, she woke up completely.

She peered over him at the clock and saw that it was after midnight. The pounding on the door had grown louder and more insistent.

"Who in the name of—" Carina sat up, about to swing her legs off the couch when Damian flung an arm possessively around her waist.

"Ignore them . . . they'll go away," he muttered.

"No, they won't, and I'm afraid they'll wake up the neighbors." Sliding out from beneath his arm, Carina reached for her robe.

"Then I'll go and…" Groggily he pushed himself up but Carina was already halfway across the room, tying her robe loosely as she walked.

She threw open the door and saw a hunched figure dressed in black. Carina staggered back a step or two, and her small scream brought Damian out of bed and to her side like a shot, hastily wrapping a bedsheet around his middle.

"Who are you?" he demanded of the visitor, shielding Carina with his body.

A small frightened voice came out from the depths of the black hooded raincoat. "It's me, Gwen Pennell. Will you please let me in?"

Chapter Nine

"Good heavens, Gwendolyn, what are you doing here?" Carina asked. "It's after midnight."

"I know," Gwen replied, "but I had to...to come and see you." She stepped inside, and water poured from her rain gear onto the hardwood floor. The black hood cast her face in a shadow, giving her a strange almost grotesque appearance. She turned and looked at Damian, who stood there yawning and rubbing the sleep from his eyes.

"Oh, dear," she said, "you have company. I'm sorry."

"No apologies necessary," Damian said graciously, "but if you two ladies will excuse me, I'm going to pull on a pair of trousers."

Carina's eyes followed him longingly, her body feeling warm and sated with the afterglow of his lovemaking. How had Gwen developed such a poor sense of timing, she wondered with acute annoyance. But there she was, so Carina decided she might as well find out why.

"Have a seat," she offered, "and let me take your coat."

Gwen sniffed loudly and pulled the hood even farther over her face. "I'll keep it on, thanks." She perched on the edge of a ladder-back chair while Carina sat down at the nearby dining table.

Gwen continued to sniffle, but since Carina couldn't see her face, it was difficult to tell whether she was crying or coming down with a cold. If she was crying, though, there was a probable explanation. "It's your husband, isn't it?"

"Carina, I've never seen him this upset. You never should have done it!"

"Done what?"

"The...press conference." Gwen snorted and wiped her nose with a crumpled ball of tissue.

"Oh, that." Carina *felt* upset that Gwen had been caught in the middle of this mess, but there was very little any of them could do about it. "So he saw the news tonight, did he?" she asked lamely.

Gwen's hood bobbed up and down. "Harland doesn't like to be humiliated. You could've just had the opening-night gala, and everything would have been fine."

"I don't think so," Carina argued. "We had to make the public aware of our problem."

"But did you have to get *them* to talk, too?" Gwen waved her arm in the direction of Damian who was standing at the far end of the room buttoning his shirt. "They made the bank sound like some kind of unfeeling monster."

Carina had to bite her tongue to keep from making the obvious retort. She was relieved when Damian came to her side, placing his hand securely on Carina's shoulder.

"What was your husband's reaction, Gwen?" he asked, more gently than Carina could have managed.

His solicitude stirred up the woman's emotions even more, and she began to cry in deep heaving shudders. He walked over to her and spoke soothingly in a low, gentle voice. "It's all right now; everything's all right. Calm down."

"He...he, um..." she spluttered, "he says he's not going to let you get away...with this. He says he's going to make you pay dearly...and...I know he isn't just talking about m-money."

Carina and Damian exchanged glances. "I'm sure Harland was just reacting in the heat of the moment," Carina said, not totally believing her own words. "No one was putting him down personally."

"Carina's right," Damian added, kneeling beside Gwen with an arm around her shoulder. "This isn't the first time a theater has had to resort to—"

"My God, Gwen, what happened?" Carina's hands flew to her face in shock. The hood had fallen back, and now Carina could see the swollen purplish bruise around Gwen's eye. She instantly understood why Gwen had refused to take off her coat.

Still sobbing, the woman dejectedly turned her head away. "I tried to tell you he was furious."

"But I had no idea. I'm so sorry," Carina said, suddenly feeling squeamish.

"There's no need to be sorry. It's not the first time he's done this."

"But if I hadn't upset him by—"

"It's not your fault!" Gwen cried, her face ravaged by tears as she looked at Carina. "He just has a...a temper. That's why I had to wait until he passed out before I came to see you."

Damian stood up, shaking his head. "That lowlife scum," he muttered. "Carina, I hope you're not going to let Gwen go back there. He might be aware that she's missing by now."

"No, of course not," Carina agreed. "You're welcome to stay here—"

"I can't stay!" Gwen wailed. "Don't you understand? He'd find me and probably kill all of us." She stood up shakily and replaced her hood. "I only came here to warn you about what he said, that's all. I ... I thought it was important for you to know. I have to go home now."

"But, Gwen, the man is no good. You've got to leave him before he does something worse." Carina's voice rose with urgency, and she put a hand on Gwen's arm to stop her from leaving.

"Don't worry about me. I know how to handle him." She touched the ugly bruise on her eye. "Good thing we're having a masquerade ball, isn't it? I'll be able to wear a mask." She laughed weakly, but it sounded more like a sob.

Carina gave up, knowing she'd be wasting her time trying to talk sense to Gwen now. "Let's get together for lunch, okay? I'll call you tomorrow."

The woman drew her coat tightly around her and thrust her hands into the pockets, her shoulders hunched. "You don't have to call me. I'll be at the Myrmidon helping out every day."

"Are you sure that's a wise idea?" Damian asked.

"Of course it is," Gwen insisted, sniffing one last time. "I have my commitments, just like Harland has. He's not going to stop me from doing what has to be done." With a hurried good-night, she was out the door.

Carina turned to Damian, feeling sad and frightened and angry all at once. He said nothing, but led her back to bed, wrapped her comfortingly in his arms and held her safe, until finally she fell into a deep, exhausted sleep.

THEY LEFT HER APARTMENT together the next morning after an intimate breakfast in bed that should have been sheer ecstasy. Gwen's visit had dampened Carina's mood, and she was still feeling subdued as they walked toward the theater.

"I'm going to have to stop off at the hotel and change my clothes," Damian said, slipping his arm around her waist. "Would you like to come up with me? We might even have time to—"

"I'd better not," Carina replied, her body craving the sensual delights he so temptingly offered, her mind resisting. "I have a thousand things to do today, and if we go to your room..." A slow smile crossed her face in spite of herself, and she reached playfully to tweak his thick blond hair. "We already know what a hard time you have dragging me out of bed."

He grinned and one hand slid down to stroke her hip. She didn't care that they were standing on Water Street, in plain sight of anyone who chose to look. She gave herself up to the sensations of his touch, his presence, oblivious to the world around her.

He kissed her deeply and then took a long moment to study her face. "You really do light up my life, sunshine," he said softly. "Save tonight for me, okay?"

She nodded and watched him take the front steps of the hotel two at a time. *If it were up to me, Damian, I'd save tonight and every other night for you.*

CARINA HAD WALKED as far as the end of the street when she heard the sound of footsteps running up behind her. She whirled around to discover that the dark-haired man in a track suit was none other than Lieutenant Chapman. She tried not to show her annoyance, but he really was the last person she cared to see—with the possible exceptions of Malcolm and Harland Pennell.

"Hello, Lieutenant," she forced herself to say. "Are you following me?"

He jogged up beside her and smiled cheerfully. "Morning, Miss Rawlins. No, I wasn't following you exactly. I like to run every day, but it gets kinda boring when you do it in the same place all the time, know what I mean?"

Carina smiled back and continued to walk. "I find it boring to run, no matter where, I'm afraid."

The policeman continued to raise his knees in an exaggerated running motion as he moved along beside her. "Actually I was hoping to see you at the theater today. Mind if I come along with you now?"

"As long as I don't have to jog," she remarked dryly.

He chuckled at her feeble joke and slowed down to a normal pace. "You know, Miss Rawlins, I've been thinking a lot about your boss since yesterday."

"Have you?" Carina wondered idly whether it was the low crime rate in the area that obliged the police to dwell on nonexistent problems.

"Didn't you say he was in Majorca?"

"That's where he is."

"Well, I checked our atlas back at the station, and Majorca's an island near Spain."

She expelled a long breath. "Yes, I know."

"So it stands to reason a person would hop a plane to someplace that far away, right?"

"Presumably," she answered.

"That's what I thought, but when I went around to check Spencer's apartment, his car was still parked at the back of the building."

"He probably took a limousine to O'Hare. There are several that leave from the Victoria daily." Anticipating his next question, she added, "Including one that departs very early in the morning."

"Yeah, I thought of that, too, but I haven't had a chance to check it out yet. But I did take a look inside his apartment, and you know what? There was a whole set of brand-new luggage in his closet.''

He'd succeeded in piquing Carina's curiosity. ''There was? How odd.''

The officer scratched his head thoughtfully. ''Not only that, his closet and dresser were full of clothes, and even his shaving kit was still in the bathroom.''

Carina had no idea how to respond to Lieutenant Chapman's observations, but she did wish he would find someone else to mull them over with. Still, he seemed to be waiting for her opinion, so she shrugged and said, ''Perhaps he wanted to buy new clothes when he got there. Malcolm has been known to live extravagantly now and again.'' She thought of the horrendous dinner tab that had arrived from the Victoria and shuddered.

''So what you're saying is the guy might have decided on the spur of the moment to fly the coop and then decked himself out in fancy new duds when he got there.''

Carina found the policeman's version of her statement rather amusing, but she didn't smile. She was too irritated with Malcolm, who still managed to torment her even when he wasn't around.

''Well, I have no proof of anything,'' she told the lieutenant, ''but knowing Malcolm, it's certainly possible.''

''There's one other tiny thing that bothers me about this case,'' he said.

''And what is that?'' Carina asked, deciding not to remind him that there was no ''case,'' as he put it.

''I found a toothbrush in his bathroom and a tube of toothpaste nearby. Some of the toothpaste was on the brush, but most of it was squirted across the counter in sort of a semicircle, like someone or something had taken him by surprise, know what I mean?''

By now they had reached the front doors of the Myrmidon. Carina, suppressing the recurring sense of unease the officer seemed to inspire, turned to look at him. "I'm not sure that I do know what you mean, Lieutenant."

He shrugged. "Me neither, but I thought I'd tell you just in case you could shed some light on any of this. I always hate to close a file until I'm satisfied."

"I understand," she said, pulling open the door.

"One more thing. Would you mind if I took a look at that telegram he sent you? Just to satisfy my own curiosity."

Carina felt needlessly relieved. "I don't mind at all. Come on in."

Nothing could have surprised Carina more than the sight that greeted her when she stepped into the lobby. Members of the stage crew were everywhere, dressed in their grubbiest work clothes. The tattered carpet was rolled up to one side of the room, wall plaster lay crumbled and broken on the floor and the air was thick with the smell of paint and varnish. Kate, in splattered overalls, was hacking at what remained of the old plaster, while Len stood on a ladder applying fresh paint to the ceiling with a roller. Everyone stopped working for a moment when Carina came in, and there were smiles and general laughter at her expression of complete astonishment.

"Good morning, dear." Kate's silver curls bobbed gaily as she set down the hammer she was using to pry off the plaster. "I know it's a dreadful mess at the moment, but it won't be long before the foyer of the grand old Myrmidon is restored to its former glory."

"I can't believe it," Carina muttered, realizing how early people must have risen to get this much done. "Why didn't anyone tell me? I could've been here to help."

"That's why we didn't tell you," Henry, the stage manager, said. "You always try to do everything yourself, and you've got enough to worry about as it is." He leaned against an electric floor sander, wearing a proud grin.

Helen, the box office manager, was also smiling broadly, her long hair tied back to keep it out of the varnish can she was holding. Even Gerry, the elusive props man, was there, a carpenter's apron around his waist. Tears of gratitude welled in the corners of Carina's eyes. People did care about the Myrmidon. She wasn't fighting this battle alone!

"I'm so...I just..." she stammered. "I don't know what to say."

Len climbed down from his ladder. "No need to say anything. If each of us can squeeze an extra hour out of our day, we'll get this place looking good in no time."

She began to unbutton her coat. "From what you've accomplished already, I can see that. And I promise to pick up a paintbrush during my lunch hour." She felt someone nudge her elbow.

"Excuse me, Miss Rawlins—about that telegram," Lieutenant Chapman said. "Could I take a look at it now?"

"What—oh, yes," she answered, realizing with surprise that she'd almost managed to forget the officer's presence. "I'll get it for you," she said quickly, and almost ran to her office.

The telegram was by now buried underneath a pile of purchase orders, invoices and assorted correspondence. She impatiently pulled it out and brought it back to the lobby for the lieutenant to read.

The lobby grew silent as people gradually became aware that the thickset, awkward-looking man was, in fact, a policeman. But they all continued to work diligently, casting him a curious glances and whispering now and then among themselves.

"Hmm," the officer said after staring at the piece of paper for an inordinately long time. "Is this *Dames at Sea* he's talking about a play?"

"Yes, it's a musical," Carina replied. "It's supposed to be our second production of the season, and Malcolm's directing." *If he comes back at all,* she added silently, *and if there's still a theater.*

"So how come he plans to stay in Majorca till June?"

"June?" Carina gave him an astonished look. "I don't know what you mean. Rehearsals start in early October."

The lieutenant held out the cable and jabbed it with a thick forefinger. "Right here, it says he'll be back June tenth."

Carina read it more closely. *Will be back 6/10,* the message read—the tenth of June. "Funny, I'd never noticed before. But it must be a misprint. Malcolm couldn't possibly afford to stay in Majorca for nine months." The last comment was a dismal attempt at humor on her part, but nobody even smiled.

The policeman rubbed his forehead intently. "I don't know. Could be a misprint, I s'pose, but normally when people send cables, the agent's pretty careful about verifying the message—especially when it's in another language. I think maybe it's not a misprint at all."

"But it doesn't make sense," Carina argued. "He wouldn't say he's coming back for *Dames at Sea* in June. Our season is over by then."

"Assuming he's the one who sent the telegram."

"What do you mean?" Carina now was thoroughly confused by what the policeman seemed to be implying. There was absolute silence in the lobby; even the plaster had ceased crumbling from the walls.

Lieutenant Chapman didn't answer right away. He took his time sizing everyone in the room, one by one, with a directness that would have been rude from anyone without a badge. "Would you mind," he mumbled to Carina out of the corner of his mouth, "if we finished this discussion in your office?"

She glanced around, her sense of disquiet mounting by the second. "No, I don't mind." She stepped gingerly over a pile of rags.

When the two of them were in her office, with the partition above the counter firmly closed, Lieutenant Chapman pointed to the numbers on the cable again. "Look here," he said. "When Americans use the short form to write a date, they put the month first, the day second, right?"

Carina agreed.

"Well, I've noticed on some of the correspondence we get at the station that Canadians and Englishmen do it the other way around—the day first, month second. See what I'm getting at?"

"Not really. Malcolm was born and raised in the United States."

"That's my point. Spencer wouldn't have written it that way, but someone who wasn't born and raised in this country would."

The palms of Carina's hands grew sweaty. "Are you suggesting that somebody else sent this telegram?"

The lieutenant nodded slowly. "If Spencer were coming back October sixth like you seemed to think, the telegram would have read ten-slash-six. Instead, it says six-slash-ten, June tenth. I get the feeling your Mr. Spencer isn't in Spain at all—someone just wants us to think he is. And if that's the case, then maybe he won't be coming back . . . at all. Get my drift, Miss Rawlins?"

She could hardly miss it. What the lieutenant was obviously suggesting was that Malcolm might be dead.

Chapter Ten

Carina stared at the policeman a long time, barely able to breathe. She felt as though a giant fist were squeezing the air from her lungs. Malcolm dead? *Murdered?* Impossible. Who on earth would want to kill him? Alarmingly, she had a sudden recollection of the many times she'd wanted to strangle him herself, but that was hardly the same thing. Dislike was a pretty weak motive for murder.

"Wh-what are you going to do now?" she asked, hoping the lieutenant couldn't read her incriminating thoughts.

"Well, for one thing, I'd like to take this telegram with me and try to trace it to the sender. And I'll want to know where everyone in the cast and crew are from—like yourself, for example."

"Born and raised right here," she answered quickly.

"Thought so. I'm also gonna check the flights out of O'Hare and find out if Spencer was on any of them." The lieutenant stuffed the cable into his pocket and got to his feet, hoisting up his track pants with two hands. "If you think of anything that might be important, you got my number. Give me a holler, okay?"

What if she couldn't think of anything important, she wondered. Was the hell-bent lieutenant going to assume she was hiding something? Carina stood up and escorted him to the door of her office. "I'll think hard," she assured him with forced enthusiasm. "And thanks for coming."

Carina stayed in her office and closed the door, hoping desperately that no one would come in to ask her what the policeman had wanted. She needed a few minutes alone to sort it all out.

She could understand why the lieutenant might think this was more than a simple missing-persons case. For one thing, they now knew that Malcolm had stolen Damian's play and tried to pass it off as his own. Then there was his reputation as artistic director. Most people who dealt with him found him egocentric, abusive and rude. Malcolm had often managed to inspire strong dislike, even rage, and more than one disgruntled theater employee had been heard to mutter angry threats behind his back.

But she still had trouble accepting the theory that Malcolm had come to a violent end. The evidence was so circumstantial. A day and a month reversed on a telegram. So what? Probably a simple clerical error made at the cable office in Majorca. If it had been sent by somebody else, then who? He didn't have any Canadian enemies that she knew of, and the only people associated with England were the Kramers, who were born and raised there. And Damian, who wasn't really English. He'd emigrated from the United States as a fairly young man. But clearly, none of them could have sent it, since they were already here.

As for the other things the officer had mentioned, the errant squirt of toothpaste and the closetful of clothes, Carina found them no more persuasive. First of all, there was his sharp-eared landlady who swore he hadn't come home that night. And then, he'd spent an entire evening with a less-than-admiring cast. So when was this imagined sneak attack supposed to have taken place? Mrs. Lucid would have heard any shouts or the sounds of a struggle, wouldn't she?

The state of Malcolm's apartment was admittedly puzzling. He had obviously entertained a woman at some point during the weekend, but it couldn't have been Judith; she despised the man. Unless she... No, she wouldn't do that. Judith was no longer interested in avenging Malcolm's betrayal of her; she'd said so. Though seducing him in his apartment would have given her an opportunity to... No, no, no. Judith would never do something as risky as commit a murder. Carina briskly dismissed the theory— but on the other hand, she didn't really know Judith well enough to know what she might be capable of doing. How much hate did it take to drive a person to murder?

Carina realized with a sickening lurch that she didn't know Damian well enough to judge, either. He certainly had reason to hate Malcolm, and he'd arrived without fanfare to appear in this play, a fact that had perplexed Carina from the start. What was it the police always looked for? Motive, opportunity... *No, it was absolutely unthinkable!* Her imagination was running away with her.

Carina yanked the filter cone from the coffee machine, emptied out yesterday's grounds and refilled it, still brooding on the policeman's dark intimations. This was all too much to take in. Perhaps there were a few loose ends, intriguing enough for a zealous lieutenant to fabricate a murder case. But the more Carina thought about it, the more she was convinced that the whole thing smacked of Malcolm Spencer's chicanery.

Any other coward would just run away when his sordid past caught up with him, but not Malcolm. He would take great delight, she suspected, in leaving behind a trail of thorny clues, just to liven things up. She disagreed with the lieutenant, who thought Malcolm wouldn't be returning in

October—or maybe not returning at all. She herself had a hunch that the man couldn't wait to get back to reveal his sick practical joke to them all, snickering at his own cleverness. As far as the lawsuit for infringement of copyright, he'd probably go to court and get off on a technicality. Or a lack of hard evidence: Damian had said it would be a question of his word against Malcolm's.

Well, even if Carina couldn't bring about a jail sentence, she could certainly ensure that Malcolm never disgraced this theater again. Once Lieutenant Chapman had satisfied himself that Malcolm was where his telegram said he was, she was going to discuss the matter with Gwen and the board of directors. Assuming the Myrmidon survived this financial hurdle, she was going to see to it that they somehow got rid of Malcolm. And if the board offered her the position of artistic director…well, she'd accept it with due modesty, of course. But there really wasn't anyone else who could do the job as competently as she could.

A WEEK FLEW BY, and Carina knew she would always look back on it as one of the happiest times in her life. Her days were long, the work hard, but there was an invigorating spirit of commitment and cooperation. Everyone involved with the theater—cast, crew, staff and volunteers—was spending extra hours on the countless tasks that had to be finished before opening night. Carina was more hopeful than ever that they could save the Myrmidon. Meanwhile, the elaborate Victorian sets were nearing completion, costumes were finished, and ticket sales, thanks to the celebrity cast and the play's notoriety, were brisk.

But her greatest joy lay with Damian. For years she'd lovingly cherished an image of him; now she knew that the real Damian far surpassed the man she'd fashioned in her mind. For years she had admired the roles he chose to play, had identified with the fragments of himself he chose to share with the public. Now, being with him was like a natural progression of all she'd known and loved before. Nothing had ever felt so right.

When they weren't working at the theater, they were always together. They took in a couple of movies and went for long walks. If the weather was mild, they picnicked in the evergreen park near the pond. For once, Dunn's Pond was not a monochrome Midwest town with nothing to offer. The skies had turned bluer, the sun brighter; everything Carina did was with newfound enthusiasm.

And then there were the nights. Soft dark nights beneath a harvest moon, when Carina and Damian came to know each other in the most intimate ways a man and a woman can. Nothing could compare to the feel of his hands on her body. There was no greater radiance than the deep ocean blue of his eyes when he held her in his arms, no sound more thrilling than the words he uttered at the climax of their lovemaking.

Carina couldn't imagine what her life would be like beyond the next two weeks; she wouldn't allow herself to think about it. For now, there was sweet solace in Damian's embrace, and perhaps when the time came for him to leave, the memories alone would be enough.

One evening, she was waiting in her office for rehearsal to finish. Only five days remained until opening night; only three to the first dress rehearsal. The cast had been putting in longer hours to ensure they'd be ready on time.

Damian would be emotionally and physically spent after ten hours of directing and rehearsing. Carina had a quiet evening planned for the two of them—a fire in the fireplace, soft music and a cheese fondue, with fresh fruit for dessert. The groceries were sitting in a plastic shopping bag beside her desk; a bottle of chablis was at home chilling in the refrigerator. All that was needed now was Damian himself, she thought with delightful anticipation.

At long last she heard the rehearsal-room door open and laughter spill out into the hall. They were finished for the day. Carina's heart began to beat faster, as it always did when she knew she'd soon be seeing Damian. He was a reward for each tiring day, an inspiration to make it through the next.

But it wasn't Damian who came to the door of her office. It was Len, natty as ever in brogues and tweed. "Ah, wonderful, you're still here," he said. "Damian thought you might be."

Might be? Why wouldn't she be here? She always waited for Damian. Or was she beginning to assume too much from their relationship? She quickly dismissed the feeling as nothing more than fatigue, telling herself that she had no reason to feel insecure. "What can I do for you, Len?" she asked as cheerfully as she could.

"Could you possibly run through some lines with me? I seem to be having a dreadful time of it." He was holding a copy of the script under one arm and smiling apologetically at her.

Carina glanced over the counter. "What, now?" she asked much too brusquely to be polite.

Len pulled out the script and sat down on the sofa. He didn't appear to have noticed her reluctance. "Kate used to say I had a mind like flypaper, but I think that over the years the glue has hardened."

Carina could hear the other three chatting as they came down the hall. "Doesn't Kate like to run lines with you?"

"Not especially, and not when we're in a play together. Our characters have a tendency to take over our lives as it is." He looked up from the page he'd been perusing. "If it's not convenient tonight, we can make it another time."

"Well, to be quite honest—" Carina began. She stopped when Damian appeared at the counter with Judith clutching his arm.

"Oh, good, you're still here," Damian said breezily. "I took the liberty of volunteering you to run through Len's lines with him. I know it's short notice, but we only have a few days left."

Carina's eyes felt like lead ball bearings as they moved from Damian to Judith. Even after an exhausting day of rehearsal, the woman looked gorgeous.

"I hope you don't mind me borrowing your man for the evening," she said. "Damian and I haven't had a real chance to talk over old times since we got here."

"No," Carina replied in a small voice, "I don't mind, but I thought that—"

"There's a good sport," Damian interjected, leaning across the counter. "I promise I'll make it up to you tomorrow night. Could I have a kiss in the meantime?"

It wasn't because of anything Damian had said or done that she felt like sulking when she stood up to kiss him. He had every right to spend time with an old friend; and Carina had often run through lines with actors and enjoyed it immensely. She was being neither ignored nor neglected; she was merely being unreasonable. Her lips brushed his, and she manufactured a winsome smile. "Have a good time, you two."

Judith wiggled her fingers in a wave. "We will. There's a new steak house in Darlington that's supposed to be good, so we thought we'd try it out."

"See you later, darling," Kate called to her husband. "Try not to wake me when you come in tonight."

Everyone exchanged cheerful good-nights, and Carina did her best to chime in. There was always tomorrow night, she reminded herself. One evening without Damian wasn't going to kill her; in fact, it would probably verify that old bromide about absence making the heart grow fonder.

Len cleared his throat delicately, as if to remind her of his presence. "Sorry to be taking you from Damian," he said. "I realize he's much more exciting than a crusty old thespian with a sieve for a brain."

Annoyed with herself for hurting Len's feelings, she turned to him and smiled. "Nonsense. I find your company thoroughly charming."

Len handed her the script, and Carina, now resigned to her fate, opened it to the first page. "Shall we take it from the top?"

"Yes, please. The first act is where I have the most lines." Wrinkling his brow, he asked, "Didn't you tell Damian you haven't read the play?"

"That's right. Why do you ask?"

Len scratched his head with a perplexed expression on his face. "Oh...it's nothing. For some reason, it came up in conversation today. I think he's a bit insecure about the play after all these years and probably thinks you'd be his toughest critic."

Carina found his remark puzzling. Damian Fleming insecure? And why would he consider her a critic? She shrugged it off telling herself she should be flattered. "All the dialogue in act one seems to be between Mr. Tiggles and Bettina, so I guess I'll be reading Bettina's part," she said as she glanced quickly at the script.

"Yes, but let me put you in the picture first. Bettina Tiggles is the daughter of a proud but impoverished taxidermist living in New York City in the latter part of the last century. She is beautiful, intelligent, headstrong and a source of great concern to her parents because she's never shown the slightest interest in marriage.''

''The whole first act is set in her father's taxidermy workshop,'' Carina remarked, reading the notes.

''That's right, and the first line is yours, so please, proceed.'' Len settled back and shut his eyes in concentration.

''Hello, Papa. I see you're nearly finished with the popinjay.'' Carina said aloud the words of Bettina Tiggles.

''Ah, you're back already, precious,'' Len replied as Mr. Tiggles, abandoning his own British accent for the broad nasal tones of New York. ''Did you remember the sodium arsenite?''

''I did,'' his daughter answered, and in the script, she set down a large glass jar.

''Be careful with it! You know it's a deadly poison, but what's this? You've bought me enough for the next fifty years, and I hardly intend to stay on this earth that long.''

''It's more economical in the long run, Papa, and despite what you say, I do intend to follow in your footsteps. Why can't I help you now? Lord only knows we could use the money.''

''Now, child,'' Mr. Tiggles countered. ''Taxidermy and the acquisition of money are not proper pursuits for young ladies. Your job is to marry, happily and well.''

Carina/Bettina wailed, ''Oh, please, don't speak to me of such things. The subject of marriage I find quite distasteful.''

Len's brow furrowed, and his English accent returned. ''Can't dredge up the next line, I'm afraid.''

''Mr. Tiggles says, 'Why don't you help your mama with her needlework?' '' Carina told him.

''Yes, that's it!'' Len exclaimed, and repeated the line.

Carina then read Bettina's reply. "You want your daughter to sit by while Mother jabs herself and bleeds all over her sampler without even knowing it? Please, Papa, I'd much rather stay here. Taxidermy is such a noble art." In an aside, she admitted, "If sorely lacking in pecuniary merit."

In the play, Mr. Tiggles was inserting tail feathers into the popinjay as he said, "How is Mama this morning?"

"As well as can be expected," his daughter answered. "Last time I checked, she was halfway through her gin, and I expect she'll be fit and ready for port by dinner."

"Bettina! I forbid you to speak thus of the woman who bore you!"

"But she does bore me, Papa!"

Together, Carina and Len worked their way to the end of the first act. Mr. Tiggles continued his fruitless efforts to convince Bettina that marriage was a worthwhile institution while Bettina, with exaggerated decorum, pointed out to her father that he was really quite henpecked and too naive to realize his marriage was a sham. Act one closed with an indignant Mr. Tiggles announcing that a distant cousin from England—reputed to be handsome, wealthy and unattached—was due to arrive for an extended visit with the Tiggles. The objective: matrimony for Bettina.

Carina had thoroughly enjoyed reading the script, surprised to find her earlier dejection lifted. The witty dialogue was fast-paced and relentless, like a championship tennis match. Anxious to learn how the play turned out, she asked, "Shall we go on to act two?"

Len stretched his arms high above his head and yawned. "No, there's no need. The first act was where I most often missed my cues, but after that, we have Mrs. Tiggles and

Jasper to help carry the load." He paused, then said, "Did you know Damian's grandfather was a taxidermist?"

"Yes, he mentioned that once."

"From what I understand, Damian became quite proficient at it himself."

"What, taxidermy?" Carina asked in surprise.

"Yes, he used to spend his summers helping his grandfather in the workshop and in the store out front. I think it must have been good for both of them. His grandfather was a lonely man, and I don't think Damian's childhood was a happy one—at least when he was home with his parents."

"Oh?" Carina didn't want to sound more than casually interested, but in truth she was longing to know about Damian's early years. Not one of the many articles she'd read on his career had delved into the family background of Damian Fleming. In interviews, he routinely refused to discuss his childhood. And even now, whenever she tried to ask him about it, he grew sullen and defensive. So she made a point of avoiding the subject, unwilling to squander the little time they had together on unnecessary disagreements.

Len rubbed his face with his hands. "I don't know that I should have brought this up at all. Kate says I have a habit of thinking out loud."

Unable to contain her curiosity any longer, she slid to the edge of her seat. "Len, please tell me what you know about Damian's past. He won't talk about it, and to me, that suggests he hasn't truly faced up to it yet."

Len studied her carefully. "I don't think Damian has trouble facing up to anything anymore, my dear, but perhaps he doesn't feel comfortable enough with you to discuss his childhood."

He must have seen the hurt look on her face, for his tone softened. "You've been right smitten, haven't you, lass?"

Carina smiled wanly. "About as smitten as one can get."

Len picked up the script on her desk and flipped through the pages as though it were a photo album. "Perhaps I'm making a mistake, but you do seem like a discreet, sympathetic young woman. And I've been impressed with the way Damian calms down when he's with you. So I'll tell you what little I know."

Carina's eyes filled with tears of gratitude. She couldn't possibly have explained to Len just how much this meant to her, or how deeply she valued being taken into his confidence. "I won't breath a word to anyone," she promised softly.

Len nodded. "The character of Mr. Tiggles is based on Damian's father."

"You said you got to know him during the war."

"Correct, and at the time, he seemed quite soldierly, but of course, I was a naive lad myself and no judge of character. What Arthur Fleming was best at, it seems, was taking orders—from his commanding officer in Europe, from his wife at home. Damian has, on occasion, referred to him as 'gifted, but spineless.'"

Carina flinched. "How could he say something so cruel about his own father?"

"I don't think he was being cruel so much as honest. His father was a talented man, like his own father, the New York taxidermist. Arthur Fleming could do anything with his hands, but despite chronic poor health, all his working years were spent at unskilled labor in the steel mills. He worked overtime constantly, did jobs no one else would do. He hardly saw his son grow up."

"There's nothing wrong with a father working hard to provide for his family," Carina argued.

"This is true, but the man was actually supporting his wife's vices. She came from a blue-blooded Philadelphia family that lost everything in the crash of '29. She was raised in poverty, but was led to believe she deserved the best. Then along came poor, unsuspecting Arthur who was so besotted he sacrificed his life trying to provide for her. Damian's mother was an alcoholic. Whatever she didn't spend on drink went to buy clothes and jewelry they could ill afford."

Carina's heart twisted with the knowledge of Damian's suffering. Her own childhood had been uneventful, but perfect, with parents who loved her and loved each other. No wonder Damian had sought the escape and the anonymity of acting. "I can understand why he'd be reluctant to marry," she said to Len, "though I used to think it was because he had too many women to choose from."

Len chuckled. "I imagine both factors have played a part in his decision to remain unattached. Anyway, I'm glad to see this play come to light at last. It should exorcise many of the demons he still carries inside, despite his outward confidence."

"I have one other question," Carina said. "Obviously the Tiggles are based on his parents, but who did he use as models for the others? Is Damian actually Jasper Garnet, the English cousin?"

"No, not at all. If Damian's character comes through at all, I'd say it's with Bettina. And once you've seen the play, I think you'll find it quite apparent that the popinjay, Jasper Garnet, is actually Malcolm. He and Damian were boyhood friends long before they went to New York."

Another significant piece of Damian's past that Carina had never known. She was trying to come up with a casual response when the phone rang. Not stopping to wonder who could be calling so long after the box office had closed, she picked up the receiver. "Good evening, the Myrmidon."

"Miss Rawlins. Lieutenant Chapman here."

Wearily, Carina closed her eyes. "Hello, Lieutenant."

"I tried calling you at home first, but there was no answer."

"That's because I stayed at the theater to help an actor with his lines." Carina offered Len a bemused smile. "Is there something I can do for you, Lieutenant?"

"Well, I've been doing some investigating," the policeman replied, "and I thought you might be interested in what I've come up with."

"Yes, by all means." Actually, she wasn't in the least interested in anything to do with Malcolm at this point. She just wished he would stay where he was.

"There's no record of your boss taking a limo to the airport, and he didn't take any flights out of O'Hare. I'm looking into the other airports, but it's gonna take a while to get the results."

"Oh, I see," Carina answered, her mind throbbing with the added worry. "That's rather odd, isn't it, that there'd be no record of his flight?"

"I'd say so." The policeman's voice was matter-of-fact.

"What about the telegram?"

"That was the other reason I called. The agent at the cable office in Spain remembers the message because it was done over the phone, and the connection was lousy."

Carina gripped the receiver tightly. "You mean as if it were long distance."

"That's right, and it means the agent never saw the sender. It took him a long time to take the message down because the caller couldn't speak Spanish—oh, yeah, he did say the caller was a man."

"So we're really not much further ahead, are we?" she asked, her fingers drumming on the desktop.

"Nope, but I'm not about to give up yet. You call me if you find anything," the lieutenant said. Carina promised that she would and hung up.

Len was buttoning his sports coat. "Problems?"

She shook her head, deciding on little more than a gut instinct that this was not a matter for general knowledge yet. "My only problem is an overzealous cop who worries Malcolm's disappearance like a dog gnawing an old slipper." She kept her tone light, almost flippant.

The actor didn't appear particularly interested. "Oh, well, I'm sure he'll tire of the sport eventually. Thanks a million for helping me out, Carina. Can I walk you anywhere?"

"No, thanks anyway. I have a few things I want to clean up here before I go home."

Len nodded carelessly, not trying to dissuade her from staying in the dark and empty theater alone. He said good night and went out the front door, whistling gaily.

In an uncharacteristic display of rage, Carina slammed her fist on the top of her desk. Damn that Malcolm! Even when he wasn't around, he was a nuisance. Either he was in Majorca, or he was somewhere else. Right now, his whereabouts didn't matter a tinker's damn to her. And she wished Lieutenant Chapman would leave her alone until he found something conclusive—like a body!

Still a little misty-eyed from her conversation with Len, Carina reached for a tissue, but the box was empty. She cursed under her breath and yanked open the bottom drawer of her desk where she kept replacements. When she thrust her hand into the back of the drawer, her fingers hit something fuzzy. Curious, she brought out a long, hard parcel wrapped in flannel.

"What on earth…" she muttered as she unwrapped the fabric. Carina stared at the assortment of metal tools in her hands. A knife, a pair of tongs, and a—no, they weren't tongs. Carina froze. What she was holding were not kitchen implements, but a scalpel, a pair of forceps and a surgical saw. And if that wasn't bad enough…the instruments were covered with blood!

Chapter Eleven

The tools fell from her hands with a clatter. Carina leaped back as though they might somehow come to life and attack her. But morbid fascination prevailed and she inched back to her desk to examine the instruments more closely. Gingerly she touched the stains on the forceps. She couldn't be sure, but it certainly looked like blood. There were dark reddish-brown smears on the flannel as well, suggesting that the instruments had been wrapped up right after they were used.

Carina's stomach gave a lurch. Used? Used for what? She recalled the day Gerry had burst into her office, worried sick about his missing props. Preoccupied with other matters, Carina had brushed him off. Now the undeniable truth hit her like a blow. These surgical tools were antiques; they hadn't been used professionally for a hundred years. There was no plausible reason for them to be bloodstained.

Icy fear rushed through her veins. The lieutenant's hunch had been right! Malcolm wasn't coming back. Someone had murdered him. And if that weren't bad enough, whoever did it had wrapped up the murder weapons and stashed them in her office. *She was being framed!*

Suddenly Carina became very much aware that she was alone in the vast theater. In her terror-stricken imagination, the squawks and creaks of the old building became lurking killers; the silences in between were listening unseen ears. With little regard for anything but escape, Carina threw on her coat and started for the front door. Halfway there, she stopped. The props! She couldn't very well leave them scattered on her desk. What was she supposed to do with them—hide them, wash them, throw them away? Whatever she decided to do, this was not the time or place to think about it. She had to get to safety first.

She dashed back to her office, rolled the instruments into the cloth and jammed them in her briefcase. She snapped the clasps shut, then hurried through the lobby and out the theater doors, into the inky darkness.

There were few people on the streets at this hour. Except for the town's two taverns, everything was closed. After running aimlessly for a block or two, Carina slowed her pace. No one seemed to be following her, and she couldn't keep running indefinitely. She had to think, think hard about who could have done this and why.

Her mind glossed over the crew. She knew them all well and knew how they felt about Malcolm, but she couldn't believe any of them capable of murder. Or of implicating her in a crime she didn't commit.

In what she realized might be small-town xenophobia, Carina's mind leaped to the cast. They were all from out of town, at the Myrmidon not as a result of normal casting procedures but by calculated design. Malcolm didn't have a friend among them. Kate and Len, though sweet and kindly on the surface, had been monitoring Malcolm's activities for the past eight years, waiting for him to stage their godson's play. Judith had been waiting even longer to tell him about her unborn child. And Damian, the most publicly celebrated of the four, had come all the way from England to expose Malcolm and to... To what? Kill him? Would someone so well known really expect to get away with it?

At first, Carina couldn't understand why her suspicions leaned most heavily in Damian's direction. All four of the cast had motives. All four of them were actors, capable of feigning innocence, masking their emotions. Why would she suspect Damian of being the most likely killer? He was the man she loved.

The man she loved. The thought suddenly leaped out like underlined words on a page, and Carina felt every bit the duped heroine from a poorly written Gothic. She loved him, yes. But what about Damian? What were his feelings?

Oh, she had been eager enough to interpret his sweet murmurings as pronouncements of love, but if she looked at it rationally, she would realize they'd known each other only a week or two. She wasn't the kind of woman men fell in love with at first sight—especially not men like Damian. He had his pick of the world's most exotic and beautiful women. Why would he suddenly fall head over heels for some plain-Jane from a hick town in the Midwest? She was deluding herself; Damian didn't care a damn about her! He needed an ally and a scapegoat, and there was none so reliable as a woman blinded by love. The annals of crime were full of such tales.

Hating herself for her stupidity, Carina turned sharply in the direction of the Victoria Hotel. She had to confront him. She'd be safe enough seeing him in the hotel if she didn't go into his room. She could stand in the hall and accuse him in a loud voice, maybe attract witnesses from the other rooms who would testify to what they heard.

Anyway, Damian wouldn't be so stupid as to kill her, too. Everyone knew they were seeing each other. He'd be the first one the police would nab.

As she ascended the steps of the hotel clutching her briefcase, Carina realized she should have called the lieutenant right away. Then she decided against it. A few more minutes wouldn't make any difference, and she wanted a chance to hear the truth from Damian's own lips. She wanted to let him know she wasn't as gullible as he thought she was. If the police came and took him away, she might never get the chance, and the rage would fester in her heart forever.

The desk clerk had seen Carina often enough that he didn't ask anything beyond a pleasant "How are you tonight" as she crossed the lobby and entered the brass elevator. The operator, who had worked there nearly as long as the hotel had existed, was perched on his little stool in the corner. He chattered all the way up, but Carina was too preoccupied to respond with more than a few nods. She tapped her foot impatiently. Wasn't there any way he could make this contraption rise faster?

At last they came to the top floor. Carina ran down the corridor and turned the corner, stopping at the first door on her left. She knocked loudly. There was no answer. She knocked again and waited. Still no answer. She checked her watch, then she remembered that Damian and Judith had gone out for dinner. *Damn!* Shouldn't they be back by now?

With a sinking feeling, Carina realized that Damian might be in Judith's room just two doors down from his. And why not? Carina had no claims on him, and Judith was not only gorgeous, but also an old friend in need of solace. Perhaps they were even involved in this mess together.

Carina knocked on Judith's door. She pressed her ear against the keyhole to listen, but there were no sounds and the room appeared to be dark. Perhaps it was just as well. Damian she could probably handle, but facing the two of them was another matter.

Carina looked up and down the empty corridor. What was she supposed to do now—sit in the hall and wait? No, her nerves couldn't take it. She could go and confront the Kramers, but what good would that do? They'd probably deny all knowledge of the crime and then run straight to Damian with the news. She didn't want him forewarned about her finding the props. Carina turned slowly in the direction of the elevator. She might as well go home; it was as safe a place as any for the time being.

"Leaving so soon?" the wizened little man in the elevator asked.

By now, Carina was near tears. "My friends weren't in."

"Too bad. I could let them know you were here if you like."

She shook her head quickly. "No, please, I'd just as soon you didn't. Thanks anyway."

Instead of cutting through the heavily treed park, she took the long way home. There were more lights and fewer shadows. Once she was inside her apartment, she shoved the briefcase into the front closet, as far back as it would go. Then she sat on the sofa and picked up the telephone to call Lieutenant Chapman. She'd already dialed the first three numbers before she changed her mind and hung up.

He was probably off duty now, and she didn't really want to discuss this with anyone else. Besides, how was she going to explain why she hadn't called him immediately from the theater? She was a grown woman. She couldn't very well tell a police officer that the creaky building had scared her to death and she'd run out from sheer fright.

His next question would probably be something like, "What were you really afraid of, Miss Rawlins—being caught red-handed with the murder weapons?"

Even the imaginary scenario was enough to make her break out in a cold sweat. She was tense and overwrought as it was; a night of questioning in a police station was the last thing she needed. It would be simpler to wait until morning to call. No one had seen her find the props, and she could reenact the discovery in the reassuring light of day. Who would be the wiser?

A few minutes later Carina was in bed with the blankets drawn up to her chin. But it came as no surprise that she didn't sleep a wink all night.

SHE WAS IN HER OFFICE the next morning shortly after dawn. Normally, the stage crew didn't come in on a Saturday, but there was still a great deal of renovating to be finished, and everyone was putting in a seven-day week. Not taking any chances, Carina made sure she was the first to arrive.

She removed her coat and hung it up carefully, determined to do things as predictably as she did every morning—with one tiny exception. Before picking up the coffee carafe to fill it with water, she opened her briefcase and took out the surgical instruments wrapped exactly the way she'd found them.

Carina glanced up at Sarah Bernhardt on the wall. "I'm counting on you to stay quiet, Sarah." The actress's response was silence. "Thanks, I owe you one," Carina muttered as she closed the drawer of her desk.

When Damian and Judith finally walked into the theater—together—Carina felt as though she'd been waiting for hours, and every nerve was jumping. She'd rushed into the lobby to avoid being cornered in the office, even though she wasn't alone in the theater anymore. Most of the crew had arrived; the set designer was in his workshop next door. If anything happened, he would hear.

Carina hoped she sounded calm when she asked if they'd had a nice evening. Neither of them seemed suspicious when they replied that they had. Then to Damian, she said, "Could I see you in my office for a minute?"

Judith waved them off and headed for her dressing room. "Call me when you're ready to start rehearsal. I could use some more sleep, so don't hurry."

Damian followed her into the office, walking with his usual fluid grace, just as if nothing were wrong. Then he touched her shoulder and Carina whirled around.

"How dare you?" she lashed out, appalled to discover a part of her still aching to be touched by him. What kind of masochist was she?

Damian looked hurt. "What's the matter?"

Carina bristled. "I think you already know the answer to that one."

His brows came together in a frown. "I hope you're not upset that I couldn't be with you last night. Judith needed to talk, and—"

"Ha! That's hardly the issue. I'm well past the jealousy stage, I assure you." Carina backed up against her desk, but Damian didn't try to approach her. He stood by the coffee machine, looking slightly lost. She should have been pleased by the effect she was having.

"Tell me what it is, sunshine," he urged gently. "I've never seen you acting like this."

Afraid she would do something stupid like cry, Carina swung around and pulled open the desk drawer. She pointed at the flannel-wrapped parcel. "I should think this would be enough to make me a little testy."

Damian peered inside. "A box of tissues?"

"Oh, for Pete's sake, cut it out!" Carina snapped. "You know perfectly well what I'm talking about."

He looked up and shook his head in puzzlement. Then he reached into the drawer and brought out the props with what seemed to her an inordinate amount of care. She watched his long slim fingers unwrap the flannel slowly. When the scalpel, saw and forceps came into view, she looked at his face.

Carina would never have suspected such a convincing look of shock. Damian's face was pale. His jaws were clenched; a muscle pulsed near his temple. He didn't touch the instruments, but he stared at them a long, long time. Then in a low, almost strangled voice, he said, "They're Mr. Tiggles's tools."

Carina folded her arms. "They certainly are, and I wonder how they got there."

Damian looked up. A thousand dark emotions seemed to be swirling in the depths of his eyes, but Carina couldn't single any one of them out. She had expected to find something identifiable like triumph or hatred, but when she found neither it disturbed her.

"Why are you showing me this?" he asked.

Carina shrugged weakly, wishing she could summon the same intensity of anger and revulsion she'd felt the night before. "Someone must have put them there, and I wondered...wondered if you knew anything about it." What was wrong with her? Why couldn't she come right out and accuse him? It had seemed easy enough when she'd imagined this scene over and over during the long, sleepless night. Now, she had him on the defensive, exactly where she wanted him. There was no reason for her to feel that if she accused him outright of murdering Malcolm and of framing her, she'd be crossing some undefinable point of no return. Did she honestly hope to salvage something of their relationship after all this? Was she so hard up that she could love a murderer?

"I don't know anything about it," Damian said.

Nearly choking, Carina replied. "Oh...I—I see." *Nice going, dishrag.* A response like that ought to send the man running away in fear. She might as well have attacked him with a feather.

For a time neither of them moved. Then Damian walked to the far end of the office. When he spoke, his back was toward her. "I don't have any idea how those tools ended up in your desk...or the blo—the stains, either. I just...I don't know."

Eight years at the Myrmidon had taught Carina that in a stage production, characters often did not speak face-to-face. But in real life, they did—unless one of them was hiding something and incapable of eye contact. "Look at me, Damian," she said with more bravado than she possessed.

He turned around slowly, almost defiantly, as if daring her to read something in his eyes. But they were shuttered, opaque. She couldn't read a thing.

"If you didn't put them in here," she said, "and I didn't, what do you suggest I do now?" She felt as though her heart were being twisted by Malcolm's icy fingers.

Damian didn't answer right away. "I suppose you have several options. You could dispose of the props, pretend you never saw them. You could wash the blood off and return them to Gerry. Or you could call Lieutenant Chapman."

What was he trying to do, Carina wondered. Was he suddenly regretting that he had tried to frame her for murder? Was he offering her a way out by suggesting she dispose of the props or return them? If she did either of those things, the lieutenant's case would be stalled until a body was found. Her mind moved to the next logical con-

clusion. If Malcolm's body *was* found and she'd obliter-
ated the bloodstains or hidden the murder weapons, she
would be an accessory after the fact. Damian wasn't doing
her any favors.

"You seem to be taking a long time to decide," he said
with a sharp edge to his voice.

Carina shook her head. "No, I had intended to call the
police all along. I just wanted your reaction first."

Damian flinched as though she'd suddenly jabbed him
with the scalpel. "Well, now you've done that, I'll leave
you to your phone call." He passed her on his way to the
door, then he stopped, without looking at her. "One more
thing. If you decide to clean up the props, I suggest you get
some new flannel. If you try to wash it, it'll shrink and that
would be a dead giveaway." Before she could reply, Damian was gone.

ALONE IN MALCOLM'S OFFICE, Damian raked his hands
through his hair, more shaken than he'd felt in years. How
could a woman he'd known for such a short time have this
effect on him? He had expected to breeze through these
few weeks with a conscience as clear as glass; now he was
wishing he had never come. No, that wasn't true at all—
meeting Carina had been worth every minute. But what
was he going to do now? Wasn't it too late to untangle her
from this mess? He reached under the phone pad for
Lieutenant Chapman's card. His hand groped for the receiver. Once the police got their hands on this latest devel-
opment, he could stop worrying. He could tell them that
his head had been turned by this lovely theater assistant,
that he had no idea the woman he'd made love to was a
killer. But when he picked up the phone, his heart froze. He
couldn't do it, not yet. He'd give it just a little more
time. Damian quietly put down the receiver and left the
office to begin rehearsal.

Chapter Twelve

It seemed as though Carina had just finished making the call when Lieutenant Chapman appeared. "I got here as fast as I could," he said, huffing as though he'd run the whole way.

"Yes, I can see that." Carina said, calmly inviting him into the office. The props were lying on her desk, on top of the cloth they'd been wrapped in, stains readily apparent.

The lieutenant bent down to study them. "When did you say you found these?"

"This morning." Until now she'd considered telling him the truth, that she'd found them the night before and panicked. But it seemed so evasive, so immature somehow, and anyway it didn't really make any difference *when* she found them.

Judging from what the policeman was wearing, she'd called him away from baseball practice. "Did you touch them?" he asked.

"It didn't occur to me not to until it was too late," she admitted sheepishly.

The lieutenant looked a little disgruntled, but he refrained from comment. "Did you say they were props for the play?"

"Yes, I recognized them right away as the ones Gerry, our property master, misplaced last week."

The look of disgruntlement intensified. "You knew all along they were missing?"

"Well, yes, but I—"

"Why didn't you tell me?"

He thought she was hiding something. Oh, Lord, this wasn't turning out to be the relief she'd hoped it would be. "I didn't think it was important, and it never occurred to me." Why was it the lieutenant always managed to make her feel as if she were lying? "Things get lost in the theater all the time," she explained. "If we weren't operating in a state of perpetual chaos, there'd be something wrong."

This time he rewarded her with a chuckle. "I know what you mean. Cop shops can be the same way." He returned his attention to the items on the desk. "Would you show me exactly where you found these?"

Carina was grateful for the change in topic. "Certainly. They were back here in this drawer. As you can see, I don't have reason to look in there very often because it's where I keep my spare tissues. But when I went to blow my nose last—this morning, the box on my desk was empty." She pointed to the empty box in the wastebasket as proof.

The lieutenant removed his baseball cap, scratched his head and replaced the cap. "Interesting."

Carina wilted. She was being framed for murder, and all he could say was "interesting." "So you think someone used my desk to stash them deliberately?" she prompted, hoping he would expand on his thought.

"Yeah, definitely. Whoever put them there wanted them to be found, but not right away. That's why they picked a spot you don't look into all the time—gives them some time to play with."

"Like time to get out of town?" Carina asked with a throat gone dry.

He shrugged. "Sure, that's a logical conclusion." He stared at her, and Carina almost hoped he could read her thoughts. She didn't want to be explicit about it, but she was trying to suggest that since the cast members were all from out of town, he'd do well to start with them. She just couldn't bring herself to mention any names.

"Do you have any enemies?" was his next, rather brutal question.

Feeling suddenly dizzy, Carina grabbed the back of her chair. "N-no, none that I can think of." Damian wasn't her enemy. Enemies were filled with hatred, and he didn't hate her. He was using her, perhaps, but that was different.

"What about Fleming?"

Carina blanched. "Damian? What about him?" Why was she doing this to herself—trying to accuse him and defend him at the same time?

"Are the two of you, uh, getting close?"

Carina paused, trying to determine how much leeway she had with this question. She recalled the time the lieutenant had walked in and found Damian kissing her, and—oh, dear—there was the morning they'd walked to the theater together and Damian stopped off at the hotel to change. Hadn't the policeman caught up to her a few seconds later? Did the man have some kind of built-in sonar?

"We're . . . close," she finally admitted.

"Are you in love with him?" followed on the heels of her reply.

"Lieutenant, I fail to see—" she began, then sighed deeply. "I thought I was . . . until I found these."

The officer's beefy face settled into something like compassion. "Yeah, I see what you mean, but look, it could have been worse."

"It could?" Carina asked doubtfully. "I don't see how."

"It could have been you whose body is missing instead of your boss."

Once again Carina had to clutch at her chair as a wave of dizziness passed through her. "What are you going to do now?"

"What a cop does most of the time when he's not filling out forms: ask a lot of questions. In the meantime, I'm going to take these props with me and have some tests done on the stains. Would you happen to know whether Malcolm Spencer had medical records on file somewhere?"

Carina thought quickly. "Yes, you should be able to find records at the county hospital. He was there for a few days after a car accident last year; I'm sure they'd have his...his b-blood type." Carina cleared her throat nervously. "Lieutenant, I guess there's not much doubt now that Malcolm is dead." She needed to hear it from someone other than herself.

The officer pushed back his baseball cap. "There certainly is a lot less doubt now than there was yesterday," he admitted. "But you know, there's something about this case that eats at my gut even worse than simple homicide."

Carina couldn't imagine homicide ever being simple, but she confined her remark to, "Oh, what's that?"

He pointed at the desk. "These instruments. There's something fishy about them."

"I'm not sure I understand," Carina said.

"Well, look at it this way. If you'd found a gun, that's one thing; a gun is a common murder weapon. A scalpel?

Okay, too—it's just a fancy kind of knife. But a surgical saw is not something I'd think of as an instrument to commit murder, and forceps? Forget it. And yet there's blood on all of them."

Carina brought a hand to her mouth to avoid retching. Her imagination was already conjuring up all sorts of gruesome pictures, thanks to the officer's insinuations. "W-what do you think happened?"

"Don't know, for sure," he said, "but one thing's almost certain. This was no crime of passion. Looks like a carefully thought out—and rather grisly—case of revenge."

"Oh." Carina's voice was little more than a squeak as she fell into her chair. She watched the lieutenant wrap up the instruments carefully and drop them into a large plastic bag.

"There's one more thing, Miss Rawlins, that might make my job a little easier."

"Yes?"

"I'd like a set of your fingerprints."

"Why?" she said with a gasp. "Am I under suspicion?"

"Nah, it's nothing like that, but you said yourself that you handled these props. I'd just like to eliminate yours right away in case we find another set of prints."

A series of terrifying images flew through her mind. Police entrapment, her attorney arguing in court that the prints were inadmissable; plea bargaining and still getting twenty-five years in the women's pen. "Shouldn't you...aren't you going to want everyone else's prints, too?" she asked hopefully.

The officer didn't appear to be aware of her terror. "I might. It's too early to say for sure right now, and hey, I'm not forcing you."

Carina realized her behavior was bordering on paranoia. She hadn't done anything wrong, and if someone was trying to frame her, then it was in her best interests to cooperate fully with the police. She stood up and lifted her coat from the rack. "Could we get this over with now?" she asked.

"Sure thing." Lieutenant Chapman was actually whistling as he led her outside to his dark-brown unmarked sedan.

LATER THAT AFTERNOON, Carina was standing on the top of a high aluminum stepladder, taking down the wine-red velvet curtain that hung behind the proscenium arch of the stage. It was long overdue for cleaning. Gwen Pennell stood below, her task to hold the heavy fabric as Carina lifted it off the rod, hook by hook.

"How many people are coming to the gala so far?" Carina asked.

"Let me think," Gwen replied. "Last count was somewhere around eighty."

"Eighty couples?"

"No. Eighty people."

Carina's arms ached with the effort of stretching them up over her head. "Eighty people are not nearly enough. We're not halfway to our goal, and it's less than a week to opening night."

"I know," Gwen said quietly. "Too bad ticket sales can't make up the difference. You're practically sold out."

"Under any other circumstances, I'd be thrilled with the ticket sales." Carina released the last two hooks, and the curtain fell onto Gwen like a huge butterfly net, trapping her underneath.

"Help!" the woman cried in a muffled voice. "Get me out of here!"

Carina came down the ladder, trying not to smile at the sight of Gwen flailing madly under the heavy folds of velvet. "I'm coming," she said. "Hang on." It took only a moment to free Gwen from her velvet prison, though she emerged looking as though she'd nearly suffocated.

Gwen patted at her lank hair. "Ooh, I'm glad we don't have to do this too often."

Carina touched the woman's shoulder consolingly. "I'm sorry. I'll try to be more careful on the second half."

"Second half? Oh dear, I'd forgotten. Why don't you let me climb the ladder this time?"

Carina could just imagine the ungainly Gwendolyn on top of a ladder. "No, it's okay, I'll do it," she countered, "and I promise to warn you when the curtain's coming down." She sat down on the bottom rung. "But first I've got to give my arms a rest. They're killing me."

Gwen sat cross-legged on the floor and began removing hooks from the curtain. Her eye was nearly healed, Carina noticed, and she didn't need to wear much makeup to conceal the fading yellowish-green marks.

"Gwen, I've been trying all week to talk to your husband, but I can't get past his secretary, and he won't return my messages."

The woman did not look up. "Oh?" was all she said.

Carina sat down on the floor beside her and picked up the other end of the curtain. "We have to know whether he's going to let us run the play or not, not to mention the gala. It's not fair of him to leave us hanging like this."

"Go ahead and continue your plans. He won't shut you down before the play is over."

"He won't?" Carina leaned closer to be sure she'd heard right. "How do you know? Did he tell you that?"

"No, Harland and I don't talk much these days, but I know he won't stop the play. I overheard him talking to our friends at the country club. Some of them are dead set against a shopping center being built in this area. They've even threatened to withdraw their money from the bank if he goes ahead with it.''

For the first time in ages, Carina felt her hopes rise. "Does this mean the deal won't go through?"

Gwen looked up, and her expression was strained. "I wouldn't say that. Harland is a very persuasive man, and he usually gets his way in the end. It's just that it won't happen as quickly as he'd hoped. The other thing is, he likes to come across as a great philanthropist, so he's bragging to all his cronies that he's decided to let the Myrmidon stage the play out of the goodness of his heart.''

Carina slumped and covered her face with both hands. "Why didn't you tell us, Gwen? We've all been on pins and needles wondering whether all this work is for nothing.''

Gwen picked up a grocery bag and dropped curtain hooks into it. "I thought my husband had already told you. Besides, what difference is one more week going to make? You can run this play, but they'll probably come and lock the doors the minute it's over.''

"I know, but at least..." Carina's initial enthusiasm faded when she realized that Gwen was right. Another week, eight more days than they had before, to be precise. It didn't mean much, but then, in one way, it did. There would be eight more days with Damian. *Damian!* She could just kick herself for wallowing in emotions that were now so irrelevant. The man was a cold-blooded, heartless criminal. Why couldn't she remember that?

"It would be nice if people worried as much about Malcolm as they did about this old theater,'' Gwen remarked sullenly.

With some difficulty, Carina pulled herself away from her own thoughts. When she finally focused on Gwen's remark, she found it puzzling. "What makes you say that?"

"Well, look at the way everyone's behaving. It's as though you never even had an artistic director who wasn't named Damian. Malcolm had his faults, but you have to admit he put on the best plays this theater has seen in years."

"No one is denying that, Gwen. Malcolm was . . . is creatively brilliant, but he's no joy to work for." The lieutenant had told her to act as if Malcolm was still in Majorca . . . and alive.

"That's because you antagonized him. You were always reminding him of the fact that everyone in Dunn's Pond liked you, but nobody liked him."

"I did not!" Carina protested. "Malcolm's problem was a great big chip on his shoulder. He never let people forget he'd rather be anywhere but here in a dusty little Midwest town, as he used to put it."

Gwen's face puckered in a pout. "You're wrong about him, Carina. You, of all people, should have understood him better. But you didn't."

Carina would never have guessed in a million years, but now it seemed do obvious. Gwen imagined herself in love with the man! No wonder she'd so willingly incurred her husband's wrath to work in a theater he was trying to close. No wonder she'd got herself elected to the board of directors and hung around every day to help out with odd jobs. She couldn't recall Malcolm treating Gwen much better than he'd treated the rest of them, but he did afford her a certain grudging respect as one of the theater's major benefactors. To a woman like Gwen, that must have seemed like a lot.

Carina's tone was sympathetic when she said, "You're right, Gwen. I should have tried to understand Malcolm better. Now why don't we tackle the rest of the this lousy job?'' She got to her feet, brushed off her skirt and gamely climbed the ladder a second time. Ironic, she thought with a twist of inner pain, how both she and Gwen had fallen for the wrong men.

"HOMICIDE SUSPECTED in Theater Director's Disappearance." Such were the headlines in Monday's edition of the regional newspaper. Damian had it tucked under his arm when he knocked on the door of the Kramers' hotel room that morning.

"Who is it?" he heard Kate say.

"It's me, Damian."

A moment later the door swung open, and his godmother greeted him with a kiss. In her dressing gown of rose satin, she looked young and fresh; he found it hard to believe she was well over sixty. Kate's gaze fell to the newspaper he carried under his arm. "I see you've read the news, too," she remarked.

Damian stepped inside. Len was sitting in an easy chair, reading the same article. "It was hard to miss," the younger man said. "The paper probably hasn't used headlines that large in fifty years."

"Would you care for a cup of tea?" Kate asked. "There's still some in the pot."

"No, thanks. I've already had coffee." Damian sat on the edge of the bed, wondering whether he'd been foolish to come to the Kramers for advice. After all, he was a grown man, capable of making his own decisions and living with the consequences.

"Something's troubling you, dear. What is it?" Kate asked gently as she sat down across from him with her cup of tea.

Propping his arms on the bed, Damian leaned back slightly. "It's funny, I thought I was going to be able to explain my problem easily, but now that I'm here, I don't know where to start."

"I hope you're not distressed by Malcolm's death," Kate declared.

Damian glanced at her in surprise. He'd never known his godmother to be callous. "Well, I . . . I'm not totally immune to it. After all, we were friends for a long time."

"What my wife undoubtedly meant to say," Len explained, putting down the paper, "is that you shouldn't allow this . . . this unfortunate incident to interfere with your work. You've waited a long time to stage *Fate of the Popinjay*. Don't let useless sentiment cloud your purpose."

Damian accepted the slice of whole wheat toast that Kate offered and munched on it absently. "You're right, I shouldn't dwell on things I can't change, but it's not really Malcolm that's bothering me. It's Carina."

Len peered over his reading glasses, while Kate's teacup paused in midair. As usual, Kate was the first to comment.

"I take it you've fallen quite hard for the girl."

Damian pushed unruly hair from his face. "She's a remarkable woman. I don't remember when I've been so . . . distracted."

"Do you love her?" his godmother asked.

"I, uh, I think so." He shied from the word as if it implied too many irreversible things.

Len's harrumph was noncommittal. Kate responded with a sharp intake of breath. "That's wonderful," she said, "but what's wrong?"

"Plenty." He shook his head. "I probably shouldn't even be telling you about it, but I have to talk to someone."

"You know you can always come to us, lad," Len assured him.

"But of course, you must," his wife agreed.

Damian had no choice but to confide in them. He'd go mad if he didn't. "All right, I'll tell you, but you have to remember this is confidential. Saturday morning, Carina called me into her office and showed me something she'd found in her desk. They were the props Gerry had been looking for—Mr. Tiggles's taxidermy tools—and they were covered in blood."

"Ah, so that's the murder weapon," Len remarked. "They were terribly vague about it in the paper."

"Until there's been an arrest, I think they have to be," Damian answered. "But what worries me is that Carina may have got herself into more trouble than she can handle, and she refuses to even talk to me. I want to help her. I need to, well, what I'd really like is for things to be the way they were before."

"It seems to me," Kate countered, "that you're asking a lot of Carina and yourself under the circumstances. Malcolm's death changes things irrevocably for all of us. But aside from that, the first thing you have to do is win back her trust. I assume that since Carina made a point of showing you the props, she accused you of planting them in her desk."

"Not in so many words, but yes, that's what she did."

"Well then, you must convince her you didn't put them there," the actress said. "Make her listen to you, make her understand, even if you have to strap her down in a chair to do it. Eventually she'll come around, and it's clear that she adores you or this wouldn't have hit her so hard."

Damian felt somewhat comforted. "You're right. I guess I haven't tried as hard as I could have, but I was so shocked that Carina could even suspect me after all we've meant to each other." This was the first time he'd admitted the depth of his feelings, and surprisingly, it felt good.

"Why shouldn't she suspect you?" Len put in. "The two of you may be rapturously enamored of each other, but let's face it, she's only known you a short while. The less appealing qualities of a person usually take time to surface, and I'm sure that's what she's grappling with now. Hence, her unhappy suspicions of you." He shook his head and sighed. "A murder is hardly conducive to a love affair, is it?"

Feeling like a schoolboy in the throes of his first crush, Damian realized how little he knew about the subtle aspects of building a relationship. When it came to women, he never gave himself a chance to get past the initial stage of raw passion. Once that dwindled, he moved on. He ought to do that now...so why didn't he?

"Carina's coolness isn't all that's bothering you, is it?" Kate observed.

His godmother, Damian realized, was a veritable seer. "No, Kate, it's not. I'm worried that I may be approaching this from the wrong angle. What if Carina's distress is all posturing, and she doesn't really believe that I killed Malcolm at all?"

"You mean, what if Carina was the killer and was trying to pin the blame on you?" Kate posed the very question that Damian couldn't bring himself to ask.

"That's precisely what I mean," he said.

Kate rose to her feet and padded softly to the large window; she pulled the curtain aside and stood there a moment, looking out onto the street, before she answered. "I would say you're worrying needlessly on that score, my dear."

"But how can you be so sure?" Damian asked.

The older woman turned to him, her light blue eyes alert and shining. "Let's just say I have an innate understanding of my fellowman. Carina, no matter how much she might have hated her boss, could never have killed him. I'm absolutely convinced."

TO HIS AMAZEMENT, Damian had discovered that it wasn't necessary to strap Carina into a chair to make her change her mind about him. Ever since he'd had that talk with the Kramers two days earlier, he and Carina had developed a cautious truce. They were far from being lovers again, but at least they were talking.

It had started off as the usual shoptalk between a visiting director and the person in charge—unimportant matters like where to find a tape recorder and what was the theater's policy on seating latecomers. But it was a beginning, and when they spoke he could tell that Carina didn't want him to rush off. Her eyes would linger, her hands would move restlessly across her desk, as if she, too, wished things were different, the way they were before. He couldn't help but feel encouraged.

Then, earlier that morning, he'd asked if he could pick up some lunch for her. She had smiled that dazzling smile, the one that crinkled her face in all the right places, and she'd said yes. It was like being a fourteen-year-old all over again, being able to please his girl with the purchase of a ham and cheese on rye. The experience thrilled him beyond belief—he, who had seen the world and engaged in all manner of reckless adventure, was overwhelmed by the chance to buy Carina a sandwich. He'd even tucked in her favorite chocolate bar and was delighted by her pleasure when she found it.

There hadn't been time for a leisurely lunch, but Carina invited him to stay in her office while they ate. For nine wonderful minutes they had basked in each other's silent company. He had to laugh, wondering what *People* would make of Damian Fleming romancing a woman who wasn't a socialite or a starlet—and romancing her in such an ordinary, unexotic way. But he couldn't expect others to understand how he felt; he barely understood it himself.

Now, in the half hour remaining, he and Carina were helping Elsie, the wardrobe mistress, drape gold-fringed valances along the ceiling of the lobby. The work was nearly complete, and the results quite spectacular. The walls were freshly plastered, the oak wainscot stripped and refinished to a smooth satin gloss. The light glowing from the burnished brass sconces was softly reflected in the gleaming hardwood floors. To enhance the turn-of-the-century ambience, lush majestic plants stood in brass planters in the corners of the foyer.

While they were hard at work, Lieutenant Chapman came in munching a sandwich. Carina saw him first and blurted out "Be careful, you're making crumbs!"

He glanced down a the floor. "Aw, jeez, I'm sorry. I should've finished my lunch in the car, I guess, huh?"

Carina came over and began picking up the larger pieces of crusty bun that lay in a trail from the door. Policeman or not, he had no right to treat this place as though it were some roadside diner. Then she remembered a promise she'd made to herself earlier—not to get started off on the wrong foot the next time she saw Lieutenant Chapman. So she brushed off her knees and stood up; she even managed a casual grin. "Go ahead and finish your sandwich. You know how paranoid people get when they've just finished cleaning the floor."

He laughed pleasantly. "I know, and I'm always doing this to the missus, too—tracking in fresh mud. She could kill me." He looked around the room as if noticing it for the first time. "Boy, I gotta tell you, this place looks great. Far cry from what it was like a few weeks ago."

Carina stepped back to eye the results proudly. "It does look good, doesn't it? All the merchants have been so wonderful about donating stuff—the whole town's pitched in. But we sure couldn't have done it without a lot of effort from all the theater staff. I just wish I could give everyone a two-week vacation and a bonus for all the work they've done." After she'd finished, she realized with a twinge that everyone's vacation could end up a lot longer than two weeks if Harland Pennell, the banker, had anything to say about it.

The policeman appeared to take his time polishing off the sandwich. Finally Damian said, "Was there a particular reason you wanted to see us, Lieutenant, or were you just looking for someplace pleasant to eat?"

His blatant sarcasm seemed to bounce right off the policeman's thick skin. "Yeah, as a matter of fact, there are a couple of things." He reached into the front pocket of his jacket and pulled out something black and silky. "I was wondering if anyone could identify this." He held out the garment, pinched between his forefinger and this thumb. It was a black half-slip with silver threads running through it.

Carina watched in horror as Elsie leaped forward to snatch it boldly from the policeman's hand. "Oh, my word, Carina!" she shrieked. "I'm so sorry. I completely forgot to look for your slip after you called me that night. I had so much on my mind. Where ever did you find this, sir?"

The atmosphere in the room was so thick, it could have been scooped up by the handful. Elsie's eyes darted from one person to another as she clenched the incriminating garment in her small hands. "Did I say something wrong?" she asked.

Carina resignedly took the slip from her and gave it back to the policeman. She had an idea he was going to want to keep it for a while. "It doesn't matter, Elsie; it's not your fault." *It's not mine, either, but since when has that made any difference?*

To Carina's amazement, Lieutenant Chapman looked almost as uncomfortable as she felt. "Where did you find it?" she asked him.

"In Spencer's apartment. It was stuffed down behind the cushions of his sofa. I, uh, I didn't realize it was yours."

She could feel Damian's eyes fixed on her steadily. They pierced like steel lances, but she didn't dare look at him to find out whether he was savoring some kind of cruel satisfaction. Things had started coming together for them so nicely until now. They'd shared a peaceful lunch.... The slip had probably ruined everything.

For the longest time, everyone stood in the lobby without moving, like some diorama Damian's grandfather might have fashioned. Finally the lieutenant said, "I'd like to talk to you alone in your office, Miss Rawlins." To the other two, he said, "I'd like to see you folks later, and would you mind telling anyone else who's here to stick around for a while?"

"Nearly everyone's out for lunch right now," the exceedingly helpful Elsie told him. Too bad there was no way of warning them to stay out, Carina thought with a fleeting sense of irony.

"No problem," the officer said. "Just let them know I'm here when they get back." He gestured with his arm, inviting Carina to lead the way to her office. She had to walk right past Damian, and for an instant she thought he might offer to be with her during what was bound to be an interrogation. One glance at his expression, however, and she knew better. Damian, in the space of a few minutes, had stopped believing in her. This, more than anything else, made a lump of terror rise in her throat.

For what it was worth, Lieutenant Chapman looked genuinely regretful when they were alone in her office. But on further reflection, she decided it was probably part of his job to feign sympathy, thereby extracting a few more drops of so-called truth from his suspects.

"Why don't you start by telling me what you were doing in Spencer's apartment the night you left this?" He pointed at the slip now lying on her desk, looking ridiculously decadent against the scarred wood.

"I didn't leave it," Carina said, "and I wasn't in his apartment whatever night the slip got left."

The officer raised his eyebrows as if truly amused at her capacity for creating weak alibis. "Care to elaborate on that?"

Carina told him the same story she'd told Damian—eons ago, it now seemed. She had lent the camisole and slip to wardrobe for a play and forgotten to get them back. The next time she'd given them any thought was the day she and Damian had gone to Malcolm's apartment and they'd found the camisole.

"So you have no idea how your lingerie got from the wardrobe department to your boss's place," the policeman repeated.

"That's right."

"What happened to the . . . whaddya call it again?"

"Camisole."

"Yeah, camisole."

Carina picked at a fraying corner of the blotter on her desk. "I found it . . . or rather, Damian found it in Malcolm's bathroom, and I brought it home that night."

"You brought it *home*?" The last word was emphasized as if she'd perpetrated something quite horrendous.

"Yes, why wouldn't I? It belonged to me."

"Even though you knew you'd be tampering with evidence?"

Something in what he said struck a faint and distant chord in Carina's memory. *Tampering with evidence.* Hadn't Damian said the very same thing when she'd begun gathering up the bedspread in Malcolm's apartment? Yet there'd been no suggestion of a crime, no evidence to consider.

"I asked you a question, Miss Rawlins."

"Uh . . . yes, I know, I was just . . . trying to think back. I brought the camisole home because I had no idea that something . . . unfortunate had happened to Malcolm. I was just annoyed at finding my clothes there in the first place."

"Did you strip the bedding?" he asked.

By now, Carina's palms were getting sweaty, and her heart was beating so guiltily she was sure the officer could hear it. "Yes, I . . . I was trying to find my slip. It was, well . . . a rather expensive set."

"But why check the bed?" Since you claim you were never in it, his silence seemed to say.

"Because it happened to be where I was standing when Damian brought the camisole out from the bathroom. If I'd been in the kitchen, I'd have probably started looking in the cupboards."

"But you must not have searched the whole apartment or you'd have found the slip, wouldn't you?"

"I would've stayed, but Damian thought we should leave before the landlady got suspicious and came to see what we were doing." A startling realization snapped into place. Damian was the one who'd discovered the camisole. He was the one who'd rushed them out of the apartment when she would have preferred to continue looking for the slip. He had followed her out the door—hands, as usual, in his pockets. How easy it would have been for him to stuff the slip into the couch on his way to the door, every bit as easy as it was to "find" a camisole in the bathroom.

"Weren't you afraid that someone would find the slip later? You could've gone back and looked for it on your own."

"No, Lieutenant, I wouldn't have done that because, you see, at that time I had nothing to be afraid of." Carina's hopes were rapidly sinking to an all-time low. Why had she wanted to mend the rift with Damian in the first place? What had she been thinking? She would have been better off keeping her distance from him after she found the props. At least it would have made this latest revelation easier to bear. As it was, she feared she might scream out loud with anguish. *How could you do this to me, Damian? What have I done to make you think so little of me?*

"Let's talk about something else for a while," the officer said. "Remember when you called me last Saturday about the props?"

"Yes," she mumbled through a fog of heartbreak.

"Didn't you say you'd just come across them that morning?"

Suddenly Carina sat up, wary of this new line of questioning. "Yes, that's what I said."

The lieutenant sucked his teeth in irritating preamble. "Funny. I talked to the desk clerk and the elevator operator, and they both saw you come into the hotel on Friday night, late. They said you seemed nervous. You were clutching your briefcase like there was something important inside, and you were in a hurry. You got off on the same floor where the cast is staying. Now isn't it true that you actually found—and I use the term loosely—the tools on Friday night and were looking for someone at the hotel to witness your discovery?''

"No!" Carina cried out. "I mean, yes, it's true that I found them on Friday night, but that's not why I went looking for Damian." Carina cursed her fair complexion for betraying her with an indignant flush, especially now that she was being honest. "When I discovered the props I was so terrified of being alone in the theater that I just ran out. I brought the props with me because I couldn't think of what else to do at the moment. Then after a few minutes of wandering around outside, it occurred to me that—" she had to say it now; there was no other choice "—that Damian might have used me, that he might have planted the murder weapons in my desk. I went to the hotel intending to confront him with my suspicions."

"Weren't you afraid that he might kill you?" the policeman asked.

Carina let out a ragged breath. "I refused to consider the possibility too deeply at the time."

"What happened at the hotel?"

"Nothing. He'd gone out for dinner with Judith and wasn't back yet."

"But you still didn't call me until the next morning. Why?"

Hoping to recover some of the crucial points she'd lost, Carina stared him straight in the eye. "Because, Lieutenant, ever since this whole business started, you've made me feel guilty as sin even though I know I haven't done anything wrong. I didn't have the nerve to call you from my apartment when I was already a nervous wreck. Then I knew that if I told you I'd deliberately waited all night before calling, you'd find something suspicious about that, too. Obviously, I was right." She sat back and, having spoken her mind, felt better.

If the lieutenant was feeling at all remorseful for making her nervous, he wasn't showing it. In fact, he looked every inch the pompous, arrogant cop. "Are you and Fleming still . . . seeing each other?"

Carina shook her head and laughed mirthlessly. "Hardly, Lieutenant. I'm not that stupid."

"Glad to hear it." He brought out his notepad and began scribbling. Carina was relieved that he had abandoned the issue of her love life for the time being. She didn't think she could stand up to any grilling about what she still felt for Damian—or rather what she had felt until a few minutes ago. After a while the officer clapped the notepad shut and got to his feet.

"I probably don't need to say this to you," he pronounced, "since you seem like a levelheaded lady, but I think it'd be a good idea if you didn't leave town for a while. Know what I mean?"

"Yes," she replied, sighing. "I know what you mean."

"Now what was that other thing I wanted to tell you— oh, yeah, now I remember. It was about the bloodstains on the props."

Carina looked up. "What about them?"

"I checked with the hospital. It's Spencers blood type all right. As for the prints, there was only one set—yours." The color drained from Carina's face as he left her with a cheerful, "See ya, Miss Rawlins."

AT LAST IT WAS THE MORNING of the final dress rehearsal; only one day remained before opening night. Tickets for the masquerade gala were sold out. It was amazing to discover the number of people willing to pay two hundred dollars to mingle at the site of a suspected murder.

Carina was to have delivered the balance of the outstanding funds to the bank the previous day, but not all the money from the ticket-buyers had come in yet. She was still well below the sum they needed to pay off the loan. Harland Pennell hadn't called, so she could only assume that Gwen had been right. The bank was going to give them a few extra feet of rope to hang themselves. But at least *Fate of the Popinjay* would have its week in the limelight before the Myrmidon closed forever.

Carina became aware of a faint memory somewhere in the back of her mind as she sat in her office thinking about the play. Something Damian had once said was niggling at her, and for some reason the play brought it nearer to the surface. *What was it?* She knew instinctively that it was vital; whatever it was, vital enough to clear her name. She had to think—

Suddenly she had it! It was the night Damian and the Kramers had come to her place for dinner. He'd asked her if she'd read the play and seemed relieved when she said she hadn't. Then, on another occasion, Len had mentioned the same thing, that Damian was still wondering whether she'd read the play yet. It had to be more than just a writer's need for praise. Heaven knew Damian got enough of that elsewhere. It was more like...dread. He was worried that she *had* read it. Why? Especially when he knew she was eventually going to see it on stage!

The dress rehearsal was still hours away, but Carina could no longer bear to wait that long. She had to find the script and read it now. She was convinced that was where the final clue lay, somewhere in the last two acts. Perhaps Damian was living out some warped fantasy by coming here, a fantasy he'd fashioned years ago in the guise of a three-act play.

She hurried out of her office and down the hall to the Kramers' dressing room. They'd have two copies of the script and probably wouldn't mind lending her one. She was about to knock on their door when she heard Len speak in a strained tone of voice she'd never heard him use before.

"I think we ought to reconsider, Kate. I'm still not sure we've done the right thing."

"What? Have you gone daft?" Kate's reply was shrill, bordering on hysteria. "Listen to me, Leonard Kramer, it's too late for either of us to back out now. Malcolm Spencer is dead; we can't bring him back. And now after all these years, we finally have the opportunity we've been waiting for."

"But what if, despite our efforts, everything falls through?" Len argued. "We've taken incalculable risks."

"Nothing will fall through," his wife insisted. "Not after all the careful planning we've done, not after all the hard work. And what could possibly happen? The only other person who knew about our plans was Malcolm—the wretch—and we shan't be hearing from him anymore."

There was the sound of a chair scraping and Len crossing the room to kiss his wife. "Of course you're right, dear, as always. The whole thing has gone off frightfully well, although I must say, that last bit of nasty business was none too good for my back."

"You'll recover, my dear," Kate said with a chuckle. "Fortunately it's the kind of thing one only has to endure once, if all goes well. Cup of tea, dear?"

Chapter Thirteen

Their argument dissolved with macabre ease into mundane matters of hotel laundry and dinner plans. Carina backed away from the door in utter disbelief. She couldn't have heard right; *she simply couldn't have*. But their conversation played and replayed itself in her head, the words uttered with such bluntness, so devoid of remorse, she knew there could be no mistake.

The Kramers: bubbly, curly-haired Kate...sweet, kindly Len—murderers! Somehow it was even harder to accept than Malcolm's death. On the verge of illness, Carina pressed her hands to her stomach and dragged herself back to her office. Her reason for wanting to see the Kramers was now irrelevant.

As she sat in her office waiting for the grip of nausea to subside, all of a sudden it hit her. If the Kramers had murdered Malcolm, then Damian was innocent. He wasn't even an accomplice. Kate had said as much when she reminded her husband that Malcolm was the only one who'd known about the their plans. Obviously the poor man had taken the secret with him to the grave.

Almost as though she'd sprouted wings, Carina leaped up from her chair and flew to Damian's office. Now they could make up for the past few intolerable days when they'd hardly spoken to each other. They could put the tension and the loneliness behind them and start over. Thank goodness that they'd both refrained from saying things they might regret later. Somehow, through all the recriminations and all the doubt, they'd remained sensitive to each other's feelings, a vestige, she supposed, of the tenderness they'd shared before. The bridges between them weren't burned, only charred. She would tell him what she'd heard; she would beg his forgiveness for ever having mistrusted him; and then she'd tell him how much she loved him. She had never stopped loving him....

Carina knocked but didn't wait for a reply before opening the door. There had been a time, not so long before, when they'd felt free enough with each other to do that, when she'd felt comfortable enough to walk into his office unannounced. Damian was stretched out on the sofa, reading a magazine. When Carina stepped tentatively in, his head shot up.

"I don't recall inviting you," he said in the cool tones she'd come to know so well of late. Ever since the lieutenant had shown up, waving that damned slip.

Carina smiled tenuously. Oh, but it felt good to smile again. "I know, but I thought once you heard what I have to say, you'll overlook my barging in."

Damian tossed the magazine aside and sat up, swinging his long legs to the floor. Though his expression was one of caution, Carina could have sworn she saw a glimmer of hope in his eyes. "Have a seat." He indicated a chair next to the sofa.

Carina sat and clenched her hands tightly in her lap. Her heart was doing silly pit-a-pats, quite at odds with the impression of composure she was trying to convey. "First of all," she said, "I've come to apologize. I was wrong to doubt you, and I should not have taken offense at your doubting me.''

Leaning back, Damian crossed one leg over the other. "I think we both had adequate reasons for the way we felt.''

She couldn't blame him for keeping his emotions in check. If the situation were reversed, she'd probably behave the same way. "I know we had our reasons, but I also believe that deep inside, neither of us was willing to accept that the other was capable of murder. Perhaps what we should have done was cling to those feelings, instead of letting external influences tear us apart the way they did.''

Damian inclined his head in a gesture of doubt. "Maybe you're asking too much of what we had. It was fabulous while it lasted—I grant you that—but it's hard to maintain passion alongside a dead man's bloodstains, isn't it?''

Carina winced at the irony in his voice, though perhaps he was right. In this, her moment of reprieve, was she reading too much into their relationship?

"Why don't you just come out with it and tell me what you have to say," Damian suggested. "You'll have to forgive me, but I doubt that you would have come to this startling revelation without some cold, hard proof.''

Carina averted her eyes. He was, as usual, unerring in his perception. She hadn't been able to rely on the strength of her love alone, and it was devastating to realize it. But she couldn't dwell on that now. She lowered her head. *Dear God, let me say this right.* She was about to accuse his godparents of murder; it wasn't going to be easy for him. Then she looked up. "I know who killed Malcolm.''

He raised an eyebrow. "Do you?''

"I overheard them discussing it in their dressing room a few minutes ago.''

Damian sat up, ramrod straight. "Them? Who's them?''

"Kate and Len." Ignoring for the moment the flash of pain that crossed his face, Carina pressed on. "I know it sounds incredible, and I never would have believed it myself, except that I heard it with my own ears. They'd been planning it for years. They must have arranged to have a telegram sent from Majorca and somehow coerced Malcolm into strewing my lingerie around his apartment. Then they killed him and left the murder weapons in my desk, hoping I wouldn't discover the things until after they left town."

The color left Damian's face as suddenly as if a curtain had been torn away. But naturally he would be shocked, Carina told herself. He loved the Kramers as if they were his parents. When he spoke, he was so racked with emotion, he could scarcely get the words out. "Do you...do you have any idea why they would want to...murder Malcolm?"

Carina shook her head, relieved that he was at least willing to discuss it. "No, not really, but I imagine they were hoping to avenge what he did to you. They're totally devoted to—"

"What about the body?" he cut in sharply. "Did they say where they had hidden the body?"

"No, I...I didn't hear anything about the body," Carina admitted.

For a long time neither of them spoke. Damian stared at the floor; his breathing was heavy and rhythmic. When he finally lifted his eyes, the shuttered look was gone, and Carina could see the raw, unbridled anguish. The sight of the pain she'd caused him was harder to bear than almost anything she'd ever endured before.

"I'm so sorry, Damian," she whispered.

He stared at her, and it felt as though he were reaching deep inside her soul to see what was really there. "I know," he said, "how desperately you've wanted to get out from under the weight of Malcolm's death, and whether or not you killed him is no longer an issue for me. I know what a worthless person he was, and I wouldn't cast judgment on anyone who'd reached their limits with him. God knows I've entertained the thought of doing away with him more than once myself."

Carina's breath caught in her throat. She had an uneasy sense that he wasn't working up to an apology. Still, she kept her silence and allowed him to continue.

"I was less than understanding when I first realized you wanted to implicate me in the murder, but after a time I could even begin to see your rationale. After all, I'm wealthy enough to retain the best attorneys, and with my public image, I could conceivably get an acquittal. The same wouldn't hold true for you."

Carina lunged forward in her chair. "But, I—"

"No, Carina, let me finish," he said, holding up his hand. "The one thing I absolutely and unconditionally will not tolerate is for you to ruin the lives of two innocent people like the Kramers. This time, you have gone too far; this time, I can't find any sympathy for you. As far as I'm concerned, you're sick, deluded...and God knows, probably beyond help."

Damian stood up, and from the contemptuous way he looked at her, Carina could tell that he was ready to throw her out of his office forcibly if she didn't leave on her own. She longed to cry out, scream, beat her fists against the wall. But Damian's words, cold and unyielding, echoed through the room like a death knell.

There was nothing she could say to bring back the hopeful Damian of a few moments ago, no gestures she could use to warm his ashen face. She had set the bridge on fire, and all she'd done was tell him the truth. Carina turned to walk away. When Damian called her name, she stopped, not daring to look at him.

"One more thing," he said, and the warning in his voice was unmistakable, "If you go to the police with your accusations, I swear you'll live to regret it."

Carina couldn't bear to stay a second longer. She fled the room as fast as her legs would take her, and she didn't stop running until she reached her own office and locked the door. Then, she fell across the couch and sobbed until there was nothing left inside her but a dull, throbbing ache.

THE FINAL DRESS REHEARSAL commenced on schedule. Carina took a seat in the back row, where no one from the stage would be able to see her. Crew members whose presence was not essential backstage sat in the front of the auditorium, and under other circumstances, Carina would have joined them. But not now. Once her tears had subsided, she'd come to realize that her only hope was to prove irrefutably who had killed Malcolm and how they'd done it. In light of Damian's threat, she didn't dare approach Lieutenant Chapman until her evidence was ironclad. She was still convinced that something in *Fate of the Popinjay* would lead her to the truth.

The set designer and his assistants had done an excellent job of creating a turn-of-the-century taxidermist's workshop for the first act. They'd painted the set in dungeonlike tones of green and gray and decorated it using a wealth of authentic detail. There were shelves cluttered with bottles of colored solution, skins of raccoon and monkey and zebra hanging over racks, and a menagerie of beasts propped and prone in various stages of completion.

At the center of it all, framed by the proscenium arch and the red velvet curtain, was Mr. Tiggles. Beakers and test-tubes of simulated acids bubbled and hissed all around him as he labored over the brightly-hued popinjay. In Len's portrayal, the taxidermist was a driven man with the total dedication of an alchemist, a man who was weak and unassertive about everything except his one obsession.

Judith was at his side as Bettina Tiggles, wearing a prim dress of black taffeta and lace. When she delivered her lines, she exuded a smoldering sexuality and a slight disdain that lent immediate depth to her character. Carina, though she was familiar with the lines, still found herself caught up in the biting repartee and the brilliant directing. It was impossible not to be entertained.

A ten-minute intermission between acts allowed for the change of sets. Carina stayed only until the curtains were half drawn, and then she slipped out the exit. As she left, she could hear Damian speaking to the lighting technician; just hearing his voice was enough to open her wounds and start them bleeding again.

But she knew it was crucial to maintain an appearance of outward calm, she chatted casually with the few stagehands she found lounging in the lobby. Then she paid a friendly visit to the box-office manager and her assistant, who were frantically answering a deluge of calls for tickets. As much as she longed to confide in someone, she didn't want to imperil anyone else in the theater. If the Kramers—or whoever—were capable of killing once, they could do it again if they felt their plans were threatened. For the next little while Carina could rely on no one but herself.

The second act took place in the Tiggleses' drawing room, where the family was entertaining their new guest from England, Jasper Garnet. Damian, in dove-gray tails and wing collar, captured the effete mannerisms of a Victorian dilettante brilliantly. His blond hair was slicked back close to his head, his upper-crust accent was flawless and when he pranced across the stage sniffing flowers and admiring his reflection, no one would have believed he was anything but a fop of the highest order. Even the crew backstage could be heard guffawing despite their best efforts at restraint.

Kate's character, the lush, blowsy Mrs. Tiggles, was every bit as comical. Her dress was a shocking chartreuse, gaudy with frills and ruffles and bows. Her jewelry was miles of multicolored beads that clacked and clattered with every tipsy swing of the arm and every doddering nod of the head. She and Damian played off each other in such a marvelously campy way that even Carina, miserable as she felt, was laughing.

Mr. Tiggles, stiff and out of place away from the comforting gloom of his workshop, clearly did not know what to make of his distant cousin. Jasper Garnet talked too much, drank too much and found his host's profession quite laughable. What disturbed poor Mr. Tiggles even more was that his adored Bettina had undergone a complete change of character; she'd become prissy and demure. And she seemed totally besotted by the man—she, who'd always rejected feminine wiles and the pursuit of matrimony.

She laughed gaily at each of Jasper's rude jokes; she batted her eyes every time her cousin could pull his attention away from himself long enough to look at her. But the deepest cut of all to the befuddled Mr. Tiggles was when Bettina refused to accompany her father and Jasper on a tour of the workshop saying, "Gracious, Papa, you know I have a delicate constitution exactly like Mother's. I couldn't possibly accompany our charming guest unless he's prepared to bring smelling salts and carry me back upstairs." Even Mrs. Tiggles, through her drunken stupor, had to sneak on a pair of spectacles to be sure it was her daughter speaking.

Scene two of the second act took place some weeks later, again in the Tiggleses' drawing room, which was now littered with glasses and half-empty bottles. Bettina wore a voluptuous scarlet gown and matching carnations in her hair. She and Jasper were alone, and the man simply couldn't keep his eyes off her as she danced about him and flirted shamelessly. After several desperate and unsuccessful attempts, Jasper finally caught her wrist as she frolicked in what seemed a gin-soaked haze. Skirts whirling, she plopped down beside him, carmine lips pursed in a pout.

"Don't you approve of my dancing?" she asked, her words just a little slurred.

Jasper took her hands and clasped them to his breast. "My lovely, bewitching Bettina, how can you ask such a thing? I love everything about you. My world revolves around your smile; my heart beats only in the hopes of your kiss." Jasper then fell to the floor on his knees. "I implore you, my delightful dancing vixen. Take this yearning from me, this incessant ache of the soul, and heal me."

"Why, Jasper, whatever are you asking of me?" Long lashes batted over eyes that seemed a trifle vacant.

"Marry me, my sweet! I can't live without you!"

Bettina brought her hands to her face as if completely taken aback by the proposal. "Dear, dear Jasper, I do love you madly, but I wouldn't make a proper wife! I haven't any money."

"But I have more than I know what to do with, my love! Whatever I have is yours!"

"I would only agree to marriage if I can be sure it will be perfect. I can't abide unhappiness." At this point, she affected a little hiccough.

"Nor can I, my love," Jasper insisted.

"I've always wanted to see the world." Bettina turned her head away loftily. "We must travel at every opportunity."

Jasper, love-struck beyond reason, craned his neck so that she would look at him. "We'll sail from Punta Arenas to Zanzibar, from Singapore to Bora Bora—wherever your heart desires."

"I can't cook," Bettina added, "and I hate to clean."

"And you never shall, my darling. You'll have all the help you need to keep your lily-white..." Jasper stumbled on his words when he looked down at her palms, stained and pitted from acid and sharp instruments in her father's workshop.

Bettina yanked her hands away with surprising delicacy. "An unfortunate childhood accident," she explained hastily, brushing an errant curl from her forehead. "There is one other tiny little promise you must make before I can hope to give my assent."

Jasper pulled a gardenia from his buttonhole and sniffed it dramatically. "You have but to name it, my pet."

"We must never, never argue with each other. I've always believed a marriage should be a peaceful, tranquil institution, a melding of compatible temperaments. If we can't give each other the things that we crave, then I say, what's the use?"

"Er...quite so, my darling." Her suitor was clearly worried. "It's a tall order, but I shall try to oblige."

"For example, dear Jasper, assuming that I am given adequate money to run our household and to travel, I shall devote myself to providing you with the luxuries of life that only I can give. In my care, darling, I promise you will forever remain young and handsome and always at the height of fashion. You will never want for anyone else but me." Bettina lowered her eyes. "Assuming I have interpreted your nature correctly."

"Oh, you have, you have! We shall make it a perfect marriage, Bettina, if you will only say yes." His head fell to her lap, and as she looked out toward the audience, it was readily apparent that Bettina was as sober as a judge and twice as shrewd.

"Yes, I shall marry you, my handsome, bright-eyed, ever-so-perfect popinjay," she said, an instant before the curtain closed.

The third and final act was set in the ivy-covered cottage at the tip of Long Island where Mr. and Mrs. Jasper Garnet spent the early part of the summer. The set was divided between the sunny drawing room of the cottage, where Bettina was pouring tea for her visiting parents, and the garden outside, where Jasper lay in a reclining rattan wheelchair, a blanket covering his knees, his eyes glassy and staring straight ahead.

Mrs. Tiggles, tipsy as usual, peered through the window at her son-in-law and said, "What was it—hic—that you said is wrong with him?"

Bettina, dressed in somber taffetas once more, replied, "Catatonic schizophrenia, Mother. The doctors in Vienna say there's nothing anyone can do."

Mr. Tiggles shook his head sadly. "Such a tragedy for a young couple. I don't know how you've managed to remain so strong and happy."

The mad and brilliant Bettina smiled. "Oh, I assure you, Papa, I couldn't be happier. I have more than enough money, I travel as often as I like, and Jasper leaves me in peace to do exactly what I choose. It's quite an ideal marriage.''

Soon after, she persuaded her parents to take a nice nap before dinner to recover from their long journey. Then Bettina went outside to her husband.

Patting him on the head, she said, "Hello, dear. I'm sorry I left you in the sun such a long time. I hope you haven't dried up.'' Jasper didn't answer, but Bettina didn't seem to expect him to. She steered his wheelchair, not to the house, but to a small building at the edge of the lawn that looked like a potting shed. She opened the door and inside were shelves of solution and skins hanging on racks to dry.

"I'll fetch you again for a little visit when the sun has gone down,'' she told her rigid husband. Then she adjusted his tie and straightened his collar. "Since you've been so cooperative, I'll buy you a new suit next week. I did do a lovely job on you, didn't I? Papa will be so proud of my work when he gets a chance to see you close up. Of course, I had to tell Mother you're catatonic, but you and I know better. Thanks to me, you'll never be ill or unhappy again. Good day, my dear sweet popinjay.'' With that, Bettina shut the door to the workshop, and the final curtain closed.

The crew in the front row applauded enthusiastically, but Carina was oblivious to the response. All she could think about was the fact that her employer had been the original inspiration for the character of Jasper. Now, it seemed the fate of the popinjay had also been the fate of Malcolm Spencer. There was only one explanation for the bloodied taxidermist's tools—Malcolm had been killed and stuffed. There was only one person who possessed the skills to do it—Damian!

Chapter Fourteen

The man was a demented genius. Horror-stricken though she was, Carina could not deny how cleverly Damian had framed her. First, by feigning an instant attraction that she was virtually guaranteed to reciprocate. After all, what woman in her right mind wouldn't fall for his expert flattery? And then, when the incriminating clues had started to appear, how brilliantly he'd played the disappointed lover, heartbroken that she could suspect him of murder after all they'd meant to each other. In some ways, the last scene he'd staged for her was the best, because he'd been caught off guard and forced to test his improvisational mettle. Obviously, what she'd overheard in the Kramer's dressing room was unrelated to the crime. But when she'd announced her discovery to Damian, he had taken her words and fit them easily into his guise of loyal godson, ready to defend the dear old couple to the very end. It was truly amazing.

Now she had to track down Malcolm's body. Having come to the unavoidable conclusion that her employer had met with the same fate as the brightly feathered bird in the play, Carina expected to find him in a similar condition. She was certain he'd escaped being dumped in a shallow grave somewhere. A psychopath who went to as much trouble as Damian obviously did would want his work displayed somewhere for his private enjoyment.

The theater was the most likely place to start looking, because aside from Damian's hotel room—which would be cleaned daily—it was where he spent most of his time. Even if he couldn't get around to admiring his handiwork regularly, he would have the satisfaction of knowing it was nearby—like Bettina keeping Jasper in the potting shed while she went about her everyday business.

The problem was when to do it, Carina thought as she sat in her office sipping brackish coffee from the morning's brew. It was essential that the Myrmidon be empty when she searched. She didn't want anyone in the cast or crew to have the slightest hint of her suspicions. For one thing, no one in the crew would believe her, and as for the cast, she didn't trust any one of them at the moment. She knew Lieutenant Chapman would be more than eager to hear her theory, but until she could point to Malcolm's body, she wasn't going to risk involving the police. All she needed was to be thrown into jail on suspicion of murder; if that happened, she wouldn't be able to do a thing to prove her innocence.

THE OPPORTUNITY to search finally presented itself the next day, a few hours before the opening-night performance. It was customary for the cast and crew to take the afternoon off to rest before the long evening ahead. When Carina arrived at the Myrmidon, she was running on nerves alone. Fortunately the outside doors were locked, which meant there was no one in the building. She was carrying her costume for the masquerade in a shopping bag, which she quickly tossed onto her own desk. Then she headed for Damian's office cum dressing room. She might as well get the most obvious place out of the way first, she decided with grim fatalism.

Doors inside the theater were never locked, so she was able to enter his office with no problem. Late-afternoon light filtered in through the windows, and Carina breathed deeply of Damian's faint but unmistakable essence—a lingering masculine scent of leather worn soft and supple against his body. *Stop it, Carina,* she told herself fiercely. That part of her life was over, and Damian was anything but the dream lover she'd once imagined him to be.

She shook her head to rid herself of memories that only served to waste time. Turning on the lights, she began to search, beginning with the closet. There was nothing, except for some of Malcolm's suits hanging in a garment bag. Next she checked the cupboards of the large wall unit. None of the sections were large enough to house an entire corpse, but she hadn't ruled out the possibility of a grisly dismemberment.

Carina avoided the tableful of framed glossies, pictures of Malcolm posing with every celebrity he'd ever met. She couldn't help feeling guilty that his death hadn't affected her more. She checked under the desk and on top of the shelves, everywhere she could think of, but found nothing.

She went next to the two adjoining nooks Judith used for dressing rooms. Carina had concluded that while Judith and the Kramers might not have had a hand in the actual murder, they were probably aware of what Damian had done and were keeping silent. Their common hatred of Malcolm would be a powerful force; Damian would surely have taken advantage of it somehow. The two rooms were so small there was barely enough space for Judith and her vast collection of cold creams and beauty treatments. The only thing that caught Carina's eye was a snapshot tucked into a corner of the makeup mirror; it was of a much younger Judith arm in arm with Malcolm and Damian. They were standing in front of what seemed to be a Greenwich Village coffeehouse; all three of them looked poor but happy. For reasons that Carina preferred not to identify, the picture disturbed her. She didn't linger, but left the room to continue her search.

The Kramer's dressing room smelled of sandalwood, one of Kate's favorite scents. Two vanities had been pushed close together, one filled with pretty porcelain pots of theatrical makeup and cleansing creams, the other cluttered with more masculine versions of the same thing, as well as the old-fashioned spectacles Len wore in the play. Two pairs of slippers lay side by side on the floor, and two matching robes were folded over the backs of the chairs.

Carina moved to the large closet and opened both doors, but except for a few sweaters and spare shoes, it was empty. She took another turn around the room. There was nothing. The Kramers were neat and tidy to a fault.

Finally, she scoured the rest of the theater. She went through rows of costume racks in wardrobe. She looked under huge sheets of plywood in the set designer's workshop. She checked every bathroom and broom closet, every nook and every cranny. The only places she didn't look were the stage and the auditorium. There was no point. The sets were shuffled around every day by the crew, and a janitorial service had come in that morning to do a thorough cleaning of the auditorium. Obviously, there'd been no sign of Malcolm's body.

Just as she was walking past the lobby to her own office, Carina ran into Kate and Len who'd just come in the front doors. Certain that guilt was creeping up her face, Carina stopped dead in her tracks.

"Um, er, hello. You're here early," she stammered.

Kate unwrapped a long silk scarf from her neck. "We always are, dear. You ought to know that by now."

You have no idea how much I know, Carina thought with a gulp as she watched Kate wrap and unwrap the scarf around her hand.

"Is something the matter, Carina?" Len slipped a hand into his pocket. "You look flushed."

Carina's hands flew to her face. "D-do I? I must be suffering pre-performance jitters." Her laugh sounded more like a gasp. What was Len doing with his hand in the pocket of his sports coat? He was fishing for something. He was taking it out. It was long and metallic, and now he was pointing it at her.

"Care for a toffee?" he asked. "I find it helps to soothe the nerves."

Carina's gaze fell to the object in his hand, and sure enough it was a roll of candy wrapped in foil. "Uh . . . no, thanks, I was just about to have some . . . gum." She made a valiant attempt to smile, then skirted past them to her office. No way would she spend another moment chatting with those two! She prayed that someone from the crew would arrive soon—someone large and muscular, like Henry the stage manager.

When she entered her office, the first thing she saw was Sarah Bernhardt's portrait hanging at an angle. But this time, instead of reacting with alarm, Carina felt as though she'd found an ally. Even an old photograph with a mind of its own was better than no confidant at all.

"I'm right, Sarah, aren't I?" she said in an effort to calm herself. "Malcolm *is* in here somewhere. I just haven't looked in the right place."

"Hello, Carina," said a voice from behind her.

She spun around to find Gerry, the props man, standing in the doorway. "Oh, hi, Gerry!" she said loudly. "I didn't hear you come in."

His leathery face creased in a grin. "That's okay. I know how it feels."

Carina thanked her lucky stars that Gerry hadn't heard her talking to herself like a lunatic. She was really going to have to renounce that habit. "Are you looking forward to the play?" she asked by way of small talk.

Gerry shrugged his hunched, troll-like shoulders. "Can't say that I am. I don't care much for opening nights. Too much tension; it's bad for the blood. And mark my words, the dress rehearsal went off without a hitch, and that's always a bad sign." With that cheery forecast, he apparently decided he had said enough and shambled off.

Carina watched him go, feeling a strange kinship with the odd little man. Perhaps she'd caught a glimpse of her own future just then, as a superstitious old crone working in a rundown theater. She would tell people she'd once had a boss who was killed and stuffed, and they'd all call her crazy. But then, perhaps, some child would take a liking to her and tell his friends, "Don't call her a witch. She may be a little crazy, but—" Oh, Lord, she had to find that body!

Like a bolt of lightning, inspiration struck. She hadn't checked the entire theater after all! The one place she'd forgotten to look was Gerry's workshop underneath the stage. Beyond the main storeroom were several other rooms that he never used, holdovers from a brief period when the Myrmidon had been more of a bordello than a real theater. The saloon girls would perform their high-stepping kicks on stage, and then bring their clients downstairs after the show for kicks of a different kind. That was back in the late 1800s, when Dunn's Pond was short of

women and long on lusty young miners and railroad nav-
vies.

Gerry's workshop. She couldn't be wrong this time.
Carina hadn't felt this sure about anything in weeks. Malcolm was down there, and she had to find him somehow.

Carina glanced at her watch. Dammit, she wasn't going
to have time before the show. Any moment, the ushers
would be arriving, and there were last-minute instructions
to give them. Then she had to get into her costume and be
ready to greet patrons as they entered the auditorium. She
had no choice but to wait. The show, as they said, must go
on.

Frustrated, Carina snatched up her shopping bag and
took it to the staff rest room. There she pulled out a long
black body stocking and began to undress. Ten minutes
later she looked into the full-length mirror and saw a black
cat that any tom would be proud to fool around with,
complete with greasepaint whiskers and a long satin tail
that curled sinuously around her legs. As a finishing touch,
she donned a black half mask that flared up at the sides,
concealing her identity and affording her a boldness of
spirit that the real Carina Rawlins didn't feel. Shivering
slightly, she went out to the lobby.

Greeting patrons in full costume was bizarre, like shaking hands at the entrance to Dante's Inferno—with the
likes of Marie Antoinette, Count Dracula and someone
who looked especially hideous draped in artificial seaweed.

"Is that you, Carina?" A scrawny Cleopatra was peering at her through a black mask on a stick.

"It's me, all right. How are you, Gwen?"

The woman dropped her mask and her mouth turned
down. "How'd you recognize me?" she moaned.

Carina glanced at the woman's knobby shoulders, sallow complexion and the ridiculous formal black gloves and

replied, "The Gucci pumps. I was with you when you bought them. Didn't Cleopatra wear sandals?"

Gwen's toes came together self-consciously. "It's too cold for sandals."

Just then, Napoleon Bonaparte came up behind Gwen and said, "Hi there, Miz Rawlins," in a thick Southern drawl.

Carina gritted her teeth when she smiled. "Mr. Pennell, how nice to see you. I tried to keep our appointment last Tuesday, but your secretary said you were tied up."

The banker brought his chestful of medals closer. "Don't worry, honey, I haven't forgotten, but I thought I'd demonstrate the depths of my generosity by lettin' you put on this play. I'm looking forward to seeing something that Malcolm Spencer didn't have his grubby hands in. Now, what say we meet the mornin' after the last performance—that's eight days away, isn't it? You can bring the money then."

At the moment, money was the least of Carina's concerns, but she made a point of purring appropriately. "That's fine, Mr. Pennell, and thank you so much for letting us put on this play."

Harland nodded, then grabbed his wife's elbow and gave her a rude nudge. "Come on, Gwendolyn, you're holdin' up the line."

Sherlock Holmes had her baffled for a minute when he said, "Good evening, Miss Rawlins."

Then Carina finally realized who was wearing the cape and deerstalker and she couldn't contain her laughter. "Hello, Lieutenant. That's quite a costume, though to be quite honest, I wasn't expecting you here tonight."

He gave her one of his hapless grins. "The department paid for my ticket, but they wouldn't spring for the missus, unfortunately. Boy, was she hopping mad about that."

Carina's smile froze. "So you're here on official police business."

"'Fraid so, ma'am," he said, doffing his hat politely and moving on.

During the play Carina realized she should have been concentrating on audience reaction as she sat in the control room next to the lighting technician. She was vaguely aware of the laughter and the audience's warm response to the actors' performances, but every nerve and fiber of her body was riveted firmly to the square panel of wood set in the exact center of the stage. She was too far away to see the actual demarcation of the trapdoor, but her mind's eye saw it clearly. Malcolm was down there; she could almost feel his presence—or that of his body, anyway. But she still had two more acts and a masquerade to live through before she could do a thing about it.

SITTING AT THE LIGHTED MIRROR in Malcolm's office, Damian removed his stage makeup with a sponge dipped in cold cream. The premiere of *Fate of the Popinjay* had been a rousing success. No one missed a single cue, their comic timing was perfect and they took ten curtain calls. He ought to be ecstatic, eager to celebrate, but all he wanted to do was go back to his hotel and polish off a bottle of something that would put him to sleep for about twelve hours.

The thought of facing a horde of partygoers revolted him. In fact, so did the idea of performing this play nine more times. Why had he ever thought he would derive some perverse pleasure out of coming here? He should have proceeded with the lawsuit from England and never set foot in this town.

For the umpteenth time he tried to imagine what life would be like if he hadn't come to Dunn's Pond—or more accurately, if he hadn't met Carina. The answer was the same as it always was. His life would continue just as it had for years; the best food, the best wine, the most beautiful women—and his work that kept him from thinking about how boring the rest of it was.

Why was he so obsessed with this freckled-nosed creature suffering from the worst case of paranoia he'd ever seen?

He didn't need a complication like Carina in his life. He'd come here to exorcise his past, not to conjure up a whole new set of demons to take back with him.

This time, it would be much worse than when that bastard Malcolm had made off with his play. There was a very real possibility that Carina could end up behind bars for murder. The cards were pretty much stacked against her.

But then, that was how things sometimes turned out when people got greedy. Carina had never made a secret of the fact that she wanted the position of artistic director. So, it really wasn't his problem, Damian assured himself again.

He tried combing the hair cream out of his hair, but without hot water and shampoo it was hopeless. Perhaps he could help Carina financially so she wouldn't be reduced to accepting legal aid. Then if she needed money when her sentence was up, he could—

Dammit to hell, who was he kidding? Tossing Carina a few bucks wasn't going to do a thing to ease his conscience. He was in love with that woman. He didn't want to see her rotting in jail all because of his stupid play and those damned taxidermist's tools. He could never live with himself.

There had to be some way out for Carina, short of turning himself in as a murderer, some other leads the police hadn't explored. Plenty of people worked in this theater and most of them hated Malcolm's guts. Couldn't any one of them have planted those props in her desk? It seemed plausible.

Damian got up and paced the room. He had to help her with more than money. He could offer to stay by her side during the trial, even it that meant breaking a few contracts. He never could have imagined that *Fate of the Popinjay* would affect so many lives, but somehow or other he had to keep it from destroying the one woman he'd ever loved.

Damian changed his mind about returning immediately to the hotel. He decided to go to the party after all, and try to get Carina alone somewhere so they could talk. He slipped off his robe and climbed into the gorilla costume. It was a dumb choice, but anonymous, and that's what he wanted for the time being. After he'd talked to Carina, he could change back into his own clothes and return to the party to sign autographs for an hour or so. He was about to put on the gorilla's head when he heard a knock on the door.

"For crying out loud, I thought I told Henry I didn't want visitors backstage," he muttered as he stormed across the room. Swinging the door open, he found himself face-to-face with Sherlock Holmes.

"Mr. Fleming?" The detective touched his deerstalker hat in greeting. "I hope I gave you enough time to unwind. That was quite a performance you put on. I tell you, I've never seen anything like it."

"Lieutenant Chapman!" Damian exclaimed. "This is a surprise." If an unpleasant one, he thought to himself.

"Mind if I come in?"

Damian considered refusing him entry, then realized that acting belligerent wouldn't do Carina's case any good at all. It was just that the lieutenant had a way of sticking in his craw like a fishbone. He stepped back. "By all means, come in. Thank you for your comment about the play, though you didn't actually say whether you liked it or not.''

The officer shrugged apologetically. "Well, to tell you the truth, I'm not much for theaters. Maybe if Charles Bronson came to town, that'd be different.''

Damian stared. "Yes, I can see it now—a theatrical production of *Death Wish*. Well, Lieutenant, what can I do for you?''

The policeman sat down, making himself comfortable. "For starters, I wonder if you could tell me where Miss Rawlins is. I haven't seen her since before the play, and I have something important to talk to her about.''

His interest piqued, Damian sat across from him. "I haven't seen her, but I came straight here after the performance. Have you checked out the party? I imagine it's well under way by now.''

"Yeah, she didn't seem to be there—oh well, never mind.'' He reached into an inner pocket and brought out his fist. "I thought I'd show this to you, see what you make of it.'' He opened his hand to reveal a fine gold chain.

Damian took it carefully and examined the locket. Feeling as though the wind had just been knocked out of him, he said, "It's monogrammed with the initials C.R.'' He looked up. "Where did this come from?''

The lieutenant held up his hands. "Where else? Spencer's apartment. It was under the bed. I imagine it got left behind 'cause of the broken clasp.'' He rubbed the side of his nose somberly. "I guess there's not much doubt about whose it is.''

Damian recalled clearly the evening Carina had told them about misplacing a locket the crew had given her. "No, I guess not,'' he agreed sadly.

The Lieutenant planted both hands on his knees and got up. "Well then, I guess that about does it."

Damian rose too, his nerves taut. "Does what?"

"Closes the case. I'll be making an arrest tonight."

"Tonight?" Damian repeated, thunderstruck. He hadn't even had a chance to warn her, to offer his help. He might be too late now. "Don't you think it's a little unfair to ruin the party with an arrest after all the work everyone's put into it?"

The lieutenant smiled. "Oh, I don't intend to ruin the party. I'm not that hard-boiled. It's supposed to finish at half past twelve, so I'd like to see you in the rehearsal hall at one."

"Me?" Damian asked, incredulous.

"You...and a few other people. I'm going out there now to tell the others." He started for the door. "By the way, if you run into Miss Rawlins, you might want to pass along the message—rehearsal hall, one o'clock sharp."

Damian escorted the policeman out the door and closed it firmly. There wasn't a minute to lose. He had to finish putting on his costume and find Carina at once.

IT DIDN'T TAKE LONG for the party to get into full swing. Champagne was being consumed at an alarming rate, and the parade of servers bearing trays of hors d'oeuvres from the kitchen seemed to be continuous. It was the kind of thing an assistant administrator was supposed to keep tabs on, but Carina was too busy looking for Damian.

Everyone was accounted for except him. Judith, in a pirate queen costume, was executing a sensuous dance with Henry, dressed as Blackbeard. Elsie, the wardrobe mistress, was decked out as Tweety Bird, and Gerry appeared to be a Prussian officer.

Carina didn't want to risk meeting Damian—or anyone else for that matter—on her way to the stage. The only way to ensure that she got into the prop room unseen was to wait until everyone was present and accounted for.

She frowned when a blue-haired lady decked out as Queen Victoria tapped her on the shoulder. "Aren't you the cat who greeted us at the door?" the woman asked in a loud nasal voice.

"Yes, I am," she answered absently, her eyes still scanning the crowd.

"I wonder if you could introduce me to Kate Kramer. I read somewhere that she loves growing African violets, and I'd like to know if she swears by sheer curtains to make them flower."

Carina stared at her. "I beg your pardon? Did you say something about Africans?"

The obviously wealthy woman assumed a we-are-not-amused look and placed her hands on her hips. "I asked you to introduce me to Kate Kramer!"

"Oh, yes, of course, I'd be happy to." She knew exactly where George and Martha Washington were standing; she'd been watching them closely all evening. "Come this way," she said and led the woman through the crowd.

Carina was grateful for the mask and the painted-on whiskers that disguised whatever expression she was wearing when she walked up to Kate. She introduced the two women and decided it wasn't safe to wait any longer. Perhaps Damian had gone back to the hotel, or else he was that tall, lean Bugs Bunny who was now dancing with the Raggedy Ann. Who could tell at a masquerade, for heaven's sake? If Damian was lurking somewhere waiting for her or disguised beyond recognition and watching her from the crowd, she'd have to deal with the confrontation when it happened.

The corridor outside the ballroom was hectic with characters coming and going to the powder room. A gorilla came out of the men's room and turned its ugly head to leer at her. Or at least, that was what its fixed expression looked like to Carina. She shuddered and backed up against the wall until the beast had passed. She knew that as long as she lived, she would never enjoy a masquerade ball again.

She hurried around the first corner, followed the length of the hall and turned a second corner that brought her to the stage wings. The set from the third act was still in place, and the floor lights were dimly lit, giving the ivy-covered cottage an ambience of twilight. Carina walked to the end of the cottage wall that marked center stage and looked over her shoulder at the potting shed that was actually Bettina's workshop. Foolish though it was, Carina had the eerie sensation that Jasper Garnet was really in there for the night, his eyes made of glass, his insides of straw or whatever they used in those days. A chill ran up her spine and she chided herself for being so susceptible. Jasper Garnet was nothing more than a character in a play, his wheelchair a mere prop for Damian to occupy in the third act.

As she knelt to lift the trapdoor, Carina became aware of the empty darkened auditorium in front of her. Why did she have the feeling someone was sitting out there watching her? Was she just being paranoid? Her nerves were strung so tight, she thought they might snap. She stared at the vast darkness for a long time, but saw nothing and except for the pounding of her own heart, there was no sound.

The trapdoor was heavy and awkward as she brought it to rest against the stage floor, but her cat costume was well suited to the task. She dropped one black-slippered foot over the edge and felt around for the top step. Then she lifted the other leg. So far, so good.

Carina saw nothing but blackness when she looked down the stairwell, but she felt reasonably confident that once she got her footing, she'd be able to find the lights. Holding on to the stage floor tightly, she descended one step and then another and another until she was waist-level with the stage. Groping with one hand along the wall of the stairwell, she found the light switch and flipped it on, not realizing she'd been holding her breath until it exploded all at once from her lungs.

There was really nothing to be afraid of in the prop room, Carina reminded herself when she reached the bottom of the stairs. Fluorescent lights banished the shadows, though they failed to dispel the macabre atmosphere. A doll with a broken neck stared blindly from her place on the shelves. A suit of armor lay in pieces on the floor, as if the knight had been dismembered. Something with noisy little claws scurried past Carina's foot, and she couldn't help but shriek though she knew it was only a mouse.

Carina had to force herself to keep walking toward the small wooden door at the far end of the room. Now that the end of her search felt imminent, she wasn't sure she had the strength to go through with it. Why hadn't she thought of asking Lieutenant Chapman to accompany her? Once he caught a glimpse of what had happened to her boss, he, too, would realize there was only one person capable of committing this murder.

Carina tugged at the door with both hands, fighting its rusty hinges and the bumpy stone floor. At last, it creaked open, and her nostrils were assaulted by the odors of dankness, mildew and cleaning compounds. Gerry only used the room to clean props, and he never ventured past the wash tub and the small shelf, both near the door. The walls dripped with moisture, and the room didn't have a floor, just packed earth. The single bare bulb hanging above the washtub cast more shadows than it did light.

Beyond that, wooden partitions jutted out from the walls at either side, creating cubicles with a center aisle between them. Carina had never found any reason to explore these nether regions, and as she walked slowly past the now-empty spaces, she tried to imagine how the saloon girls had entertained their men in this dungeon. Even though there was evidence that curtains had once hung for privacy, it must have been a hideous place.

There were at least a dozen partitioned sections, and Carina had no choice but to proceed slowly and feel her way through each one. As she groped through the semidarkness, she wished she had thought to bring a flashlight and worried that she'd trip over something and hit her head against the wall.

At one point she did stumble, and when her hand flew out to grab a partition for support she caught a thick handful of cobweb. Whimpering softly with revulsion, she tried unsuccessfully to shake it off.

There were only four cubicles left to search, and Carina began to wonder whether her theory would fall flat. By now the light at the far end of the room was of little use except as a guide to find her way back. Her feet shrank from the sensation of the cold dirt floor through her slippers as she turned into the nook on her left. She followed a pattern of feeling along the wooden wall nearest her, then the stone outer wall, and when she turned to the third wall, her shin hit something hard and she cried out with pain. But it was nothing except an empty bench built into the partition. On second thought, she realized it might have been a cot and felt even sorrier for the poor girls in the dance hall.

The cubicle across from her was empty, and so was the one adjacent to it. There was only one left, and because Carina's eyes had adjusted to the darkness, she was able to make out a large irregular object in the corner.

Her heart was in her throat as she inched slowly closer, one hand on the wall for balance, the other reaching out. She had to remind herself that however hideous he might be, Malcolm was dead and couldn't hurt her. Her hand hit something cool and tube shaped, like a handle. Feeling around with the other hand, she found a second one; they were spaced like a wheelbarrow but higher. Carina wrapped her fingers securely around them and tugged hard. She heard the sound of wheels, but they were too rusted to do much more than jiggle. She tried again. This time, she was able to pull the contraption a few inches. Sweat beaded on her forehead from exertion. Several more tugs and the wheels released, though they still wobbled and jerked as she pulled the object into the dim light of the central aisle.

Now Carina could plainly see that it was a wheelchair, covered over with an old woolen blanket. Every cell in her body was screaming with fear, every nerve set to snap, but she couldn't run away. Terror had effectively paralyzed her, and she couldn't have escaped now, no matter how much she wanted to.

Cautiously she lifted an edge of the blanket, using her thumb and forefinger. She could distinguish the shape of a man's head, but she was still behind the chair so she moved around to the front for a better look. The blanket slid down of its own accord, and in the space of an instant, Carina recognized the dark hair, the mustache and the glassy eyes staring straight ahead.

It was Malcolm!

Chapter Fifteen

For an excruciating length of time, Carina gaped at a nightmare more hideous than the most psychotic of imaginations could have conjured. But the sightless eyes, the rigid body of what had once been her employer was no dream. When the grisly reality seeped through her mind, Carina screamed and tore out of the room. She fled through the prop room and raced up the stairs two at a time. Then, her pulse thrumming loudly, Carina spun around to slam the door shut, but as she did, a pair of strong hands clamped onto her shoulders.

"So there you are," Damian said from behind her.

Carina's first thought was that he intended to push her down the stairs. A cry of panic raked her lungs. Thinking no further than her immediate escape, she lunged across the opening and grasped the stage floor on the opposite side. Damian lost his grip on her shoulders but regained a hold on her ankles, leaving her helpless and spread-eagled over the gaping stairwell.

Her back arched high like the feline she portrayed, Carina kicked one slippered foot and then the other. "Get away from me, dammit!" she snarled. "Let go or I'll scream even louder!" Hanging her head down and peering under her arm, she could see that Damian was wearing a furry suit minus head and paws. So he was the gorilla she'd seen earlier!

He was having a hard time holding on to her ankles, and she could see that occasionally she pinched his fingers against the doorframe. "Stop it, you stupid...for God's sake—Carina, listen to me! You're going to break your neck if you don't settle down!"

She *was* stupid! In the split second when his warning gave her pause, Damian got a better grip on her legs, this time so merciless that his fingers dug into her flesh. Already the blood was rushing to her head, making her dizzy, and her arms ached with the effort of holding herself up on all fours. But she'd never let him know it. "Isn't that what you want—for me to break my neck?" she argued. "Or do you have something more elaborate in mind?"

Damian ignored her outburst and to her surprise, released her legs. "Now whatever you do, don't move!" He leaped over the edge of the stage door to the third step, then tucked his arms around her waist and lifted her from danger. But even as he deposited her on the reassuring firmness of the steps, Carina flailed and kicked with all her might. Damian wasn't fazed in the least. He let go of her waist to avoid one of her better aimed kicks, and in the same moment, caught hold of her ankles again. He yanked so hard that she slid between his legs like a rag doll, her arms limp at her sides. Then he promptly straddled her with enough weight that she was pinioned beneath him, unable to move.

"All right, my little black panther, that's enough!" he ordered. "Stop fighting and talk to me!"

Though her strength was diminishing quickly, Carina continued her futile struggle. "Like hell!" she tossed back.

He held up his powerful hands. "If you prefer, I can pin your shoulders to the floor, as well, but I'd rather not." This was said as calmly as one might speak to a child.

Fatigue forced Carina to lie still, but every cell was poised for escape. "You can spare me your smooth delivery. I've fallen for every one of your lines so far, but not any more—now that I know what you've done to Malcolm."

"What is this thing that I've done?" he asked evenly.

The pressure of Damian's weight on her pelvis caused an erratic jumble of sensations, most of them irrelevant to the terror that still coursed through her veins. "Why should I spell it out? Are you that proud of your handiwork?" To avoid lying flat and vulnerable, Carina was propped on her elbows, but teetering over the stairwell had taken its toll, and her arm muscles were trembling.

Damian's brows contracted. "My handiwork? God, woman, what are you accusing me of?" The thread of anxiety in his voice seemed strangely out of place, under the circumstances.

"You did the...the same thing to Malcolm that Bettina did to J-Jasper," Carina stammered, her mind recoiling from the memory of it.

His reaction was the last thing she expected. He squeezed his eyes shut and a low moan escaped his throat. "Oh, Lord, I was afraid it would be something like this."

"That's why you didn't want me to read the whole play, isn't it?" Carina thrust her retort like a lance. "You knew I'd been putting the pieces together all along and that as soon as I saw the play, I'd figure it out."

"Carina, I—" he implored.

"Oh, no, you don't, Damian. It's too late to play the wounded lover now. I just saw Malcolm's body, and if you intend to try anything like that with me, I swear I'll ... I'll scratch your eyes out.''

Ignoring her feeble threat, Damian rested his hands lightly above her hipbones with a gentleness that was both soothing and unnerving. "Where is the body?"

"Downstairs in the back room...right where you left it, of course." Why did he have to wince every time she brought out another fact? Did he think she would be impressed with a display of remorse?

Finally Carina couldn't bear the weight of her upper body a moment longer. Her arms gave out, and she collapsed, flat on her back. If ever there was an ideal time for Damian to strangle her, this was it, she thought with exhausted resignation. But instead of attacking her, he got up. Her eyes widened in surprise. "What are you going to do now?" she asked in a hoarse whisper.

"I'm going downstairs. The lieutenant is still at the party, so if you want to go and get him, by all means, do so. But I'd prefer if you stayed right here and waited for me." He disappeared down the stairs before Carina could think of a thing to say. Exhausted, still frightened and totally befuddled, she remained where she was, lying motionless to get her breathing under control. Damian's behavior made no sense. His expression before he left had been so woeful, almost as though he were in mourning, somehow. But even if he was suffering an acute attack of conscience now, she could hardly forgive him....

It seemed that a long time passed, but finally Carina heard squeaky wheels moving across the floor below. Good heavens, she thought, her stomach heaving, he was bringing that frightful thing out into the prop room. She rolled over onto her side and covered her mouth as the bile rose in her throat.

"It's all right, Carina!" Damian called up. "It's not Malcolm. Come down and see for yourself, please. I promise I won't hurt you!"

The wave of nausea sudsided and Carina sat up. Did he think she was crazy? He was asking her to go down into that dungeon with him where no one would ever hear her cries for help. The rational thing to do would be to slam the trapdoor shut and drag something heavy over it. Then she could fetch the lieutenant, he would arrest Damian and that would be the end of it. Oddly, Carina felt as though she'd suddenly come to a crossroad after an endless journey of blind curves and dead ends. And worse, she felt that by trapping Damian downstairs, she would be shattering something infinitely precious. What? His love? His trust?

It burst from her thoughts like a firecracker. *Trust.* That was the key word. Damian knew she could run away, but he trusted that she wouldn't. Trust was a virtue shared by friends . . . and lovers, not homicidal maniacs.

With a fresh reserve of inner strength, a new resolve, Carina called down, "I'm coming." Then she descended the stairs.

Damian was standing by the wheelchair, his eyes glistening. Were they tears, Carina wondered in amazement. She forced herself to look at Malcolm, and she saw right away that something wasn't right. Then, thunderstruck, she realized it wasn't Malcolm's dark hair, mustache and glassy eyes staring straight ahead. It was a mannequin, a dummy, no doubt sequestered from Gerry's prop room.

She looked up. "What on earth is going on?"

Damian shook his head and when he spoke, his voice quavered. "I don't know...but all I can say is that I'm glad you don't know, either." He opened his arms and Carina, needing his embrace more than she'd ever needed anything in her life, rushed into them.

She sobbed with relief and confusion and a thousand other emotions too complex to name as Damian held her tight. She was smearing black greasepaint from her face onto his furry chest, but he hardly noticed. He stroked her back and whispered soothingly. "It's all right, love. Everything's going to be fine."

At last, the tears eased, and she looked up at him, mindless of her ravaged face. "Wh-what do we do now, and where *is* Malcolm?"

He touched her cheek, and he smiled. "First, we have to repair your whiskers, then there's a masquerade ball that still requires our presence—"

"No, I couldn't possibly—"

"Yes, you will, because you've worked so hard to make it happen. And besides, we have to do something to kill time. The lieutenant wants to see all of us in the rehearsal hall at one o'clock. He claims he's ready to make an arrest."

Damian's expression was grim and Carina wondered why. "Do you have any idea who could have killed him?"

He looked away, but not quickly enough for Carina to miss the flicker of anxiety. "I don't know, but I'm almost afraid to find out." Then he took her hand, and together they climbed the stairs. He couldn't bring himself to tell her about the locket.

THE REHEARSAL HALL was nothing more than a large room with hard-back chairs and a single table. Its starkness was conducive to the function it served. Here, actors developed their characters without distraction or external influence. One could almost feel the creative energy crackling in the atmosphere. But there was something else in the air, Carina thought as she sat beside Damian and surveyed the others who had gathered. There was a gritting, skin-prickling aura of tension.

Kate and Len sat across from her. Len, in powdered wig and breeches, was drumming his fingers on the table. Kate, as Martha Washington, toyed nervously with the lace trim of her apron. Even Judith, stunning as she was in scarlet skirts and peasant blouse, looked pale and uneasy—a captive pirate queen.

It was two minutes after one, and the lieutenant hadn't arrived. Then the door opened, and in walked Napoleon Bonaparte and Cleopatra, followed by Lieutenant Chapman. Carina glanced at Damian questioningly. *What was the banker doing here?* Damian replied with a shrug.

Harland took a seat without acknowledging anyone else in the room. His expression suggested that he was barely tolerating the lieutenant's effrontery in asking him to be there, just as Napoleon himself would have reacted under similar circumstances. Gwen sat pigeon-toed beside him, an Egyptian caricature. Together, they made an absurd pair, and Carina wondered why they were there. She was prevented from pondering the question further by the lieutenant's opening remarks.

"I'd like to thank all of you for coming here so promptly. I know it's late and you've had a busy day, so I'll try not to keep you any longer than necessary." The lieutenant leaned against the back of a chair, his stance casual. Then he took off his hat and cape and tossed them aside. "Darned costume weighs a ton. I don't know how Sherlock could stand it."

Carina couldn't bring herself to smile even though he'd looked straight at her. She turned her gaze to Damian, who reached over and took her hand.

Judith waved her fingers in the air, an unlit cigarette between them. "I have a question before you start. Why are there only seven of us? There are at least a dozen other people who work in this theater."

The lieutenant smiled. "Because, Miss Deveau, none of those people had anything to do with Spencer's murder."

The cigarette fell from her lips, and she issued him a haughty look. "What are you trying to say, Officer Chapman, that all of us in this room did?"

He reached over to light her cigarette. "In a way, yes."

Gwen gasped, and Harland leaped up from his chair, his uniform medals clinking. "Now wait just a darned minute. I didn't come here to—"

"A figure of speech, Mr. Pennell!" Lieutenant Chapman spun around to face the banker. "It was just a figure of speech. Now if you will kindly let me continue. The main reason I asked the seven of you here tonight is to reenact the crime. That way, when the time comes to make my arrest, all of you will understand how I reached my conclusion." He grinned affably. "It'd make me feel a lot better, too, knowing I got it figured out right."

Looks of paranoia passed around the room but no one spoke, so the officer went on. "First of all, I'd like to establish that all of you had motives for killing Spencer. The man was a no-good snake, and the world's probably better off without him, but as you know, the law doesn't make allowances for humanitarian murder." He turned to George and Martha Washington. "Let's take the Kramers, for example. What did they stand to gain by killing Malcolm Spencer?"

Everyone seemed to stop breathing as they stared at the kindly older couple. Len looked close to fainting, but the plucky Kate matched the lieutenant's gaze eyeball-to-eyeball. Carina silently applauded her bravado, certain she could never emulate it herself.

"Why don't we begin by going back eight years to the first time they visited Dunn's Pond?" Lieutenant Chapman addressed the others as though the Kramers weren't even in the room. "When they came to the Myrmidon, they hadn't worked together for nearly a year, and since then, except for a couple of seasons in New York, they've had to commute across the country or the Atlantic just to see each other. That's gotta be rough after forty years, and apparently they thought so, too. Eight years ago, they approached a local realtor about investing in retirement property."

"What could that possibly have to do with Malcolm?" Kate demanded.

"Nothing, but the agent recently happened to recall your interest in the Myrmidon. You were thinking about managing a theater and drama school. It makes sense, an active couple like yourselves, buying a theater that's already operational and fixing it up the way you'd like."

"Yes, that's quite true," Kate conceded, "we did approach Mr. Spencer on both occasions, and he turned us down flat."

"Not only that," Len added, "he was unforgivably rude. He swore he'd never work for—and I believe the term he used was—a pair of senile geriatrics."

"That's why we decided on a stronger tactic this time," his wife said, "but I don't mean murder. I mean via the bank."

The lieutenant turned to Harland Pennell. "Did the Kramers approach you about buying the theater?"

The banker squirmed like a pinned worm. "I don't rightly recall; they might have."

"We did!" Kate rose from her chair with her hands on her hips. "How dare you try to deny it!"

"It doesn't matter!" The deeper timbre of the policeman's voice easily overpowered Kate's, and he threw Harland a threatening look. "You, sir, I will get to in a moment. In the meantime, I think it'd be smart for you to work on telling the truth."

Len scooted his chair closer to his wife's to comfort her, the two of them looking more persecuted than presidential, despite their attire.

Carina had been trying to imagine the Kramers going to prison and found the prospect unthinkable. Malcolm wasn't worth losing one's freedom for, she thought, and was immediately shocked at her own callousness about her employer's fate. But Harland Pennell's strange behavior had her baffled. What could he have had to do with all this?

"And now we come to the second reason the Kramers might have had for disposing of Mr. Spencer—revenge for the theft of their godson's play."

Damian dropped his face into his hands and groaned. "Dear Lord, I never should have told him about that."

The lieutenant heard his comment and whirled around. "But I'm glad you did, Mr. Fleming, since I specifically asked you during one of our discussions what your relationship was to the Kramers. You'd have been foolish to cover it up, even to protect them."

"But they wouldn't kill Malcolm for me!" he protested. "They wouldn't do it for anyone!"

"No one is saying they did! I am only laying out motives, but since you and I are already on the topic of your play, let's stay with it." Lieutenant Chapman strode across the floor to stand before the handsome blond actor. "Seems to me a play written by Damian Fleming could break all box office records, especially with the added notoriety of a lawsuit, the betrayal of an old friend...his

mysterious disappearance. Being one of the world's most
famous actors, you could make quite a killing—if you'll
pardon the pun—on Fate of the whatever-it-was." He
leaned closer in an attempt to intimidate, though Carina
noticed that it didn't work. "Who knows, Fleming?
Someday you could write a book about how Spencer
duped you; it'd make a hell of a movie, too."

Damian fought to control his expression, but his forehead was beaded with sweat. He yanked down the zipper
of his gorilla costume. "That's ridiculous, Lieutenant.
Everything you're saying is total fabrication."

"Maybe yes, maybe no, but it's hard to ignore the press
coverage you've gotten so far, and the play isn't even on
the road yet." Lieutenant Chapman stopped just short of
accusing Damian outright of murder. Then he turned to
Judith. "Miss Deveau, we come to you." His tone of voice
was entirely different with the actress—affected, almost
cloying. Carina was both offended and impressed by his
methods.

Judith stubbed out her cigarette and reached for another. She kept her eyes downcast. "Lucky me," she
muttered to herself.

The officer swung his gaze slowly around the room.
"I'm not sure how many of you are aware that Mr. Spencer and Miss Deveau were once engaged—"

"Not officially!" Judith cut in.

"Sorry—almost engaged. Then one day, her ambitious
boyfriend took off for California with five thousand dollars of her money and his best friend's play." There was no
visible reaction from anyone, so he continued. "Since Miss
Deveau never heard from the creep again, she never got the
chance to tell him he was going to be a father." His tone
grew gentler. "Unfortunately, she lost the baby, and for
eighteen years she's been waiting to tell Spencer what a no-

good bastard he was." The officer cast a sympathetic eye toward the actress. "Wounds of the heart can fester a long, long time, can't they, Miss Deveau?"

She didn't answer, but dark hatred glistened in her eyes. Carina couldn't tell whether the emotion was directed at the policeman or at the memory of Malcolm; perhaps it was a bit of both.

"And next we have Mr. Harland Pennell," the lieutenant went on to say, "bank president and esteemed community leader. What could you gain by knocking off the artistic director of this theater?"

The man gave a snort of nervous laughter. "Why, Lieutenant, there isn't anythin' of Mr. Spencer's that could possibly be of interest to me." The Southern drawl coming from a man dressed as Napoleon made the denial sound ludicrous and implausible.

"I wouldn't be too sure about that," the officer countered. "I understand you've been meeting with a group of real-estate developers about a proposed shopping mall for this town."

"That's right," he answered cautiously.

"None of your colleagues in this town are keen on the idea—what with the traffic problems, increased property taxes and the like—but you don't see it from their point of view, do you?"

"Well, I—"

The lieutenant had no intention of allowing him to speak yet. "No, your main interest in the mall is to lure all those retailers into your bank. Why, I understand the principals even offered you a prime location in the mall for a new branch of Merchants' and Farmers'."

The banker jumped up onto patent-leather feet that looked too small for his girth. "Listen here, Lieutenant, what I do in the interest of this community don't have nothin' to do with Malcolm Spencer. He may run this theater, but I own it, and I don't have to kill the caretaker when I can just as easily burn down the shed, if you know what I mean.''

The officer chuckled. ''You're right on that count, Mr. Pennell. However, I suspect you do have one other motive for killing the caretaker, as you put it—which ties into why you chose to ignore the Kramers' offer to buy the place. New owners might not have served your purpose.''

Gwen Pennell was gnawing on her nails. Carina was watching her when she heard her own name mentioned, and she jumped at the sound of it.

''Miss Rawlins, you could probably do a better job of running this theater than Malcolm Spencer ever could, am I right?''

Carina considered denying it, but what good would false modesty do her now? Confidence was no crime. ''I believe I've already proven that in the past few weeks,'' she answered simply.

''Yes, and very well, I might add,'' Lieutenant Chapman concurred. ''It's no secret, either, that you and your boss have never gotten along.''

''I wouldn't say never, but . . . well, Malcolm is—was a very unreasonable man, at times.'' It was a horrible feeling to know he was setting her up and that she couldn't do a thing about it. Carina clenched her fists and tried to stay calm. Even the knowledge that Damian was at her side wasn't enough to quell her anxiety completely.

The policeman grabbed a chair a few feet away from her, turned it the wrong way round and straddled it, his forearms resting across the back. ''Seems to me you couldn't pick a better time to murder your boss—assuming you were so inclined—than right now, while you have the biggest assortment of his enemies ever assembled. With a bit of planning and luck, you could knock him off, and the chances are good that Mr. Fleming, whose play was stolen, or the betrayed Miss Deveau would take the rap.''

"But I didn't know that then!" No sooner had the words flown from her mouth than her face flooded with color.

"You couldn't know what, Miss Rawlins?" he asked carefully.

Carina's shoulders sagged. "That...that everyone else disliked him as much as I did."

"Guess not." To her amazement, she watched the lieutenant stand up and walk away from her as if she hadn't practically admitted to murdering Malcolm. "We've established motives," he said, "so now let's look at the evidence."

An assortment of sighs and nervous gestures filled the room when it became apparent that the lieutenant wasn't ready to let anyone off the hook quite yet. Carina felt the knot of apprehension pressing against her rib cage and hoped the evening would end soon.

"In Spencer's apartment, we found lipstick on a wine glass, remnants of food, an incense burner near the bathtub. Then I found the silky black slip and eventually discovered that it belonged to Miss Rawlins, who admitted removing a matching camisole from the apartment a few days earlier."

Carina sensed that everyone was trying too hard not to stare at her. She could almost feel the morbid fascination slithering along her skin.

"But it bothered me," the lieutenant continued, "that she had loaned the same lingerie to the wardrobe department and never got it back." He reached into his pocket. "Then I found this under Spencer's bed."

Carina recognized it at once as her own gold locket, and she gasped out loud. For a moment the room swayed dizzily before her eyes, as though she were about to faint. She looked at Damian; his head was down.

Then he glanced up, his eyes full of pain, and he whispered. "I'm sorry."

Sorry? Had he done it, she wondered with a sinking heart. Now everyone was staring at her openly.

"Yes, folks," Lieutenant Chapman said, "the locket with Miss Rawlins's initials was found in his apartment, but the clasp is broken. She could have lost it anywhere." He paced the room slowly. "If the lady were going to go to the trouble of murdering her boss, would she leave behind two identifiable pieces of lingerie *and* a monogrammed locket? I think not."

"Then there are the little clues," he went on to say. "The fact that none of Spencer's clothes or luggage was gone, the squirt of toothpaste across the bathroom counter, suggesting he was startled by an intruder. But then there's his landlady, Mrs. Lucid with the sharp ears. She never heard Spencer come home at all after the hotel dinner party that Sunday evening, and if he'd had a visitor intent on killing him, she'd have heard *something*—a shot, a scuffle, the sound of a body being dragged. Would this mystery lady friend have had the strength to murder her lover and dispose of him without making a sound?"

No one answered, but the banker yawned loudly. "Could you get to the point, Lieutenant? I've got an early golf game in the morning."

"I'm getting there, Mr. Pennell, and I appreciate your patience."

Gwen touched her husband's arm consolingly. "Calm down, Harland." But she seemed unsurprised when he merely ignored her.

"Then there is the matter of the flight record," the officer pointed out. "There were no records at O'Hare of Spencer taking any international flights. His car was at home, and he didn't take a limo to the airport. Assumption? He never left."

"Of course he never left!" Len erupted with a rare display of impatience. "The man was obviously snuffed out sometime Sunday night."

Lieutenant Chapman issued him a barely tolerant look. "I realize that, Mr. Kramer, but we had no way of knowing it at the time, did we?"

The actor sat back, remorseful. "No, forgive me; please go on."

"Finally we have the bloodied props—a scalpel, a pair of forceps, a surgical saw. Only one set of prints, belonging to Miss Rawlins; the blood, positively identified as matching the blood type of the presumed victim."

Again Carina felt the movement of eyes in her direction, but she was too distraught to acknowledge them. Was Lieutenant Chapman getting some sort of perverse pleasure out of building a case against her in front of all these witnesses? Couldn't he just make the arrest and let her call an attorney?

Still the officer continued. "At this point I had a lot of questions. If she'd been clever about hiding the body, why leave all the other stuff behind? And why not hide the murder weapons with the corpse instead of in her desk drawer?"

"All right, Lieutenant," Damian interjected, "you think Carina couldn't have done it. Who did, and who framed her?"

"I'm coming to that. The guys in forensics helped me out. The bloodstains weren't right. If the tools had been used to slice the body open or even just to stab it, the blood would have smeared across the scalpel blade. But there were no smears on the instruments; only the cloth was smeared. The instruments were covered with spots that had well-defined, rounded edges, meaning the blood was dropped onto the metal surfaces from a vertical position of less than two feet.''

''Are you suggesting they weren't murder weapons?'' Damian asked, after exchanging quizzical glances with Carina.

''Most likely, they were not. Then there were the hair samples we found in Spencer's bed—some of his own, and some from a woman—definitely not from Miss Rawlins.''

Carina closed her eyes and allowed herself the first small glimmer of hope since she'd come into this room. Then she opened them again and found the lieutenant looking at her, and she saw deep sympathy in his gaze. He smiled before he went on with his exposé.

''I guess what I ought to tell you first is that Malcolm Spencer isn't dead at all. He's alive and well in a swank Majorca hotel. But he wanted all of us to think he'd been murdered, and he actually wanted to see one of you charged with the crime. I should tell you, too,'' he continued, ''why I've gone on with this charade, this pretense of Spencer's murder. For several reasons. One, to test my own thinking against your reactions. But mainly to show all of you how you provided Spencer with his raw materials, so to speak, in this deception—the hatred each of you felt for him. As I've proved, each of you had a motive. And his hatred for most of *you* was strong enough to make him want to see your lives ruined by suspicion—and maybe even a charge of murder.''

The sounds of shock through the room were unanimous. ''That bastard!'' Judith cried, speaking for all of them. "Why would he do that? Why would he bother? Why not just disappear quietly?"

Lieutenant Chapman shrugged. "Maybe he wanted to prove how clever he was, or he figured it'd be more fun to make a dramatic exit. He must have known the theater was in hock, that it was just a matter of time before the bank moved in. So why not take the chance and stage Damian's play and get the hell out before the heat got him. Bailing out of a sinking ship, in other words, but doing it on his own terms. A guy like him likes to have the last laugh over his enemies."

"How did he manage it?" Kate wanted to know.

"Well, first of all, he had someone rent a car for him in Chicago on Sunday, the day he took the four of you out to dinner. That night, he pretended to get plastered, but actually he'd been drinking mineral water all evening, prearranged with the waiter on the pretext that he was an alcoholic. Even Fleming's surprise arrival wasn't enough to make him panic, 'cause he already had everything planned. The presence of Damian Fleming—the man whose stolen play was being staged as Spencer's own work—just added an extra twist to the confusion. Anyway, sometime after two, he staggered home alone."

"But his landlady said he didn't come home," Carina said.

"He didn't use the front door. He used the fire escape at the far end of the building. There wasn't much he had to do since the apartment was already an incriminating mess from his pajama party that probably took place the night before. He scattered the slip, camisole and locket, the clues that were intended to implicate Miss Rawlins, obviously the easiest person to frame. Then he squirted some toothpaste and left the apartment the way he came in, no doubt carrying just a single change of clothes."

"He walked to the theater parking lot, where the car had been left, and drove to Milwaukee. He dropped off the car—prepaid so there were no questions asked—then flew to Detroit. From there, Spencer bought a ticket to London, England, and in London, he hopped a charter to Barcelona. That's where he would have been when he phoned the cable office in Majorca."

"So it was a long-distance call," observed Damian, "just as the agent had claimed."

The lieutenant nodded. "And the agent would have had no way of knowing whether the call came from the Spanish mainland or Timbuktu."

"Why wouldn't he have waited until he got to Majorca to send the telegram?" Judith asked.

"Because he wanted to maintain an element of suspicion. I'm positive that the reversal of the day and the month was as deliberate as the roundabout itinerary, meant to throw us off the trail."

Damian's face was twisted by an inner rage that Carina could well appreciate, since she was feeling the same way herself. "What about the blood on the props?" Damian asked. "How did he do that?"

"He must have slashed his arm and let the blood drip onto the instruments," the policeman replied. "I guess he figured he could stand a little pain in the interests of his goals."

Carina had been wondering when or if she should mention the incident earlier that evening and decided this was a good time. "Lieutenant, I found a mannequin tonight—"

"Oh, yes, the dummy," he said. "I found it myself when I searched this place a few days ago."

"You knew?" she asked. "But why didn't you say anything?"

His smile told her there was no more ill will between them; perhaps there never had been. "I was conducting a police investigation. A guy's gotta keep some secrets to himself." Oblivious to the curious expression of the others, he went on to explain. "Spencer went to a lot of trouble to set up this whole bizarre hoax. First, he got the propman to dig up an extra wheelchair to resemble the one in the play. Then he made use of a dark-haired mannequin, applied the appropriate facial hair and set up a reasonable fascimile of himself in the storeroom below the stage. Now that I've seen the play, everything has fallen into place. I'm convinced Spencer was hoping someone would suspect he'd come to the same gruesome end as Jasper Garnet. I take my hat off to you, Miss Rawlins, for picking up on that clue. You're a clever lady."

"I should've known. Let's get out of here, Gwendolyn." Harland pulled his wife roughly from her seat, though it was evident she didn't want to go anywhere with the man.

The lieutenant observed Harland dragging his wife across the room and then said, "Excuse me, Mrs. Pennell, but those shoes aren't exactly the kind Cleopatra would have worn, are they?"

Despite her husband's forceful grip, Gwen came to an abrupt halt and looked down at her feet. She glanced askance at the police officer. "It's nearly October, too cold for sandals." She tried to giggle, but it was a choked kind of laugh.

Lieutenant Chapman raised his brows. "Is that it? Or did you find it more convenient to use the shoes you were planning to wear on your morning flight to Madrid?"

"What? I don't underst—"

"I've seen the passenger list, ma'am. One-way for a Mrs. G. Pennell, Chicago-Madrid."

Gwen yanked her arm from her husband's grasp, and her voice rose half an octave. "So what? If you must know, I'm leaving Harland! And after twelve years of hell, why shouldn't I?"

The lieutenant was unmoved. "You also have a connecting flight from Madrid to Palma. That's in Majorca, isn't it? And that garment bag that's been sitting in Spencer's office closet for a couple of weeks? It now contains a wool traveling suit and ladies' resort clothes. They weren't there yesterday." He paused. "Are they yours, by any chance?"

Goose bumps broke out on Gwen's sallow arms. "Yes ... but I still don't see what business it is of yours. Malcolm has offered emotional support while I ... put my life back in order. Just because I choose to tell no one where I'm going doesn't make me a criminal."

Harland's mouth curled into a snarl. "So you were planning to leave me, you adulterous little—"

Lieutenant Chapman moved a step closer. "I'd be careful, if I were you, Pennell. Your wife filed charges of assault and battery this afternoon, and while I intend to read you your rights, I'd like to clear up this Spencer case first." He indicated a chair. "Mind taking a seat for a minute?" Then he glanced at Damian. "As you've no doubt guessed, this is the arrest I was talking about."

The banker turned white and without another word, skulked back to where he'd been sitting. Gwen remained where she was in the center of the room. The officer turned to her. "Now, Mrs. Pennell, it was you who rented the car in Chicago, wasn't it? You paid for it, and you drove it back to Dunn's Pond. After Spencer left the country it was your job to make sure all the clues he'd planted came to light at the proper time—and most of them did." To the others in the room, he said, "The man was far from stupid, recruiting a woman who was not only in love with him, but wealthy enough to keep him in clover the rest of his life.''

Gwen's chin was stubbornly set. "You have no proof of any of this! Just because I rented a car—how was I to know he'd do all those awful things?''

"Oh, I think you knew," the lieutenant said in a soft voice. "Lovers tend to share things like that with each other.''

"We were *not* lovers! We were just friends!''

"I don't think so, ma'am. The hair samples we found in Malcolm's bed are a lot like yours—fine, light brown and straight. Of course, we'll need to authenticate it with a sample of yours, but..."

Gwen's face turned from ashen to beet red. "And how do you suppose I could conduct an such affair in a small town like this?''

"It wouldn't be easy, I'll grant you that, but you found a way. Remember that night you showed up at Miss Rawlins's apartment during a rainstorm?''

It looked as though she were going to deny it, but then she caught Carina's eye and knew she wouldn't get away with it. "Y-you followed me, Lieutenant?''

"Let's just say I was keeping an eye on things. Seems your husband's a pretty sound sleeper, considering you can leave the bed, drive away and he doesn't even know it. Maybe you slip him a Mickey Finn every night—''

"You bitch!'' The banker lunged across the room to his wife, but Lieutenant Chapman instantly whirled around, pointing a threatening finger.

"Get your butt back into that chair, Pennell, or I'll add obstruction of justice to the charge of assault.'' Reluctantly the baby-faced man complied.

The policeman continued. "I don't know quite how you did it, ma'am, but I do know that you used the fire escape to visit your lover and sneak away before dawn. There was a hair sample lodged in the railing that matched the ones found in the sheets."

Before Gwen could reply the officer turned to Harland. "Now we come to the real reason you wanted to close the theater and get rid of Spencer. You knew about your wife's philandering, but you couldn't very well toss her out. She was your goose who laid the golden egg, wasn't she, Pennell?"

Harland seemed to deflate by a third. "But I love my wife, Lieutenant. That's the only reason I wanted Spencer out of town."

"I won't get into an argument about that, but I know the real-estate deal isn't anywhere near resolved, and there are plenty of ways to get around demolishing the theater. You were just too spittin' mad to consider them."

Gwen began to sniffle loudly. Kate, perhaps taking pity on her, asked the lieutenant, "What now? Surely, Malcolm won't be allowed to continue his exploitation of this poor woman."

"No, Mrs. Kramer, " he assured her. "There's Fleming's lawsuit, for one thing, and we've got a fistful of other charges besides—fraud, misrepresentation, fabricating evidence, to name just a few. We've already started extradition proceedings."

In a gesture of concern that touched Carina to her very soul, Damian got up and put his arm around Gwen's shoulder. He guided her to a chair beside him. "Things will be fine, Gwen," he whispered. "You've already started in the right direction by pressing charges and leaving your husband."

"He's right," the policeman agreed. "I'll have to book you as an accessory, but it's a first offense and there are extenuating circumstances. My guess is, the judge'll go easy."

At this, the wretched Gwen burst into tears, but to Carina they seemed like tears of profound release, an emotion that echoed the sentiments of nearly everyone in the room.

EIGHT DAYS LATER, Carina sat at her desk going over a column of figures a third time. "Damn," she muttered. "I was so sure we could do it, but we're still four thousand dollars short."

Damian was sitting nearby, reading the reviews of *Fate of the Popinjay*. The final performance had played to a full house the night before. Some critics were calling it the finest social comedy in years; others compared it to Oscar Wilde's *The Importance of Being Earnest*; and hoped there would be more forthcoming from this brilliant actor-director-playwright.

"Aren't you even listening to me?" Carina demanded. "Here I am, bemoaning my failure, and all you can do is lap up reviews. Talk about your typical, egotistical actor!"

Damian looked up, saw the teasing in her eyes and tossed the paper aside. "Sorry, sunshine, but I've been waiting nearly two decades to read this stuff. I can't seem to get enough of it." He held out his hand for her to join him. "Why are you worried? The Kramers are at the bank this very minute signing papers to buy the Myrmidon."

Carina snuggled beside him, resting her head on his shoulder. A solid week of bliss had banished all worries about what would happen when the play finished its run. Damian hadn't even hinted at the future, and Carina—determined to squeeze every bit of happiness she could from the week—hadn't brought it up, either. Now, suddenly, it was over. Damian's flight left from O'Hare late that afternoon.

"I know I don't have to worry," she said, "but it was important to me to show the bank what we could do."

Damian touched her cheek tenderly. "And you did that, love, and quite remarkably when you consider there was a murder investigation going on in the middle of everything. There's something I've wanted to talk to you about—"

A hysterical voice sliced through his words. "We did it! It's ours!" Kate came rushing to the counter, waving a document in her hands. Len, as usual, trailed quietly behind her, but he too was beaming.

Carina got up to hug them both across the wooden counter. "Congratulations, both of you! The Myrmidon couldn't be in better hands."

"Thank you, dear. Your confidence means a great deal to us."

"Was Harland still there?" Damian asked.

"Oh, no, Gwen is managing things until they elect a new president. All charges against her have been dropped in exchange for turning state's evidence, and she's filed for divorce. I understand Harland is out on bail, staying in some seedy hotel outside town. It's all worked out so marvelously," Kate said with characteristic enthusiasm.

"Don't you think we ought to tell her now?" Len said in a low voice to his wife.

"What? Oh yes, that—I'd almost forgotten."

Carina's smile of anticipation faded when she saw their expression grow serious. "What is it?" she asked.

"This probably isn't the ideal time to discuss it," Kate said, "but it's about your job here at the theater."

She felt her throat tighten. "Yes?"

"Well, Len and I were hoping to run the theater ourselves, in addition to simply owning it . . . to be quite honest, we won't be requiring three of us to do a job customarily done by two. Of course, we'd like you to stay for a few months to help us get organized…if you could." She clasped her hands. "Oh, dear, Carina, I do hope you understand."

She hadn't thought about it before, but it made sense. Why should the Kramers pay her to hang around when they could fulfill the duties admirably themselves? They probably wouldn't take out much of a salary, either, and the place would be profitable in no time. "Yes, yes, of course, I understand," Carina said weakly.

"Uh…Kate, Carina and I hadn't had a chance to discuss her options before you came in," Damian said with an obvious wink and a nudge.

Kate lifted an eloquent hand to her face. "Oh, no, haven't you? Len, we missed our cues for the first time in years."

Len offered an arm to his wife, and it was readily apparent that they'd rehearsed the whole scene. "Then let's get out of here at once, my dear, and let the two young people have their little chat." He waved to Carina and Damian. "See you both for lunch. We can celebrate then."

Carina forced a smile to her face. "It was nice of them to give you advance notice of my layoff," she said. "There probably isn't another actor alive with as many contacts in the theater business as you."

"You're right. I do know everyone worth knowing, but I won't let them know you're available until you've considered my offer first."

Carina looked up. "Your offer?"

"I need someone with experience to run my theater. I'm not cut out to be an artistic director, and I'd rather concentrate on playwrighting and the occasional film. *Fate of the Popinjay*'s success has inspired me—"

"But your theater's in England!" Carina blurted out.

"Yes," he replied, quite serious. "Does that pose a problem?"

Carina threw her hands up in the air with exasperation. "Yes, it poses a problem! Good jobs in theater are hard to get everywhere. I can't just go to England and snatch the position of artistic director. The immigration authorities wouldn't let me out of the airport."

Damian took her hands and steered her back to the sofa. "You're absolutely right. The only way they'll let you work there is if you're my wife."

Carina gave a disbelieving chuckle. "Your wife, right. I should think they're onto marriages of convenience by now."

"Who said anything about convenience? Being married to me will be anything but. I'll be away on location part of the year, while you're tied up with the theater. Then I'll be writing while you learn your way around the city...."

Carina felt as though she were soaring straight to the heavens at breakneck speed. "Are you actually—honestly—proposing to me?"

"Oh, yes, quite," he said, assuming a convincing upper-crust British accent. He reached into a front pocket and pulled out an envelope. "I trust this will prove my sincerity."

Carina took the thick air-mail envelope and saw that it was addressed to Damian. Puzzled, she looked up at him. She could tell that he was having difficulty containing his exuberance. Carina squeezed the envelope. It couldn't be a ring. She opened it and out fell a handful of tickets. "What is this?" she asked in amazement.

"Every play that's running in London as of January. You'll have to wait until spring to buy tickets for the summer season, I'm afraid."

Carina riffled through them. "There are two of everything."

"Yes, well, I thought we could make a honeymoon of it, unless you'd rather go somewhere tropical right away."

Carina looked up into fathomless blue eyes blazing hot with desire. Who needed the tropics? "Oh, Damian!" She flung her arms around his neck. "You can't imagine how much I love you!"

He crushed her to him and laughed deeply. "Yes, I can, sunshine, because I love you at least as much—probably more. Does this mean you accept my proposal?"

The hint of insecurity in his voice made Carina's heart swell with emotion. She pulled away and stared at him with sober conviction. "Yes, I'd be happy to accept the position of artistic director for as long as my services are required."

His grin, a combination of dry wit and roguishness, thrilled her to the core as always. "And the other proposal, Miss Rawlins?"

She pretended to think a moment. "I'll accept that one as well, but only on one condition."

"What's that?"

"It will have to be for life."

Damian took her swiftly into his arms. "For life, it is," he vowed, then sealed the pledge with another kiss.

Sarah Bernhardt observed the goings-on from her framed perch on the wall, and she didn't budge an inch. After all, nothing this perfect had happened at the Myrmidon since the time she'd graced the place herself, seventy-five years before.